PRAISE FOR NE
KNIGHT

"Fast-paced and crisply sty

"[The Nessen and Neuman team] is rapidly making a place for itself in the mystery genre."
—*The Washington Times*

"Yes, they do more in Washington than spend your money and make you mad. They also commit murders and have a great time solving them. Join the excitement and fun by reading *Knight & Day*. It's a treat of a story. . . . "
—Jim Lehrer, co-host of the MacNeil-Lehrer News Hour

"A cute premise. . . . Well-plotted. . . . "
—*Publishers Weekly*

"*Knight & Day* is a story as current as today's headlines, with characters as contemporary as tomorrow's news. The gender chemistry of Knight and Day and their needling banter give verbal foreplay a whole new meaning. A great mystery."
—Steve Martini, author of *Prime Witness*

"We bid a warm welcome to Ron Nessen and Johanna Neuman's exciting first Washington mystery."
—Margaret Truman

"It's too bad we no longer have the Hepburn-Tracy combination out there acting up a storm. They would be just right to play the leads when *Knight & Day* gets made into a movie."
—*The Washington Times*

"You'll learn much more about Washington from reading Nessen and Neuman than from six months of watching the 'McLaughlin Group' or 'Capitol Gang'—and you'll have a hell of a lot more fun, too."
—John Weisman, *New York Times* bestselling coauthor of *Rogue Warrior*

"The debut of *Knight & Day* is especially good news for mystery lovers who are also political junkies, and who equate heaven with insider knowledge of Washington, D.C. Nessen and Neuman have a great deal of fun with their story and you will, too."

—*Mystery Scene*

"Full-contact government, the way they play it in the big leagues. They're all here: the media, the lobbyists, and the politicians for whom the buck stops . . . somewhere in their vicinity. Just when you thought it was safe to go back in the voting booth . . . "

—Jim Bohannon, host, "All-Night Network Radio Talk Show," Mutual Broadcasting System

"*Knight & Day* is sprightly, charming, and great entertainment. Knight and Day are terrific characters, and it's fun to watch them exploding each other's political pomposities, even as they're working together to track down a deadly killer. First-rate."

—Warren Murphy, two-time Edgar Award winner

"Husband and wife Ron Nessen and Johanna Neuman bring impressive credentials to their first novel, a witty and entertaining story of murder in Washington, D.C."

—*Sunday News-Globe* (Amarillo, TX)

"A spark-striking detective duo. Washington chicanery, authentic radio talk-show background! Great stuff! You'll love this one."

—Barbara D'Amato, author of *KILLER. app*

"Fascinating . . . written with Inside-the-Beltway insights that few writers bring to a story. . . . Extraordinarily fast-paced."

—William Harrington, bestselling author of the Columbo series

PRESS CORPSE

A KNIGHT & DAY MYSTERY

RON
NESSEN

AND

JOHANNA
NEUMAN

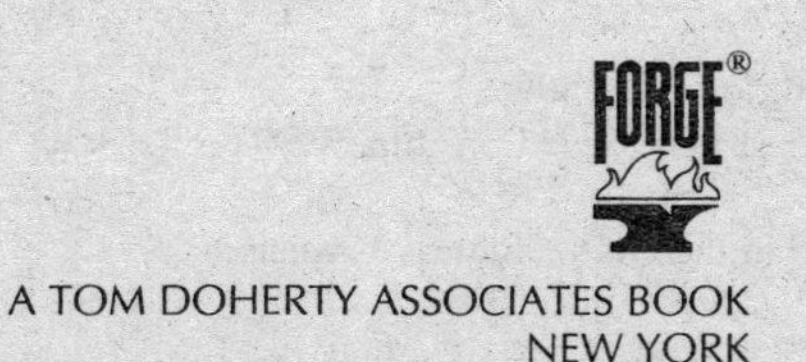

A TOM DOHERTY ASSOCIATES BOOK
NEW YORK

PRESS CORPSE

Cover art by Paul Stinson

A Forge Book
Published by Tom Doherty Associates, Inc.
175 Fifth Avenue
New York, NY 10010

Forge® is a registered trademark of Tom Doherty Associates, Inc.

ISBN 0-812-56793-5
Library of Congress Catalog number: 95-53233

First edition: May 1996
First mass market edition: June 1997

Printed in the United States of America

0 9 8 7 6 5 4 3 2 1

A NOTE TO THE READER:

This is a work of fiction. All of the characters and events portrayed in this novel are either products of the authors' imaginations or are used fictitiously.

To Caren and Edward.

CHAPTER ONE

"LADIES AND GENTLEMEN, the President of the United States and Mrs. Hammond!"

The anonymous public-address announcer's voice boomed through the gigantic ballroom of the Washington Hilton Hotel.

"That's *Ms.* Grady Stein Hammond to you, buster," the First Lady muttered under her breath.

While the Marine Band played the "Ruffles and Flourishes" fanfare, Secret Service agents held open the green curtain from a backstage holding room. President Dale Hammond and his wife—Grady the First Lady, the news media had dubbed her—stepped onto a raised platform behind a long headtable. Blinking into the spotlights, they waved to the two thousand guests standing at round tables below. The red-jacketed band blared "Hail to the Chief."

The President and his wife had arrived to participate in an annual Washington ritual of spring, the black-tie dinner of the White House Correspondents Association.

The applause for President Hammond was tepid, at best. He was the first conservative elected to the White House since George Bush. Not many of the Washington reporters, editors, and producers crowded into the Hilton ballroom shared his views on family values, individual responsibility, and small government.

"Pigs!" Grady Stein Hammond mouthed her opinion of the audience to her friend Jerry Knight at a table in the front row.

Jerry winked and grinned at the First Lady's famous outspokenness. No wonder her enemies called her "Grate-y." The First Lady turned away, executing a mocking curtsy to the unenthusiastic crowd.

Jerry Knight was one of the few media people in the audience who did share Hammond's views. Jerry was the aggressively conservative host of the *Night Talker* show on ATN, the All Talk Network, the most popular radio call-in show in America.

"What did she say to you?" reporter Jane Day asked Jerry from her seat at the adjoining *Washington Post* table.

"She said you media people are pigs."

With a jerky motion Jane wrote this down in her reporter's notebook, open on the table.

Jerry Knight and Jane Day had developed a prickly relationship since they'd teamed up a year earlier to expose the murderer of environmental activist Curtis Davies Davenport, a friend of Jane's who was clubbed to death in ATN's parking garage after an appearance on the *Night Talker* show. They periodically had dinner together or attended some Washington VIP soiree, usually spending the evening sparring over their political differences.

Jerry and Jane were truly an odd couple, opposites in every way. He'd been divorced three times; she'd never been married. He was fiftyish; she was nearly twenty years younger. He was supremely egotistical; she was full of self-doubts about her looks and her future. She was as far over on the liberal side of the political spectrum as he was on the conservative end.

Even their working hours were in conflict. He slept all day and showed up at the ATN studios at ten P.M. for his midnight show. As a White House correspondent for the *Washington Post,* her working day began at ten A.M. And she often fell asleep at night fuming over some right-wing outrage Jerry had uttered on his program.

"Please stand for the presentation of the colors and remain standing for the National Anthem," Dorothy Swisher, the president of the White House Correspondents Association, directed from the headtable. Dorothy, a reporter for the Knight-Ridder chain of newspapers, had chosen an unfortunate, overly elaborate red taffeta gown for her big night.

"Oh, dear," Jane's fashion-conscious mother would have sniffed at the creation.

The ballroom lights dimmed. The spotlights picked up the Marine Color Guard, resplendent in dress blue uniforms and gleaming boots, holding their satiny flags aloft. They marched down the center aisle between the tables at an impossibly slow, synchronized cadence. The leader barked a command and they snapped to attention directly in front of the headtable.

The Marine Band struck up "The Star-Spangled Banner." The sound from the drums and brass echoed off the ballroom's domed ceiling, blasting the close-packed attendees.

Jerry Knight sang the words loudly. He did it deliberately to irritate the reporters around him who stood silent. Damn liberal media. He believed they declined to sing the National Anthem because they were afraid of being regarded as patriotic zealots.

One of those irritated by Jerry's loud singing was Jane Day at the next table.

"Don't strain your voice," she hissed out of the corner of her thin mouth. "You don't want to disappoint all those kooks out there in your listening audience."

"At least I know the words," Jerry retorted between stanzas, "unlike your liberal ilk."

"Ilk? Very good. What did you do, buy one of those 'Learn a New Word a Day' calendars?"

Jerry let it pass.

"Speaking of giving proof through the night, you're going with me to the ATN hospitality suite after the dinner, right?" Jerry asked Jane as the last notes of the anthem faded away.

"Aren't you going to the party for Rush Limbaugh?" she responded. "I thought he was your idol."

"You've got it backwards," Jerry said. "I'm *his* idol."

"Ahhhh. He must admire your humility."

"Okay, then, I'm going to put you down as 'tentatively yes.' "

In fact, Jane had decided to accompany Jerry on the post-dinner round of receptions staged by various news organizations. He was old for her and a Neanderthal in his politics. But he could make her laugh, and he wasn't at all threatened by her career, as most of the men she met were. Besides, what else did she have to do? Go back to her apartment in Adams Morgan and talk to her cat Bloomsbury?

Jane dragged her fingers through her tangled orange hair. Two hours that afternoon at George's hair salon in the Four Seasons Hotel in Georgetown. And it was already frizzing up. A wasted $75.

What a difference a year made. A year ago she was an unknown reporter writing routine environmental stories for the *Post.* Her role in catching the creep who killed Curtis, and her related exposé of questionable campaign contributions to Senator Barton Jacobsen, had won her a promotion to the newspaper's prestigious White House team. And a primo front-row seat at the Correspondents Association dinner.

Come to think of it, her exposé was indirectly responsible for Dale and Grady Hammond having good seats at the dinner, too. When the campaign contribution scandal scuttled Senator Jacobsen's White House hopes, the party had turned to the innocuous Hammond.

The Marine Color Guard marched out. Next up at the podium was the pastor of a local church to deliver the invocation. Seizing his moment in the spotlight, the pastor prayed for every one of the President's domestic and foreign initiatives, called for divine retribution against the nation's enemies, and concluded with a pointed request that God give the assembled reporters the wisdom to report the facts and not just their opinions, the good news as well as the bad news, the uplifting as well as the debasing. Amen.

Long, but on the mark, Jerry thought. He was confident that God was a conservative.

Jane paid no attention to the lengthy invocation. She used the time to scan the ballroom and scribble notes in her pad.

She'd have a tight deadline to dictate a story for her newspaper's final editions after the President's traditional post-dinner remarks. Since no hard news was expected, she needed color—gaffes, garb, and gossip that, hopefully, would embarrass the high and mighty.

The White House Correspondents Association annual dinner was an A-list event. News organizations competed fiercely for the distinction of having Cabinet members and other movers and shakers as guests at their tables. It gave the bureau chiefs and reporters the opportunity to impress the home office by casually dropping, "As I was saying at dinner the other night to the Secretary of . . ."

Jane spotted Maud Downy, White House correspondent of the *New York Times,* turning her famous adoring gaze on the White House chief of staff, Aaron Strauss. He seemed to be falling for it. Jane was always amazed at how many powerful men blurted out every secret they knew when Maud turned on that idolizing look. Well, Jane knew from her own experiences, sometimes women reporters had to use their wiles, because male sources didn't take them seriously. To flirt, perchance to scoop.

Jane noted another VIP couple two tables over and jotted it in her notebook: self-absorbed CBS correspondent Sandra Winchell and her constant companion, the taciturn and hound-dog-faced chairman of the Federal Communications Commission, Simon Simpson.

A lot of male guests seemed to have found an excuse to drop by a table near the center aisle, Jane observed. The attraction was Glory Justice, a stunning anchor for local TV channel 7, wearing an extremely low-cut strapless white gown and what Jane guessed was a WonderBra.

Jane giggled. Too bad her father wasn't there.

"You'd think, with all the money that woman must make, she could afford the *rest* of the dress," Lester would have joked. Corny. She'd heard it a hundred times. But it always made her laugh.

Jane checked out the less-desirable tables at the back and along the sides. That's where the association usually placed the guests who were more infamous than famous.

One newsmagazine delighted in annually inviting "this

year's blonde," the bimbo then in the headlines for some titillating scandal, usually involving sex. And there she was, Jane noted. Tawnee Wooten, former Miss Alabama, former *Playboy* centerfold, who had recently traveled at taxpayers' expense to a conference in Rio as "personal assistant" to a very senior, very married, very much older United States senator.

Tawnee was the focus of a half-dozen TV Minicams. The previous year's blondes in the audience could have advised her to enjoy the attention while she could. Her fifteen minutes of tabloid fame would soon be gone.

Next, Jane checked out the Hollywood contingent. A half-dozen movie stars turned up at the Correspondents Association dinner every year, usually the ones involved in political causes.

The Hollywood guests and the Washington guests were easily distinguishable by their clothes.

Ninety-nine percent of the Washington men wore traditional black tuxedos, black bow ties, black shoes, and white shirts, looking like so many penguins. Here and there a nonconformist sported a midnight blue tux, and a couple of really daring revolutionaries showed up in red cummerbunds or plaid bow ties. By contrast, the Hollywood men wore velvet tuxedos, gold lamé tuxedos, opera capes lined with red satin, jogging shoes, black shirts, or, in one case, no shirt at all.

Jerry Knight leaned over and read the names of the movie stars Jane Day had scrawled in her notebook.

"The Hollywood people are awed by the power of the politicians and the politicians are dazzled by the glamour of the Hollywood people," Jerry pontificated. "Mutual admiration. It's disgusting."

Jane made a note of his comment for inclusion in her story, attributed to "one veteran Washington observer." She quoted Jerry anonymously often. It was one of the things she liked about him, his acerbic insights, based on years in Washington. Except when his comments were too politically incorrect or too far-out conservative.

"Okay, time to eat," Dorothy Swisher announced from the podium.

An army of waiters and waitresses swarmed in from the wings, bearing huge trays of soup bowls on their shoulders.

Jane turned her attention to the headtable, scratching in her pad without looking down at the pages.

Dan McLean, an aggressive CNN reporter with devilish eyebrows and a bad toupee, was clowning for the photographers with the President's national security adviser, Gregor Novasky. The two men bore a resemblance to each other and had once appeared in the *Spy* magazine feature *Separated at Birth.*

McLean was shouting to the photographers that he was really Novasky and had ordered the bombing of Havana to start in fifteen minutes.

Jane checked out the rest of the headtable.

Heddy Kirkland, the ancient wire-service correspondent, sat silently, her hooded eyes taking in everything. Heddy hadn't written a story in years. The younger reporters handled that. Her role now was to shout quarrelsome and outrageous questions at whoever happened to be President and to appear as a celebrity on TV talk shows.

But in years past, Jane knew, Heddy had blazed a trail for her and other women reporters. Heddy had been the first woman president of the White House Correspondents Association, the first woman to break into the rolls of the all-male National Press Club, the first woman admitted to the even more exclusive all-male bastion of the Gridiron Club.

"Mr. President, are you going to break off diplomatic relations with Vietnam?" Heddy shouted up the table. "Are you knuckling under to the MIA families and the ultra-right-wing veterans groups?"

Hammond smiled and pointed to his ear, pretending he couldn't hear her question in the din of the banquet.

Jane wrote down the exchange in her notebook.

The rest of the headtable lineup consisted mostly of arrogant pundits and arrogant White House officials, Jane noted. In fact, some of the pundits used to be White House officials, and vice versa.

The evening's entertainer, Chad Bartlett, a comedian from *Saturday Night Live,* was seated at Grady Hammond's right, talking animatedly with the First Lady.

Jerry Knight, following Jane's gaze, watched the pair. They were laughing at something. Grady put her hand on Chad's arm, and kept it there. Jerry felt a twinge of jealousy.

He'd become smitten with Grady during the presidential campaign when she and Hammond had appeared several times on the *Night Talker* show because it was one of the few programs that offered a non-hostile atmosphere to a candidate with conservative views.

What the hell were she and Bartlett laughing about? Jerry wondered. Didn't she know the comedian had made his reputation by ridiculing her husband? In accord with the dinner's ritual, Bartlett would stand at the microphone after the meal and tell twenty minutes of jokes making fun of the President. Hammond would then reply with some self-deprecating humor drafted for him by the White House speechwriters, before winding up with a few serious sentences about how he and the reporters might disagree but he still respected them for their role in the great American system of a free press.

What blather, Jerry fumed. Hammond shouldn't praise these liberal jerks. He should hate them for putting him down every chance they got. And Jerry didn't like Grady acting so friendly toward Chad Bartlett, either!

Jane also watched the First Lady and scribbled notes. Her dress—copper-colored satin with black boa feathers—hadn't she worn it before, at a state dinner for the visiting president of some Latin American country? Jane would nail Grady in her story for having a limited wardrobe. And for flirting publicly with Chad Bartlett. Jane always made a point of referring to Grady in the *Post* by her real name—Gertrude—a name she knew the First Lady hated.

Grady was a different kind of First Lady. Statuesque, svelte, stylish, self-assured, outspoken, outgoing, always willing to argue her views on issues, even when they were at odds with her husband's views. Jane had witnessed the famous episode when the First Lady whacked a TV panel moderator with her purse for introducing her as "a conservative Bella Abzug."

Grady was the first President's wife ever to hold a paying job of her own outside the White House. George Will had once referred to Grady Hammond in a column as "foxy."

Jane shifted her gaze to Dale Hammond. He looked morose and uncomfortable, studying his notes and making desultory conversation with his dinner partner, the flamboyant Dorothy Swisher.

What had Grady seen in him? Jane wondered. He was such a wimp. They'd met and become engaged in college, so she couldn't have latched on to him as a ticket to the White House. Jane had heard her colleagues snickering that the Hammonds' daughter was born seven months after the wedding. So, she guessed, in those days before legal abortions were available and acceptable, it must have been a shotgun wedding.

Jane had also heard the rumors that Grady wasn't exactly Pat Nixon or Nancy Reagan when it came to marital faithfulness. Some of the gossip about affairs mentioned the moneybags behind the computer service company the First Lady ran. But other persistent rumors said Grady's "close personal friend" was a woman.

Jane had a folder in her file drawer at the *Post* where she saved such tidbits. One of these days . . .

But right now, her problem was finding a lead for her story for the next morning. She had only ninety minutes before she'd have to phone the *Post* if she was going to make the deadline for tomorrow's Sunday paper. Jane flipped through her notes.

About a hundred demonstrators had heckled the President and the other guests as they arrived, waving hand-lettered signs demanding that Hammond break off diplomatic relations with Vietnam because of the discovery of a mass grave of American prisoners outside Hanoi a month earlier. A possible lead, but not exactly the killer copy Jane was hoping for.

Grady wearing a gown she'd worn before might make it. Or Grady calling the audience "pigs." But Jane was hoping for something nastier.

Usually some guest at these dinners did something really stupid and provided copy for a few days of media frenzy. One year, a second-level White House official, after too much to drink, had stuck his hand down the front of the dress of a congressman's wife. Another time, a Redskins quarterback made an indecent proposition to a female Supreme Court justice. Last year, a Cabinet member had thrown up on the Brazilian ambassador.

But this year, Jane fretted, nothing had happened to make a story. The dinner was dull. She decided to lead with Grady calling the audience of hostile reporters "pigs."

A sudden movement at the left end of the headtable caught Jane's eye. She turned to see Dan McLean, the CNN reporter, half-standing, clutching his chest. His mouth worked but no sound came out. His face was gray, contorted in pain. Then he toppled forward onto the table, his head in his soup bowl.

A Cabinet member sitting next to McLean laughed, thinking the reporter was pulling one of his famous tasteless pranks.

"Doctor!" a Secret Service agent shouted, moving toward McLean.

The President's doctor, always close at hand, groped through the green curtains onto the platform. He leaned over the correspondent.

Jane scribbled frantically in her notebook, never taking her eyes off the scene at the headtable. This was an outlandish performance, even for McLean, she thought. The guests in the ballroom buzzed with puzzlement.

In a moment, the doctor straightened up, smoothing his blue Navy officer's uniform.

"The son of a bitch is dead," the doctor pronounced.

Dwight Longstreet, the agent in charge of the Secret Service detail, sprang at Hammond, shielding the President's body with his own.

"Let's go! Let's go!" Longstreet shouted to the other agents. "We're moving Teddybear back to Homeplate! Now! Get Manhandler! Move it! Move it!"

Longstreet had no idea what—or *who*—had killed McLean. Maybe a heart attack. Maybe an assassin. But he wasn't going to wait around to find out. In Secret Service code, he was ordering his agents to rush the President and First Lady back to the safety of the White House. The detail responded instantly.

A wedge of agents screeching "Move it! Move it!" half-dragged, half-carried the couple off the platform, through the holding room, and down a corridor, knocking over two hotel employees who got in their way. In less than ten seconds Hammond and Grady were on the floor of the presidential limousine, agents on top of them, racing down Connecticut Avenue toward the White House at fifty miles an hour.

Four Secret Service agents left behind roamed the platform, peering into the audience, agitated and confused, but alert, trying to figure out what the hell was going on.

What was going on was pandemonium.

A paramedic crew from the ambulance that was discreetly parked near every event attended by the President rushed onto the headtable platform lugging their folded gurney and equipment. They confirmed that McLean was dead, covered him with a gray blanket, and loaded him onto the stretcher.

Dorothy Swisher, seeing her big evening disintegrating, chirped nervously into the microphone, "Okay, folks, a little excitement here. No big deal. Let's just take a couple of minutes for things to calm down, then we'll resume the festivities. It's going to be a fun night!"

"Like hell," growled the police captain in charge of the detachment of uniformed D.C. cops assigned to the dinner.

Lieutenant Mike Pickett pushed through the crowd to the headtable, where he introduced himself to the agent in charge of the remaining Secret Service guards, Lawrence Frieze. They immediately began arguing about how to proceed.

A man had died, cause of death not yet known. Could have been a heart attack, choking, drug reaction, any number of routine causes—routine in law-enforcement parlance—Pickett declared. Therefore, it was a matter for the Metropolitan Police to investigate, the lieutenant insisted.

But suppose McLean was murdered, the Secret Service agent replied, and suppose the President had been the intended target. After all, he had been seated only four places away from McLean at the headtable. Therefore, the Secret Service should conduct the investigation, Frieze argued.

"That's a lot of supposes," Pickett retorted sourly.

While they bickered over jurisdiction, the two men agreed on one matter of investigative procedure: If McLean *had* been murdered, the perpetrator might still be in the room.

Nobody would be allowed to leave until Pickett and Frieze figured out what had happened and screened the crowd for suspects.

The lieutenant made the announcement over the PA system.

It set off a frenzy in the ballroom.

Many of the tuxedoed and gowned banquetgoers had reverted to being reporters. Something had happened. They weren't sure exactly what. But it was bad enough to require the hurried exit of the President and First Lady. They were scrawling notes on the backs of their programs, shouting questions at the bewildered Secret Service agents on the platform, and interviewing each other.

They urgently needed to get to the pay phones in the lobby to call their newspapers and networks. And this fat cop was telling them they couldn't leave!

"Let us out!" the mob howled. "We're reporters!"

Lieutenant Pickett and Agent Frieze ignored them.

All over the room pagers on belts and in purses chirped. The word was seeping through Washington that something had happened at the White House Correspondents Association dinner. News desks were beeping reporters. But the cops were preventing the reporters from responding.

Except for the reporters carrying cellular phones.

Jane Day yanked a tiny black fold-up model, barely larger than a pack of cigarettes, from her beaded evening bag and frantically punched in the phone number of the *Post.* She ducked under the table for privacy.

"What the hell's going on?" Jerry Knight shouted at a Secret Service agent he knew from the Hammonds' visits to his show.

"We can't let anybody out until we check the audience for suspects!" the agent shouted back.

"Suspects?" Jerry repeated. "Are you kidding? I first met Dan McLean thirty years ago when we were both war correspondents in Vietnam. McLean started making enemies then and never stopped. Between the politicians McLean scalded on the air and the reporters he scooped or stole stories from, *everybody* in the place is a suspect."

CHAPTER TWO

THREE BLOCKS AWAY, at the 7-Eleven on Columbia Road in the Adams Morgan neighborhood, D.C. Homicide Detective Abraham Lincoln Jones was having dinner—a burrito and a can of root beer. Jones was hungry. He'd spent the afternoon investigating the murder of a pizza deliveryman on Maryland Avenue NE, near the Hechinger Mall. The deliveryman had been lured to an apartment building by a pizza order, stabbed twelve times, and robbed of the $7.50 he was carrying.

The Adams Morgan 7-Eleven was a favorite hangout for cops because the manager fed them for free. It was cheap insurance against robberies. There was almost always a police cruiser parked outside. That made the residents of nearby apartment buildings and row houses—once elegant, now faded—feel safer.

A. L. Jones, squat, chunky, his mahogany-brown face grizzled with a straggly gray mustache and gray stubble, confronted a teenage boy in the soft-drink aisle. The boy wore baggy black shorts past his knees, a Shaq T-shirt, and elaborate black sneakers. His head was shaved, except for a greasy tuft on top.

"You seen LaTroy?" Jones demanded.

"I ain't seen him," the boy mumbled.

"You sure?"

"Sure I'm sure."

"You see him, you tell him I'm looking for him," A.L. ordered in a deep rumble. "Hear?"

The boy grunted and scuttled out of the 7-Eleven, not stopping to shoplift a bag of potato chips as he'd intended.

Damn drug boys, Jones cursed to himself. Didn't give props, proper respect, even to a cop. Probably packing a piece in those baggy pants. The detective was weary and depressed, and it was still early on a Saturday night. He anticipated the drug boys would chop a few—themselves and some innocent folks—before the night was over.

Jones was looking for LaTroy Williams.

Two days before, the fifteen-year-old boy had watched as two gang members broke down the door of his apartment and wasted his mother with their Nines. Jones first thought it had been a mistake. Wrong apartment. But maybe not. Popping witnesses was standard procedure for drug boys. And the mother, a high school dropout trying to make a living cleaning offices at night, had witnessed a killing in the alley behind her apartment one morning as she returned home from her job.

Jones suspected LaTroy was out somewhere in the city trying to buy a piece to drop the drug boys who'd dropped his mother. Probably he could. Then the relatives or fellow crew members of the drug boys would chop LaTroy. Then the friends he hung with would chop the crew members who hung with the drug boys.

And so on, blood without end.

Something about LaTroy had touched A.L., something about him that suggested the boy, if encouraged, could escape the killing streets and make something of himself.

LaTroy reminded the detective of himself. He'd had plans to make something of himself. He'd wanted to be an architect, until his father lost his job at Amtrak and couldn't afford to pay his tuition at Howard after the first year.

After that, A.L. had hung with a bad crowd, got in trouble, got arrested. His own brother was killed holding up a liquor store. The draft and Vietnam saved A.L. from going down that path. Back from the war, he'd decided to become a cop, to save his city from the bad boys, to save the boys from going bad.

He snorted. After what had happened to D.C. in the past twenty years, he had adopted more modest goals. He just wanted to stay alive long enough to retire.

"You see LaTroy Williams, you tell him I'm looking for him," Jones instructed the convenience store's Asian manager in a hoarse, tired baritone.

"Okay." The manager grinned. "You want more root beer? You take."

"Okay." A.L. helped himself to another can and started out.

The walkie-talkie on his belt crackled.

"Say again," A.L. spoke into the device.

"You still at the 7-Eleven, honey?" asked the voice of Michelle, the Homicide dispatcher.

"Yeah. What's up?"

"You better get yourself over to the Hilton Hotel. You right near there, right?"

"Yeah. What's going on?"

"They got some kind of big banquet, the President and all is there, and some white dude is dead."

A. L. Jones was on the bubble, meaning he was the homicide detective designated to investigate the next killing in D.C. on this shift.

"Yeah? What else you know about it?"

"Nothing. All I know is sounds like there's a lot of people running around in circles, all worked up, yelling and screaming at each other. You better get yourself on over there, honey."

"On my way."

A.L. lumbered to his vanilla-colored detective's car, hit the blue light on the dash, made a U-turn on Columbia Road, drove down the wrong side of Connecticut Avenue, hung a left on T Street, and braked to a stop under the portico of the Hilton's lower driveway.

Like Michelle said, A.L. found a lot of people running around, all worked up, yelling and screaming at each other.

Officers from a half-dozen different law enforcement agencies scurried about: D.C. uniformed cops, hotel security guards, uniformed Executive Protective Service cops, plainclothes EPS agents, Secret Service agents talking into their cuffs, even Park Police in crisp white shirts.

A man in a blazer with a Hilton Hotel nameplate pinned over his breast pocket was proclaiming to the TV Minicams that the hotel was not a jinx for Presidents.

"It could have happened anywhere," the man said. "It's just a weird coincidence."

A.L. recalled that John Hinckley had shot President Reagan in the very same Hilton Hotel driveway. No wonder there were so many PR guys in Washington, the detective thought.

Jones flipped his detective's badge out of the breast pocket of his rumpled sport coat and let it dangle to identify himself. He went looking for Lieutenant Mike Pickett.

"You on the bubble tonight, A.L.?" the beefy lieutenant asked when Jones found him in what had been the presidential holding room behind the headtable.

"Yeah. Whatta we got here?"

Pickett filled him in on what had happened. A.L. dug a bent notebook and a cheap ballpoint pen from his jacket pocket and scribbled notes.

"How come the Secret Service looks like they're running things?" Jones asked.

"Ask them yourself," Pickett advised.

Lawrence Frieze, a tall, silver-haired Secret Service agent, had just entered the holding room. Pickett introduced him to Jones.

"You're welcome to observe, Detective," Frieze advised him in a distracted manner. Someone apparently was talking to him in his radio earpiece. "We may need you to coordinate our investigation with the local police."

"The President's all right, isn't he?" Jones asked. "I thought the dead guy was a newsie. How come the Secret Service is in it?"

"He *was* a newsie," Frieze replied. "Dan McLean of CNN. But he was seated close to Teddybe . . . to the President.

We're treating it as an attempt on the life of President Hammond until we determine otherwise."

"Attempt on? You're assuming—what's his name? McLean?—was whacked?" Jones persisted. "Lieutenant Pickett says there wasn't any shots. No apparent perp. Whatta you got as the cause?"

"We don't know that yet," Frieze responded impatiently.

"Well, if you don't know what killed him, how do you know he was busted? Maybe it was natural."

Jones hoped it was natural. Then he wouldn't have to get involved.

"We're treating it as an attempt on the President until we determine otherwise," Frieze repeated astringently. "Okay? I appreciate your cooperation, Detective . . . ?"

"Jones."

"Detective Jones."

Somebody spoke to Frieze in his earpiece. He hurried away.

Pickett shrugged at A.L. "I got plenty of guys here if you need help," the lieutenant offered. "I think it's going to be a long night."

A.L. thought so, too. He went to look at the scene of the crime.

CHAPTER THREE

BY TEN P.M., Jane Day was back in the fluorescent-lit *Post* newsroom, pounding out the story of Dan McLean's death at the White House Correspondents Association dinner on her computer, looking incongruous in her black evening gown. She'd spotted Detective A. L. Jones, whom she knew from her coverage of Curtis Davenport's murder a year earlier, and cajoled him into letting her slip out of the ballroom through an obscure passageway.

With the streets around the Hilton blocked by police vehicles, she'd run through the traffic on Connecticut Avenue toward Dupont Circle barefoot, carrying her black high heels in one hand and her cellular phone in the other. She'd jumped in front of the first taxi she saw and refused to move until the driver agreed to take her to the *Post*.

Normally at this hour on a Saturday night, the newsroom was an acre of empty desks and cubicles. A few news assistants would be checking area police departments for late crimes or accidents, and the editors would be scanning early copies of the *New York Times* to make sure the great rival had not scooped them.

But now the newsroom was filling with *Post* reporters and editors who had escaped from the Hilton. It was too big a story to leave to the usual Saturday night skeleton crew. After all, the reporters and editors flocking in had personally witnessed the story. That made it *big*.

Russ Williamson, the editor in charge of the newsroom Monday through Friday, stripped off his tuxedo jacket and undid his black tie, like some late-night lounge singer, and took over from Jeff Plotnick, the steady and reliable veteran editor who was entrusted with deciding what went into the newspaper during the hours when no one else wanted the job.

But tonight, Russ Williamson wanted the job, wanted the chance to impress Kirk Scoffield, the legendary managing editor.

"How you doing?" Williamson asked Jane, leaning over the reporter, staring at her computer screen. He moved closer until his hip rested against her shoulder. "How much longer? We're holding the press run for the final."

"Soon!" the reporter snapped. "I'll get it done faster if you stop breathing on my neck!"

She was stressed from the pressure to write her piece in a hurry while half the paper's brass looked on. She was trying to write, decipher her scribbled notes, keep an eye on CNN, and ignore the editors and reporters in formal clothes huddled around her.

The phone on Jane's desk chirped.

"Yeah?" she answered, propping the phone against her ear with her shoulder while continuing to type.

"Honey? It's your mom. Are you all right?"

"Of course I'm all right," Jane answered, only half paying attention to her mother's call from Los Angeles.

"I was worried," Mavis Day explained. "I just saw on TV that someone died at the correspondents dinner and I wanted to be sure you're okay."

"I'm okay," Jane assured her mother, nervously twisting a strand of orange hair around her finger.

"Parents worry, you know. No matter how old their children are, parents worry."

"I'm okay," Jane repeated.

"So, how was the dinner other than that?" her mother asked.

"Mom!"

"What did you wear, honey?" Mavis continued, ignoring her daughter's rising exasperation. "Your black long dress?"

"Mom, I've got to go."

"Did you have a date, honey?"

"Mom! I'm on deadline. I'll call you later." Jane hung up.

Russ pointed at her computer screen, brushing her breast with his arm, seemingly by accident.

"How come you're not leading with the White House saying Hammond was the intended victim of an assassination attempt?" the editor demanded.

"It's just spin," Jane replied, nodding toward CNN's live coverage on the TV set hanging from the newsroom ceiling. The picture shifted back and forth between a spokesman in the White House briefing room and a correspondent at the Hilton.

"The White House spin doctors are trying to generate sympathy for a President who's going nowhere except into early retirement," Jane said, talking and typing at the same time. "The conservatives had their chance and Hammond screwed it up. We shouldn't let the White House use McLean's death to generate a sympathy vote for a failed President."

"Isn't it much more likely that someone would try to kill an unpopular President than an unpopular TV correspondent?" Williamson argued.

"No," Jane said. "Dan was a tough investigative reporter. Maybe he dug up something that someone didn't want him to broadcast."

"McLean had a lot of enemies," the editor agreed. "But that's because he was a shit. If every journalist in Washington who's a shit was a target for murder, there'd be damn few journalists left."

Yeah, and you wouldn't be among them, Jane thought.

"We don't even know if it *was* murder," she argued. "McLean could have choked on his food or had a heart attack."

"You've got to quote the White House," Williamson instructed her.

"Russ," Jane snapped, "isn't it a little far-fetched to believe that some would-be assassin was smart enough to get past all the security, get to the headtable without being seen, and then by some incredible act of stupidity at the last minute killed McLean instead of the President? Really? You believe that?"

"The White House says it could have happened," Williamson responded without conviction.

"Come on, Russ!" Jane was on the brink of losing control.

"Write it straight," Williamson ordered, noticing that Kirk Scoffield was following the debate. " 'McLean dead at correspondents dinner. Cause of death unknown. Secret Service says it may have been an attempt to assassinate Hammond.' "

"Fine!" Jane angrily hit the PAGE UP key on her computer and deleted the first five paragraphs of her story.

"We'll follow up later and if—" the editor cajoled.

"You want me to make deadline?" Jane interrupted. "Get out of my face and let me write. Or maybe you'd rather let the White House write it *for* us!"

When Jane got home to her apartment in the Adams Morgan neighborhood at three A.M., she found three yellow roses wrapped in a cellophane cone and stuffed through the door knocker. A note scribbled on the back of Jerry Knight's business card read, "You're good at what you do, even though you work for that liberal rag. I missed doing the parties with you. Another time? J."

She bristled at the "liberal rag" crack, but liked the rest.

CHAPTER FOUR

At the Hilton Hotel, the deserted headtable for the White House Correspondents Association dinner was fenced off with yellow police tape. So was the kitchen.

The dinner guests had complained so persistently, and had invoked their VIP credentials so threateningly, that they had finally been allowed to depart the ballroom after giving police officers their names and phone numbers and promising to be available for questioning later. The last to leave was Dorothy Swisher, weeping and crushed, finally accepting that her big dinner could not continue.

The ballroom doors were shut and police stood guard to keep out the curious and the news media. Police officers combed the area, looking for clues.

The banquet tables were now occupied by policemen and policewomen patiently interviewing dozens of waiters, kitchen workers, and other hotel employees, one after the other. The questioning went slowly because the interviewees spoke Spanish, Korean, Vietnamese, Arabic, Cambodian, Farsi, Swahili, and a half-dozen other languages.

Inspection of the trash cans in the lobby had turned up a

pocketknife, apparently dumped there by someone who must have realized it would trip the alarm on the metal detectors through which all the dinner guests had to pass before being allowed into the ballroom. Detective Jones placed the knife in a plastic evidence bag.

The trash can search also found a pair of woman's black bikini underpants. The find produced many surmises, as well as snickers, from the officers conducting the search. Secret Service Agent Frieze, who did not share their humor, ruled that the panties were unconnected with McLean's death.

Frieze and Jones had worked out an accommodation of sorts on jurisdiction. Pending a determination of whether McLean's death was natural, accidental, or murder, the Secret Service agent would be in charge of the investigation on the possibility that someone had tried to kill the President but got the TV correspondent by mistake. Jones was consigned to assisting Frieze, primarily supervising the personnel from the Metropolitan Police Department.

Jones and Frieze could not have been more different. Frieze was tall, athletic, and polished. Jones was short, tubby, and uncomfortable. Frieze wore an immaculate well-tailored tuxedo and glistening black patent shoes. Jones wore a wrinkled plaid sport jacket too light for the season, and scuffed, clunky brogans.

The only thing that marred Frieze's suave appearance, A.L. noted with satisfaction, was that his teeth were crooked and discolored.

About one A.M. Clifford Wolfe, assistant director of the FBI, arrived at Frieze's holding room command center, further complicating the jurisdictional jockeying.

Jones had worked with the FBI official once before when a member of Congress was stabbed to death in a gay theater. The detective noticed that Wolfe's hair was uncombed and his suit jacket and pants didn't match. Rousted from bed by an FBI watch officer, no doubt.

Lot of firepower up in the middle of the night because some TV newsie bought it, Jones thought. Might have been just a heart attack. Would have been a simple and routine case, if the President of the United States hadn't been sitting ten feet away when McLean died.

Shortly after two-thirty A.M., an unintelligible voice spoke on Jones's walkie-talkie.

"Say again?" the detective spoke into his radio.

"A.L.? That you, honey?" asked Michelle the dispatcher.

"It's me. What's up?"

"Your friend Willie Wu—at the Medical Examiner's Office?—called you."

"Yeah?"

"Yeah. He said tell you that boy died at the Hilton—at that dinner, you know?—Willie says looks like he was poisoned. Said tell you it's preliminary and all. But looks like he was poisoned. Got that?"

"Yeah. I got it."

So much for simple and routine. So much for natural.

A.L. reported this development to Frieze and Wolfe.

With poison as the tentative cause of death, the questioning of the waiters and kitchen help took on new importance. Jones summoned the uniformed D.C. policeman supervising the interviews to report on the findings so far.

While the names and social security numbers of everyone in proximity to the President had routinely been run through the Secret Service computers before the dinner, the check apparently had been cursory. The more detailed examination of the hotel staff had turned up two people using "borrowed" green immigration cards, one wanted on a warrant for car theft, and a few with old drug possession and DWI arrests.

None of the hotel employees acknowledged seeing anything unusual prior to McLean's death. Nevertheless, Frieze directed that the Salvadoran waitress assigned to McLean's end of the headtable be brought to his command post.

Clara Henriquez was short, wiry, and very scared. Her interview form showed she was a legal immigrant, an employee of the Hilton for twelve years, lived in an apartment in the Petworth section, and supported three children without a husband. She had never been in any kind of trouble.

Using the rudimentary Spanish he'd picked up on the streets, Jones translated the questions of Frieze and Wolfe for the waitress and translated her imperfect English for the Secret Service and FBI officials. The many hand gestures that accompanied the exchange needed no translation.

"Ask her where she got the food she served to McLean," Frieze directed.

"She says only the soup had been served when McLean collapsed," A.L. translated her answer in his deep, gruff voice. "There was already a soup bowl at his place when she got there with her tray, so she figured another waiter had served him. She went on and served the other guests at her end of the table."

"Did she serve him water?"

Clara understood the question, and answered "No" in a trembling voice. "*Agua* there before. Somebody else do."

"Did you serve him wine?"

"No *vino.*"

"Did you also serve the President?" Frieze asked.

Jones translated that one.

"No. She says someone else was assigned to wait on him."

They went over the same questions again and again. Clara gave the same answers every time. Finally she was sent away.

Jones dispatched a policeman to retrieve McLean's dishes, glasses, and silverware so they could be tested for poison. The cop returned to report that in the confusion after the correspondent's death, the headtable had been cleared and everything had been run through the kitchen's industrial-size dishwasher.

"Goddamn it!" Wolfe exploded, looking accusingly at A. L. Jones. "What a fuckup. That will certainly give plenty of material to the conspiracy nuts."

The detective stared back at the FBI official's accusatory eyes with a blank expression. But Jones understood the reference.

Thirty years after JFK's death, conspiracy theorists were still minutely examining police procedures on November 22, 1963, in Dallas, creating fantastic scenarios of plots and coups, of evidence missed and evidence suppressed. Hell, Jones thought, 130 years after his namesake's death, some people were still concocting conspiracy theories for Lincoln's assassination.

A.L. knew he'd screwed up by not confiscating McLean's place setting as evidence. But he hadn't known about the poison when he first arrived. He didn't even know then that it was a murder case. Still, he was going to catch a lot of shit over it. And, as Wolfe predicted, the nutcases would use his mistake to support their conspiracy theories.

The police continued questioning the waiters. None admitted serving McLean. And if any had seen who did serve him, they wouldn't admit it.

The waiter who had been chosen to serve the President had worked at the Hilton for thirty years, often was hired to help at White House state dinners, and was known and trusted by the Secret Service. No traces of poison were found in the kitchen or elsewhere in the area. Traces of white powder found in a stall in the women's restroom near the ballroom turned out to be cocaine. That, the black underpants, and the pocketknife were the only things out of the ordinary uncovered by a careful search.

"Maybe McLean wasn't poisoned at the dinner at all," Wolfe suggested. "Maybe he ate or drank something with poison in it *before* he got to the dinner, and it only took effect after he was at the headtable."

"In which case it could have been accidental," Frieze suggested. "Maybe he accidentally ingested pesticide or rat poison."

"Maybe." Jones grunted wearily. He'd been up for twenty-two hours. He scribbled a reminder in his notebook to trace McLean's activities before the dinner.

It was four A.M. Jones, Frieze, and Wolfe were out of ideas.

The Secret Service agent asked for privacy so he could phone his director for instructions. Jones and Wolfe stumbled toward the kitchen in hopes that someone had made coffee.

Frieze gave his report to Secret Service Director Colbert Clawson.

At the other end of the line, Clawson did not respond immediately. Frieze could hear his heavy breathing over the phone.

"I say we drop out of the case," Clawson spoke at last. "It's a no-win for us. If someone poisoned McLean—God knows plenty of people had reason to—or if he *accidentally* poisoned himself, it's a case for the D.C. cops. If Teddybear was the intended target, it's not going to make the Service look good to publicly acknowledge that we let someone get that close to the President. Plus, sounds to me like it's not going to be easy to find out what really happened there. You see my reasoning?"

"Sure," Frieze said. Clawson was much better than he was with the politics and the PR of these situations.

"So, unless you've got evidence that McLean's death was an assassination attempt gone awry, I'm going on CNN and announce that the Secret Service is out of it," Clawson concluded. "Got a problem with that?"

"Not really," Frieze replied. "But what if the D.C. cops find out that Teddybear *was* the target?"

"Then we jump back in, arrest the assassin, take credit, and look like heroes."

Frieze agreed to the strategy. He went in search of A. L. Jones to tell him McLean's death was his case. He found the detective in the stainless-steel hotel kitchen drinking coffee from a thick mug.

Jones was not happy to hear the news.

A.L. found himself in the middle of another case involving a whole lot of uptown big-name white dudes—more even than in that Davenport case. It was high profile. Every damn body would be looking over his shoulder, second-guessing him. The Uncles—Secret Service and FBI—the newsies, the mayor, the police brass. And McLean's network, CNN, for sure.

A.L. thought of homicide cases as jigsaw puzzles. He kept collecting pieces and moving them around, seeing what fit together with what. When he had collected most of the pieces and put them together in the right order, they made a picture and he knew who the perp was.

This was going to be one of those *big* jigsaw puzzles, one of those five-hundred-piece jobs. Maybe a thousand.

Jones decided to go home, sleep for an hour, shower, change clothes, and then return to the investigation. He dispensed instructions to his troops in an exhausted growl, got into his dirty vanilla Ford, and drove into the feeble dawn.

On the way home, Jones decided to stop at the top-floor apartment of LaTroy Williams's sister in a run-down building near Kingman Elementary School in the northeast section of the city. The detective thought LaTroy might be staying with her since their mother's killing.

He tapped softly so as not to disturb the neighbors sleeping in the other apartments. No answer. A. L. Jones thought he heard a noise inside. But it might just be a rat.

"It's Detective Jones," he whispered, tapping again. Still no answer.

If LaTroy and his sister were inside, they were afraid to open the door. And Jones couldn't blame them.

He shambled down the stairs, which stank of urine, and drove home.

CHAPTER FIVE

"COLBERT CLAWSON COULDN'T find his ass with two hands. And you just smile and let him treat you like dirt."

It was Monday morning in the private living quarters of the White House. First Lady Grady Stein Hammond was telling her husband what she thought of the Secret Service's decision to turn over Dan McLean's death to the D.C. Homicide Squad rather than investigate it as a possible assassination attempt against the President.

"Now,. Grady," Dale Hammond said soothingly, not putting down the commentary section of the *Washington Times,* the *Post*'s once-scorned conservative rival which had enjoyed a burst of popularity since the voters gave the Republicans control of the White House and Congress. "The Secret Service knows what it's doing," the President continued, pouring fresh coffee into his china cup from an ornate silver pot. "If they say Dan's death didn't have anything to do with me, well, I just have to accept their judgment."

"The hell you do!" Grady protested. "You're supposed to tell *them* what to do. They don't tell *you* what to do. You're the President. Act like it for once."

The couple was eating breakfast, reading the morning newspapers, and arguing in a bright chamber at the west end of the long central corridor which ran the length of the third floor of the White House. It was a clear spring morning. Sunlight streamed in through a great fan-shaped window.

The third and fourth floors were the Hammonds' home—"public housing," Ronald Reagan had joked—furnished with a combination of historic antiques assembled by the White House curator and their own quirky things trucked down from their former residence, the governor's mansion in Hartford.

On the two floors below were the public rooms—the State Dining Room, Blue Room, Library, etc.—open to tourists and rarely used by Dale and Grady except for formal occasions. The offices of the President and his staff were next door in the West Wing.

Traditionally, First Ladies had maintained offices and a staff in the adjacent East Wing. But Grady Hammond scorned that tradition—and most other traditions—in favor of a full-time paying job outside the White House.

And she was late for work.

"I've got to go," she exclaimed, slurping a last sip of coffee and stuffing the unread newspapers into her red leather briefcase. "I've got a second breakfast with a potential client. *Big* client."

"All right, hon, have a good day," Dale Hammond said, without looking up from the *Washington Times*. "See you tonight. Don't forget I've got that speech to the mayors group. Eight o'clock."

"Go without me, Dale," Grady replied. "I've got a West Coast trip at the end of the week and I'll be in the office late getting ready."

She rose and smoothed her suit, a bright red number with pants instead of a skirt, a man's dress shirt, and a black patterned tie. In dress, too, the First Lady was unconventional.

She bent over and kissed the President on top of his head, with considerable affection.

He absently patted her bottom.

"Talk to Clawson," Grady urged, moving toward the elevator. "Tell him you're not satisfied with his decision to drop the Secret Service investigation. Okay? You'll talk to him, right?"

"I will," the President assured her.

But Grady didn't think so.

When she launched her computer service company and leased office space in a modern building near Dulles Airport, Grady had refused any Secret Service protection. But Dale and Clawson argued so long and strenuously, and bombarded her with so many warnings of nutcases just waiting to take a shot at the President's wife, that she'd eventually relented. But she insisted on limiting her detail to only three agents—a driver and two guards—all women. And she rejected being driven in an armor-plated black Lincoln behemoth from the White House fleet. She wanted a white Mercedes.

The Detroit automakers had screamed. The Secret Service had screamed. The editorial writers and TV pundits and columnists had screamed. But she ignored the outcry, bought the car with her own money, and promised to drive herself to work if the Secret Service didn't like her choice of transportation. The Secret Service gave in.

So here she was, in the front passenger seat of the Mercedes being driven to her office.

Grady was still fuming over Clawson's decision not to investigate the death of Dan McLean as a possible attempt on Dale's life. How could Clawson be sure that Dale wasn't the target?

Even if it turned out that McLean had been the intended victim, not Dale—and Grady knew dozens of people in Washington with good reasons to bump off the nasty TV correspondent—she guessed that Clawson didn't want a Secret Service investigation that might focus attention on how lax his agents had been to let a killer get so close to the President. An investigation by the overworked and incompetent D.C. cops would move the episode onto the back burner—and off the front page.

Clawson was a Washington survivor, Grady knew. He'd held his hot-seat job since the last years of Reagan's administration, through Bush, Clinton, and now Dale. You didn't hang on that long in this league without finely honed political instincts. With Dale's public-opinion ratings dropping, Clawson must have calculated that he'd be gone at the end of his first term, so why risk tarnishing the Secret Service's reputation—and Clawson's own—by undertaking a difficult and unpromising investigation?

Grady was sure Dale wouldn't insist that Clawson determine whether the poison had been intended for the President. Dale was so accommodating. He was maddening sometimes!

Well, if Dale wouldn't take action, she would.

The First Lady removed the cellular phone from its cradle on the console, checked the number in her Filofax, and called Jerry Knight's apartment.

"I'm sorry," the desk clerk informed her, "Mr. Knight is sleeping right now."

"Well, wake him up!" the First Lady shouted. "It's the White House!"

CHAPTER SIX

"It's midnight, and ATN, the All Talk Network, presents radio's most popular all-night talkmeister, Jerry Knight, and the *Night Talker* show, live from Washington, D.C.," the announcer intoned.

"For the next five hours, sit back and listen while Jerry entertains, informs, and sometimes enrages you. Tonight, with a very special guest—the First Lady of the United States, Grady Hammond—ladies and gentlemen, here is Jerry Knight, the Night Talker!"

The theme music blared. The red ON AIR sign on the studio wall lit up. Sammy, the Vietnamese technician on the other side of the glass wall in the control room, jabbed his finger at Jerry.

Airtime! The moment Jerry Knight lived for.

"Hello! Hello, you night people, favored yet again by my presence. The world's greatest living talk-show host comes amongst you. No! Not the *world's* greatest talk-show host. The *galaxy's* greatest talk-show host! Certified and guaranteed! Ready for another night at battle stations against the forces of liberalism, political correctness, and cultural mumbo-jumbo! I'm girded—I am GIRDED—against the billowing hot air, the hypocrisy, the plain old baloney emanating from this, your nation's capital!"

The woman Secret Service agent listening to the broadcast in Grady's Mercedes, parked on M Street outside the ATN headquarters, spoke into her wrist microphone.

"What bull."

The woman agent standing guard just outside the studio door heard the comment in her earpiece, grinned, and replied into her sleeve, "That's a roger."

Jerry's tiny producer, K. T. Zorn, at her position next to the technician, rolled her eyes. She was familiar with colossal egos, having worked previously for Phil Donahue, the *Today* show, and Rush Limbaugh. But Jerry threatened to break the ego-meter for talk-show hosts.

"Tonight we are honored to have as our guest a real freedom fighter against those forces of liberalism," Jerry informed his two million listeners. "She is none other than the First Lady of these United States, Grady Hammond, the wife of President Dale Hammond, and a very outspoken and feisty and powerful voice in her own right for conservative values. Welcome, Grady."

"Jerry, you just don't get it," Grady chided from across the baize-covered table. "Why do you introduce me as 'wife of'? You wouldn't introduce Dale as 'husband of' the CEO of H-Drive Computer Services."

"See, folks, I told you she was feisty." The host laughed cluelessly.

The President's wife, dressed for the late-night interview in satiny purple-and-black jogging pants and warm-up jacket, stuck her tongue out at the host. That was one thing she liked about radio. No one could see you.

K.T. checked her phone console. All fifteen lines were already flashing and Jerry hadn't even gotten to the first commercial break. Lots of fanatical followers and fanatical detractors waiting to express their views to Jerry and the First Lady. K.T. ran her hands over her iron-gray crewcut. It was going to be another wild night.

"When you phoned me this morning, Grady—you don't mind if I call you Grady, do you?—you said you were concerned that the Secret Service isn't investigating the poisoning of Dan McLean as a possible attempt to assassinate your husband—to assassinate the President. See! I'm getting it! Tell the listeners about your concerns."

"There are a lot of angry liberals in this country, Jerry," the First Lady explained. "They've led this country in the wrong direction for a long, long time. Now they see Dale Hammond leading this country back in the right direction, toward personal responsibility, toward treating people as individuals instead of members of favored groups, toward the values that made America great. And the liberals just can't stand it! One of the things they're angriest about is that Dale opposed Clinton's decision to grant diplomatic recognition to the repressive and outlaw regime in Vietnam. Dale insisted then that Hanoi should first demonstrate it's ready to enter the family of nations by allowing its people to enjoy democratic freedoms, and by accounting for the American soldiers still missing in Vietnam. And now, with the discovery of the grave site of the American prisoners in North Vietnam, the whole world realizes that Dale was right. As you know, Jerry, some of our experts who have examined that grave site believe those prisoners died long after North Vietnam claimed it had released all the American soldiers it was holding. The liberals just can't stand that Dale was right all along and that Clinton and the whole crowd of apologists for Hanoi turned out to be wrong. Liberals get very angry when you expose their stupidities, Jerry. I think some of them are angry enough to try to get rid of Dale any way they can. I can't tell you for sure that whoever poisoned Dan McLean actually intended to kill Dale. But I believe the Secret Service ought to investigate and find out."

"Why won't they investigate?" Jerry Knight asked in a sympathetic tone. The usual barrage of sarcasm and disbelief he aimed at his guests was absent.

"Why *won't* they?" Grady repeated. "Because they're a bunch of incompetents!"

"Do you believe this?" the Secret Service agent waiting in the car radioed to her colleague.

The agent outside the studio door grunted in response.

"Look at their record," Grady continued. "They let

Kennedy bring a mobster's girlfriend—and God knows who else—into the White House. Then they let Lee Harvey Oswald assassinate Kennedy. They let incredibly unsavory people into the Nixon White House. It seems like every other week someone was taking a shot at Jerry Ford. They let a nutty kid shoot Reagan. Then they *really* got incompetent. When Clinton was president, people were crashing planes into the White House, shooting through the front fence, shooting through the back fence, climbing over the fence! I mean, these clowns are giving incompetence a bad name."

"I can see why you're upset." Jerry clucked fawningly. "Does the President agree with your complaint?"

"Jerry, why does the media make such a big deal if presidents and their wives don't agree on everything? We're two separate people. Why should we be expected to agree on everything? Do you and your wife agree on everything?"

"I've had *three* wives and I didn't agree with *any* of them on *anything,*" Jerry exclaimed.

Grady Hammond had to laugh at that, despite her intensity.

K. T. Zorn put down her omnipresent clipboard and laughed, too. She got along better with Jerry than his ex-wives or his many ex-girlfriends. Ever since he'd come on to her when she first joined the program, and she informed him that men weren't her thing, they'd gotten along fine.

"Dale Hammond is a serious, focused, and self-effacing man," Grady continued. "He's totally concentrated right now on getting this country back on the right track. He just doesn't have the time or the temperament to get involved in a mud-wrestle with a bureaucratic pigmy like the head of the Secret Service. That doesn't mean *I* don't have the time or temperament to take on Colbert Clawson."

"So what do you want done?" Jerry asked the First Lady.

"I want the Secret Service to get off its butt and find out if the poison was intended for Dale! Is that such a big deal? I'll tell you what I think. I think Colbert Clawson is afraid he won't be *able* to find out. He's ducking an investigation so he won't be publicly embarrassed."

"And if Clawson won't . . ."

"Maybe *you* ought to look into McLean's death," Grady

suggested, only half-jokingly. "You figured out who killed Curtis Davenport after he was on your show last year. You ought to be able to figure out what really happened at the correspondents dinner. You're smarter than Colbert Clawson."

K.T. held her hands up where Jerry could see them through the glass and pantomimed the motion of breaking a stick. Time for the first commercial break.

"Great show tonight, folks!" the host proclaimed. "The First Lady takes on the Secret Service! Only Jerry Knight brings you this kind of dynamite radio! We'll be back in a moment, and we'll take your phone calls for Grady Hammond!"

Sammy the technician killed the microphones and hit the button to play the recorded commercial.

In her triple-locked apartment in Adams Morgan, Jane Day sat at the chipped wooden table in her tiny kitchen, listening to Jerry Knight's interview with Grady Hammond, scribbling notes, and directing snide remarks at the radio.

Bloomsbury, her cat, sensed that his owner was not in a good mood. Assuming she was unlikely to offer him a midnight snack or even rub his head when she was in such a mood, Bloomsbury sauntered into the bedroom, hopped up on the bed, draped his paw over his eyes, and went to sleep.

Russ Williamson, the night editor at the *Post,* had phoned Jane at about ten P.M. He'd instructed her to monitor Knight's interview with the First Lady and file a story or an insert for the newspaper's late editions.

Jane despised the First Lady for her politics. But she was great copy. A public fight between the President's wife and the Secret Service would keep Jane on the front page for days. It must have been like this when Martha Mitchell made her midnight phone calls to UPI's Helen Thomas during Watergate, confiding in her Deep-South drawl John Mitchell's latest dirty trick to assure Richard Nixon's reelection.

Based on Grady's allegations on the *Night Talker* show, Jane dictated a new lead for the *Post*'s follow-up story on McLean's death. She managed to imply that there was no evidence to support *Gertrude* Hammond's charge of Secret Service foot-dragging. And she quoted an unidentified "observer" as clucking that the First Lady's performance on

Jerry Knight's show demonstrated again that she was the real power behind a weak and tottering President.

Williamson came on the line and suggested that Jane treat more seriously the First Lady's suspicions that the President may have been the target of an assassin.

"Goddamn it, Russ," Jane flared. "I don't buy it. It's just spin, trying to win sympathy for a conservative President whose ratings are in the toilet. That's what these people do best, spin. It's the *only* thing they can do."

It was too close to final deadline for Russ to continue the debate. He'd tone down Jane's skepticism in the editing.

"Hey, since you're up, why don't I stop by for a nightcap after I finish here," the editor proposed.

"Sorry, not tonight, Russ. I've got Robert Redford staying over. Maybe another time."

She hung up.

Almost instantly, she thought of calling Russ back and telling him to stop by. At least he'd be somebody to talk to. She felt restless, lonely, in the empty apartment.

No. No more married men. They never left their wives. And she always ended up feeling angry at the husbands, guilty toward the wives, and disgusted at herself.

But who else was awake at this hour for her to talk to?

Jerry Knight. She knew he was up. Jane hadn't thanked him for the roses he left the night of Dan's death. That could be the excuse to call him during the next newsbreak. Jerry had given her the private phone number in the studio, and Jane was sure K.T., the producer, would put her through.

Jane was ambivalent about Jerry.

In a town of temporizing, compromising, vacillating, and hypocritical centrists, Jerry had a loud and clear voice. He knew what he stood for, and was comfortable expounding his viewpoint. Of course, his viewpoint was 180 degrees opposite from hers. She thought he was misguided, maybe even dangerous. But what he said in public was the same as what he believed privately. Jane found that rare and refreshing among Washington's programmable mush mouths, who changed their opinions as easily as they changed their neckties.

Physically, she got no vibes from Jerry. No buzz like she felt sometimes when she spotted a cute man in a bar or on the street. And she didn't seem to turn Jerry on, either. They'd seen each other periodically for a year, and he hadn't made a serious move on her. Jane had heard plenty about Jerry's reputation, that he came on to everything in a skirt. But not her. Some leering innuendo, but no real groping. Maybe he didn't find her attractive.

Jane unconsciously rubbed the end of her nose, as if trying to reduce its size.

She decided not to phone Jerry. His newsbreak had passed. Anyhow, she needed to sort out her mixed feelings about him before taking the next step in this—this what?

Jane went into the musty bathroom and turned on hot water for a bubble bath. She left the radio in the kitchen on so she could listen to the *Night Talker* show.

K.T. had been right. Things got wild when Jerry Knight started punching up phone calls from his listeners for Grady Hammond.

"Hey, you dyke!" the very first caller shouted on the air before Sammy could hit the censor button. Jerry glanced through the glass window toward his lesbian producer to see if she was offended by the slur. She seemed oblivious.

The second caller, a woman with a deep Southern accent, suggested the First Lady was suffering from PMS.

One caller accused Grady, the President, Newt Gingrich, and all other conservatives of being heartless fat cats who were willing to allow poor children to starve to death in the streets in order to give tax cuts to the rich.

Another caller suggested that Grady used her marriage to the President to influence the award of government contracts to her computer service company.

The First Lady, relishing the verbal jousting, gave as good as she got.

"Listen, buster, maybe you don't read the papers," she retorted. "Maybe you *can't* read the papers. My company accepts *no* government contracts. Federal. State. Local. County. None. Zero. Zip. Plus, I publish my tax return every year. And my company's tax returns. I hate to bust your bubble, fella. I got where I am on my own talent, not because I'm married to Dale. I worked my way up to vice president of management information systems at Citibank before Dale even thought of running for President. I busted right through that glass ceiling on my own. So *please* don't give me that nepotism crap."

Jerry was in full cry, too, denouncing hostile callers as ultra-libs eager to redistribute *his* money and the money of middle-class working women to lazy welfare queens who had one child after another without the benefit of marriage so they could collect a monthly government check.

Finally, at the three A.M. newsbreak, in accord with the format of the *Night Talker* show, Grady left.

Jerry walked her to the elevator. Just before the doors closed, he leaned in and kissed her on the cheek. The Secret Service agent tightened her grip on the 9 mm Sig-Sauer in her open shoulder bag. She didn't draw when Jerry lunged to kiss the First Lady. But she was tempted.

The remaining two hours of the *Night Talker* show were dubbed "Talk Back, America." Just Jerry and the callers, whispering and shouting some of the weirdest and angriest exchanges on radio, in the darkness before dawn.

"Talk Back, Nutcases" was a more appropriate title, K.T. thought, as she transmitted the name and location of Jerry's callers to a computer monitor facing him in the studio.

And nuttier than usual tonight.

The two most interesting calls never got on the air.

One was from Detective A. L. Jones of the D.C. Homicide Squad. A year earlier Jones had concealed himself in the corridor outside the studio to capture the environmental guerrilla Drake Dennis after he had been tricked, live on the air, into confessing to Curtis Davenport's murder.

Now, during a commercial break, Jones was calling about Grady Hammond's comments.

"You're up early," Jerry greeted him.

"Up late, you mean," Jones corrected in his rumbling baritone. "Just picked up a drug boy near Thomas Circle killed that woman and two kids in the carjacking on Suitland Parkway. On my way home I heard Mrs. Hammond suggesting you get yourself involved in the McLean case."

"Is that your case?" Jerry asked teasingly, knowing it was

from news reports. "Great! We'll be working together again!"

"Stay out of it this time, Mr. Night Talker," Jones instructed. "You don't know what you're messing with. Leave it alone, you hear?"

"Detective Jones, you need all the help you can get. The D.C. police department couldn't find a murderer if he was riding down the middle of Pennsylvania Avenue on a camel. Oops, got to go. Commercial's almost over."

"I'm not in the mood for your 'cops ain't worth shit' jive—"

But Jerry had hung up.

The other interesting call came during the four A.M. newsbreak.

"Pick up line seven," K.T. typed on Jerry's computer screen.

"Hello!"

"You son of a bitch! I heard what you told her about me! I'm seeing my lawyer! I'm suing you for slander!"

Jerry grinned at K.T. through the glass and mouthed the words "The Bitch."

The caller was Lila, Jerry's ex-wife number three.

"Why, Lila, how nice to hear from you," Jerry crooned insincerely into the phone. "And what keeps you up so late tonight? Are you having a nice visit with Mr. Booze?"

"Shut up, you bastard! I heard you tell Grady Hammond that I'm stupid! I'm suing you for ten million dollars!"

With each sentence, Lila's voice got louder and louder. Jerry held the phone at arm's length and he could still hear her. He could picture her in their old house in Chevy Chase, spittle collecting in the corners of her mouth, spraying the phone with each word. It was a habit that had irritated him when they were married. Now he found it hilarious.

"You weren't listening carefully, Lila. I didn't say you were stupid. I said I didn't agree with you or my other wives on anything."

"You said I was stupid!" Lila insisted. "And I'm suing!"

"Okay. But before you run up a lot of legal bills, I should tell you that truth is an absolute defense against slander."

"Twenty million!"

"Good night, Lila. Sweet dreams."

"I think you're in love with her is what I think! Are you having an affair with Grady Hammond, too? It sounded like it! You sounded like you were practically doing it with her in the studio!"

"Lila, you're a disgusting drunk."

Actually, Jerry *was* half in love with Grady Hammond, he acknowledged to himself. What red-blooded conservative man wasn't?

"Got to go, Lila. Newscast's almost over."

"Yeah? Then I guess you don't have time to hear what happened to your precious son."

"Marty . . . ?"

But she was gone. And he knew she wouldn't answer the phone if he called her back.

"Marriage must be hard," K.T. messaged to his computer.

"Marriage is easy. Divorce is hard," he messaged back.

Jerry was an expert on both marriage and divorce. Lila was his third wife.

He sometimes thought he'd still be married to his first wife, Marion, if he hadn't been so young and stupid. Nobody had told him what marriage meant—the commitment, the responsibility, an ever-deepening relationship.

Jerry's relationships seemed to be best at the beginning, then steadily deteriorated until they evaporated altogether. For a long time he thought that was the normal course for men and women. Eventually, he realized from observing the lives of his friends that becoming involved with an appealing new person wasn't the first step on an inevitable path to disaffection and separation. He saw that a man and a woman could entwine their lives in a strong, growing, happy—and permanent—relationship.

It wasn't a lesson he'd learned at home. Jerry's parents married just before World War II. His father was drafted and spent four years with an artillery battery in Europe. After the war, his father stuck around just long enough to impregnate his mother. Three months after Jerry's birth, his father took off for California. Jerry and his mother were left to fend for themselves in Baltimore. She never remarried, although various "uncles" and "friends" stayed with them periodically when Jerry was growing up.

With Marion, Jerry had repeated the pattern of his parents almost exactly. Married less than a year, Jerry took off in 1968 for Vietnam as a radio correspondent for ABC. High on the excitement of war, his new celebrity, and a paycheck bigger than he'd ever dreamed of, he filed distinctive broadcast reports by day, and drank and screwed by night. When his one-year tour was up, he volunteered to stay. As many Western reporters had before him, Jerry became addicted to the seductiveness of Vietnam and its star-crossed people. An old French correspondent told him he'd come down with the *mal jaune,* the yellow sickness.

By 1970, Jerry was living at the Caravelle Hotel with Sophie, an Italian photographer for the Gamma agency. He flew home long enough to go through the mechanics of an uncontested divorce from Marion. Two months later he married Sophie during an R and R trip to Singapore. And eight months after that, she decamped for South Africa with a BBC correspondent. Jerry barely noticed. By then, he'd moved in with a Vietnamese woman who ran a floating restaurant on the Saigon River.

Jerry met Lila in the early eighties in San Diego, where he was a rising star in the conservative radio talk show world. Ronald Reagan himself appeared twice in his studio. Jerry responded to Lila's lush curves, wild white-blond hair, and movie actress past like a dog in heat. They had sex on their first date. Actually, before their first date.

They stayed together for ten miserable years. Within months of the wedding, Lila turned to vodka to blur the humiliation of her thickening body and Jerry's constant philandering. And when she came home unexpectedly and found him in bed with her best friend, she finally threw him out.

Since he turned fifty, Jerry more and more often rehashed his history with women. He wasn't proud of it. And it hadn't made him happy. What was the matter with him? He was sure his attitude toward women had something to do with his father abandoning him and his mother, and with his mother's string of boyfriends. Maybe his inability to commit to one person was inherited, something in his genes. Other times he blamed his constant pursuit of sexual conquests on a sense of entitlement. He was different, better, more famous than others. He was entitled to more women than ordinary men.

On the air, Jerry frequently scorned the claims to special entitlement by the baby-boomer generation. He was born in the earliest days of the postwar baby boom. Could his womanizing be just another exercise of yuppie privilege? No, he rejected the notion that he behaved in any way like the yuppies.

Jane Day, born in the last days of the baby boom, was Jerry's idea of a yuppie.

Why had he thought of her?

Actually, Jerry thought of Jane Day frequently. He wondered why she was one of the few women he had not tried to take to bed on their first date. Or before their first date. There was something about her that caused Jerry to treat her with respect. She wasn't that great looking. And she was a knee-jerk liberal who worked for the despised *Washington Post.* But she was smart, with an appealing touch of vulnerability. And she wasn't afraid to put him down, which was an intriguing challenge after a lifetime of adoring and witless bimbos.

Since turning fifty, Jerry acknowledged to himself that he didn't really understand women, despite having chased—and caught—hundreds of them. But Jane seemed different. He thought their slowly unfolding relationship might teach him to understand.

"Stand by, Jerry," Sammy alerted him in his earphones. "Coming out of commercial."

CHAPTER SEVEN

THE PHONE RANG just as Jane Day was leaving her apartment the morning after Grady Hammond's appearance on Jerry Knight's program. It was a producer from CNN inviting Jane to serve as a panelist on a special edition of Bernie Kalb's *Reliable Sources* show devoted to McLean's murder.

"We're calling it, 'Does the public hate the press enough to kill?' " the producer informed her. Jane stifled a giggle at the tabloid title. But she readily agreed to appear. In Washington, TV exposure translated directly into lecture fees, book contracts, and returned calls from hard-to-reach sources.

The other panelists were a columnist from *Time,* a media critic from *USA Today,* and an investigative correspondent from NBC-TV. The producer had seen Jane's byline on the *Post*'s stories about McLean's death and figured she might have some views on the subject.

She did. Jane was sure that Dan McLean had been targeted for murder because he'd stumbled onto a scandal that someone was anxious to keep off the air. McLean had been a bulldog of a reporter who made plenty of enemies with a manner that was nasty and tenacious, and eyes that glared accusingly.

Jane had admired and envied him. She was outraged by the sympathy-seeking White House effort—now led by the First Lady—to spin McLean's death into an attempt on President Hammond's life.

The first thing Jane did after accepting the invitation to appear on CNN was notify the *Post* that she couldn't cover that day's White House briefing.

The second thing she did was phone her hairdresser, Turgot, at George's in the Four Seasons Hotel. She apologized for the short notice. But this was an emergency. Her tangled orange hair, bad enough for daily appearances in the briefing room, would be a disaster on TV. Turgot understood. He received such emergency calls all the time. Few reporters, politicians, pundits, or advocates—of either gender—would appear on television without visiting their hairstylist first.

Before leaving for George's, Jane changed into The Uniform for TV: plain dark suit, silk scarf of a complementary color at the neck, unobtrusive pin on the lapel.

The cab let her out under the hotel's canopied driveway. Even without the presence of George's, the red brick hotel beguiled Jane as an oasis of calm refinement in the chaotic city. On the east edge of Georgetown, it backed up to the incongruously pastoral meadow where the C & O Canal began in Rock Creek Park. While the Four Seasons was favored by visiting show-business celebrities and big-money Wall Streeters, the hotel reminded Jane of a quiet hostelry hidden away in a London mews.

She hurried through the brick courtyard to the right of the main entrance toward the hair salon. Slender trees grew through the red paving blocks. As always, Jane couldn't resist stopping at the strange two-part Raymond Mason sculpture. She touched the cream-colored bas-relief frieze of stylized human figures affixed to the wall near George's. She followed the gaze and the pointing fingers of the figures to another three-dimensional frieze near the top of the opposite wall, at the sixth-floor level. Amid carvings of billowing clouds emerged the heads of George Washington and his horse and his revolutionary soldiers.

Jane didn't understand the sculpture, but it never failed to draw her attention whenever she visited the hair salon.

George, the Turkish immigrant owner, welcomed Jane with a kiss on both cheeks. She had been bringing her unruly locks to George at the Four Seasons—the official name spelled out in gold letters on the window—ever since she'd moved to Washington from Atlanta, where she had been a junior reporter on the *Constitution.* George's was one of the best tips she'd gotten from an older woman reporter at the *Post.*

For a while George himself did her. But when he became too busy handling richer, more famous, and more demanding customers, the owner had shunted Jane off to Turgot, recently arrived from George's hometown in Turkey.

Jane didn't mind the switch. Nobody gave blow-dry like Turgot. Besides, he liked to talk politics with her, and to whisper the latest gossip.

After the shampoo, wrapped in the black smock given to each customer—to match the black-white-and-gray decor—Jane nestled into Turgot's chair and studied herself in the tall mirror. She needed to shed the ten pounds that made her hips bulge, even under the smock. On TV, it would look like twenty pounds.

While Turgot stretched her hair and directed the hot blast of air from the nozzle of the dryer on each small cluster of strands, he asked Jane about the McLean case. She recounted her theory of the case, that McLean had been working on a big story which some Very Important Person didn't want aired.

Turgot, blow-drying the hair over her left ear, told Jane she had it all wrong.

"I don't think you have the right answer, Jane," the hairdresser whispered. "But *she* might." Turgot pointed with his blower toward a flashy blonde two chairs over with wet hair clinging to her head.

"Who is she?" Jane asked sotto voce.

"Kristi Thatcher."

"Senator Thatcher's daughter?"

"His *wife.*"

"Wife!"

In her surprise, Jane spoke louder than she intended to. The blonde glanced at her guardedly.

Norton Thatcher was in his mid-sixties, Jane guessed. The

blonde was probably in her thirties and looked even younger with her hair plastered down.

"Why would she know the answer to Dan's murder?" Jane asked Turgot, lowering her voice.

"Mrs. Senator was a *very* good friend of Dan McLean," the hairdresser confided. "But you already knew this, of course."

Jane smiled and assured Turgot that, of course, *everyone* knew the senator's wife was carrying on with the CNN correspondent. It was the way Turgot salved his conscience. He could pretend he had not violated a customer's confidences because Jane already knew about Dan McLean and Kristi Thatcher.

Jane closed her eyes and tried to picture the two together. The tall, dark, and satanic McLean and the compact, golden-haired Kristi Thatcher. Having an affair. Cheating on their spouses.

People thought Washington was such a proper town, everyone working long hours, doing the peoples' business, too busy for sex, workaholics gone amok. And that was true. Then, periodically, Jane stumbled onto the Illicit Affair. She wondered how people found the time.

"How long were Dan and Mrs. Thatcher"—she groped for the right words—"*very* good friends?" Jane asked the hairdresser softly. She had the uncomfortable feeling that Mrs. Thatcher was reading her lips.

"More than a year. I remember because she wore her hair longer then."

Turgot finished Jane's styling by pushing her head down over her lap and blowing her temporarily straight hair forward over her face. He liked that part, his fancy clients made to bow before the greatness of his hair-blowing.

"Did Dan's wife know?" Jane asked.

"No."

"How can you be sure?"

"I know."

Turgot yanked Jane's head up and blew back the hair near her temple. The orange frizzes now looked calm and immaculate, laying down neatly one on top of the other.

Jane looked in the mirror and sighed. If the fates had given her straight hair instead of curls, she could have gone into television and become rich and famous. Of course, other customers at George's were paying to have their naturally straight hair made curly with permanents. Well, if the fates had given women the hair they wanted, people like George and Turgot would still be back in Turkey.

"How you like?" Turgot asked, swiveling Jane's chair around and showing her the back of her head with a handheld mirror.

"Great," said Jane. But not for long.

"How can you be so sure Dan McLean's wife didn't know about his affair?" Jane persisted.

Turgot smiled enigmatically and put one finger to his lips. With the blower turned off, their voices carried in the salon.

Wait a minute. Jane got it.

"You do Patricia McLean, too, don't you?"

The hairdresser's black eyes twinkled. "All the beautiful women come to Turgot."

He handed Jane a receipt to take to the cashier at the front desk and kissed her on both cheeks.

Jane allowed the gray-uniformed Four Seasons doorman to usher her into a taxi. She directed the driver to the CNN studios behind Union Station for the taping.

Could her theory that Dan McLean was poisoned to stop him from exposing someone's dirty little secret be wrong? Jane pondered as the cab headed east, past the ever-changing string of trendy restaurants lining Pennsylvania Avenue in the West End. Could his death have had something to do with his own dirty little secret?

A jealous husband?

A jealous United States Senator?

Wait a minute. She was getting way ahead of herself. She didn't know for sure that Dan McLean and Kristi Thatcher *were* a dirty little secret.

Jane dug her cellular phone out of her oversized tapestry shoulder bag. She called Jessie Bell, the *Post*'s gossip columnist. Jessie was in. Her nightly crawl through the capital's receptions, dinners, openings, and assorted soirees wouldn't begin for hours.

"Jessie, I need to check a tip with you," Jane explained.

"Glad to help you, if I can," the gossip columnist replied. "It's so terrific to see a woman promoted to the White House beat."

"I'm looking into Dan McLean's murder," Jane announced. She glanced at the driver. No need to be discreet, she decided. Ninety percent of them didn't speak English well enough to understand street directions. So he wasn't likely to understand illicit Washington social relationships.

"Somebody just told me Dan was carrying on with the wife of Norton Thatcher," Jane spoke into her phone. "Is that true?"

Jessie laughed wickedly. "Where have you been, dearie?" the gossip columnist asked with mock astonishment. "In Mongolia? *Everybody* knows they were an item."

"Well, *I* didn't know," Jane said. "I never saw anything in print about it."

"Of course not. He was a TV correspondent, not a politician. We protect our own, don't we? You know the rules."

"I didn't know there were any rules for reporting gossip," Jane said, wondering whether Jessie was putting her on.

"Oh, sure," the columnist teased. " 'The Official Rules For Reporting Gossip, Sex, and Sleaze.' I'll send you a copy."

Now Jane knew Jessie was putting her on.

"The rules are we never report on anyone's sex life unless it affects his or her official duties, unless we have clear photos, or unless the man is a Republican."

The columnist cackled at her own bon mot.

"Seriously, Jessie, were they having an affair?" Jane asked.

"Seriously, I never saw them in bed together. But sources I trust tell me they were, for about a year and a half."

Jane didn't reply, pondering the implications for her quest for Dan McLean's poisoner.

"Thanks, Jessie, for the confirmation," she said after a moment.

"Don't sound so shocked, dearie. Welcome to the big, wicked city. People fuck people they're not married to. It happens. It keeps me in business."

"I know."

Jane pushed the END button and folded up her phone.

The taxi slammed into a particularly large pothole, nearly throwing her off the seat.

After the CNN taping, Jane decided, she'd pay the widow McLean a visit.

CHAPTER EIGHT

PATRICIA MCLEAN LIVED in Spring Valley, an affluent but not ostentatious neighborhood of eclectic homes bordering Massachusetts Avenue just before it crossed into Maryland.

After the CNN program, Jane had phoned the *Post* library for information about Pat McLean. *Doctor* Patricia Ferris McLean. In the cab, the reporter reviewed what the librarian had found.

Pat McLean was born in Rochester, New York. Forty-five years old. Daughter of a Kodak executive. Undergraduate degree from Columbia. Masters in social work from Penn. Peace Corps volunteer in Africa. Medical school at Georgetown. Specialty in tropical medicine. Worked for the CDC in Atlanta, where she apparently met McLean when he came to interview her about the Ebola virus. When CNN transferred him to Washington, she followed. Got a job as a lecturer at the Georgetown Medical School. A Nexis search showed she was interviewed occasionally as an expert on diseases of the Third World. Once she wrote a study for the National Institutes of Health on the geographic evolution of AIDS. She and Dan had two children, a boy and girl, both teenagers.

The only quirky item in the otherwise unexceptional file was a clipping from a *Washingtonian* magazine gossip column in the early 1990s reporting that Patricia and Dan McLean had engaged in a loud argument in the Palm Restaurant, but denied reports they were separating.

The cab driver followed Jane's directions to the McLean house. Out Mass Avenue, past the National Cathedral, around the circle at American University, left at Sutton Place Gourmet. Right at the first street. Then left. Third house on the right, a brick home painted white, with a basketball backboard in the driveway and a seasonal flag fluttering on a pole beside the front door.

Jane could never figure out what such flags were for. The one at the McLean house was emblazoned with an Easter bunny and some carrots. A block away Jane had seen one bearing a birthday cake and candles symbol. She'd seen others featuring a giant pineapple motif, an iris flower, and a multicolored squash. Jane wondered if there was a hidden meaning to these decorative flags. Perhaps they were some secret suburban code. Definitely a suburban thing.

Patricia McLean answered the door. Her eyes were red. But her posture was erect, as if she had been practicing a brave demeanor.

Jane introduced herself and watched Patricia McLean sag. Clearly she was not in the mood for an unannounced visit from a reporter. But manners prevailed. She invited Jane in.

"I don't know what more I can tell you," said Pat McLean, her arms folded protectively across her chest. She stood facing Jane in the spacious foyer. She didn't offer the reporter a seat. "I've talked to so many reporters already. And to the police. What is it you want to know?"

Jane studied Dan McLean's widow. She was very thin, almost birdlike. She wore a plain dark skirt, a muted flower-patterned blouse, and an unbuttoned cardigan sweater. Her hair was dark auburn, pulled back tightly and knotted in a bun. Her brilliant blue eyes were beautiful, but rimmed in dark and puffy circles. The look in her eyes was guarded and a little frightened.

She looked like a dowdy professor. She did not look anything like the dazzling Kristi Thatcher.

"I'm sorry to intrude like this, Mrs. McLean," Jane apologized. "I'm here more as an admiring colleague of your husband than as a reporter. Dan was a hell of a correspondent. I was a great fan of his ability to expose wrongdoing by government officials and business executives. I have to believe he was on to a big story and somebody wanted"—how did she say it without being insensitive?—"somebody wanted to stop him from broadcasting it."

Pat McLean stared at Jane, unblinking, with her bright blue eyes.

"I don't buy Grady Hammond's story that Dan was just an innocent victim of an attempt on the President's life," Jane continued. "Whoever killed Dan *meant* to kill Dan. I came here to find out if you know what Dan was working on. It might point toward whoever wanted to stop your husband from blowing the whistle on some scandal."

"I know who you are now." Pat McLean smiled for the first time. "You're the *Post* reporter who helped catch the man who killed Curtis Davenport, aren't you?"

"I am," Jane acknowledged.

"And now you think you can catch the person who poisoned Dan?"

"I'm trying."

Pat McLean smiled more broadly. When she smiled, she was not dowdy, Jane noted. A handsome woman. Jane could see why Dan had been attracted. Definitely not dowdy, but even smiling, Pat McLean was no Kristi Thatcher.

"Come in." The widow steered Jane out of the foyer toward the kitchen at the back of the house. "Would you like something to drink?"

The kitchen had a sleek, modern look, with a black-and-white tiled floor, green granite countertops, and the high-gloss white cabinets Jane admired when she saw them in magazines. One of these days she'd graduate from her minuscule scruffy apartment to a real house like this. She hoped.

Patricia McLean opened the refrigerator and leaned in. "Is ice tea all right?"

"Great."

The widow brought a frosty pitcher and two green-tinted glasses to the kitchen table. The glass-topped table, decorated with black-and-white cloth placemats and matching napkins, overlooked a deep garden. Jane never would have guessed that such a large sanctuary of flowers and shrubs was hidden behind the unassuming brick colonial house.

Jane sampled the ice tea. It had a pleasant, herbal taste.

"I appreciate your efforts," Pat McLean told her. "I don't have a lot of faith in the Metropolitan Police. Oh, I hope that didn't sound racist. . . ."

"I know exactly what you mean." Jane waved off her concern. "Without help, they never would have caught the man who killed Curtis, either. And it's especially important to find out who poisoned Dan. I mean, if it looks like you can get away with killing a reporter to stop him from broadcasting some embarrassing story, it'll be open season on reporters. None of us will be safe."

"You remind me a little of Dan." Patricia smiled. "So determined. So outraged by wrongdoing. So sure you've been anointed to expose the evils of the world."

Jane sipped her ice tea modestly and didn't reply. Was there an edge of mockery in Mrs. McLean's remark? If so, was she mocking Dan? Or Jane? Or both?

Jane found that people trained in the precision of the sciences often disdained the undisciplined ways of reporters.

Jane wondered if Pat McLean knew her husband had been fooling around with a senator's wife.

Jane prided herself on being an aggressive reporter. But she couldn't bring herself to ask the question of this grieving widow, sitting at her own kitchen table, extending her hospitality to a virtual stranger.

Jane knew that other reporters would ask the question without qualms if they thought Dan's affair might have something to do with his murder. In similar circumstances, Dan himself would have asked, and gleefully. A colleague of Jane's at the *Post* once asked Gary Hart at a news conference during the New Hampshire primary campaign whether he'd ever cheated on his wife. That episode just about eliminated any boundaries on prying into the private lives of public figures.

But Jane didn't have the stomach for it. She wondered whether she possessed a sufficient amount of the killer instinct to succeed as a reporter.

A fluffy white dog bounded into the kitchen. He sniffed Jane's shoes, his stumpy tail wagging a fast metronome beat.

"He must smell my cat on me," Jane said, running her fingers through the dog's silky coat. "What kind of dog is he?"

"A West Highland Terrier," Patricia McLean explained. "His name's Scoop. He misses Dan terribly. And he misses the children."

The dog bounded into Patricia's lap and nuzzled his head under her sweater.

"How are the children taking Dan's death?" Jane asked.

"As well as can be expected," the widow replied. "They went to stay with their grandparents after the funeral. But I miss them. The house is so quiet without them. Scoop is my only company. You know, when you're not a couple anymore, your friends stop . . ."

She didn't finish the thought.

"Mrs. McLean . . ."

"You call me Pat. I'll call you Jane. Okay?"

"Okay," Jane agreed. "Pat, did Dan have an office at home? Where he might have kept files or notebooks from the stories he was working on?"

"He has—had—an office upstairs. It's got a file cabinet. But I have no idea what's in it. Dan didn't talk to me much about his work. He didn't include me."

Another ironic put-down of Dan by his widow? Jane wondered.

"Why do you ask about his files?" Patricia asked. "Do you think there's something in there that might help you find out who poisoned Dan?"

"Maybe."

And maybe it's a threatening note from a jealous United States Senator, Jane added to herself.

"Well, then, let's go look," Pat McLean invited.

The second-floor office was bathed in sunshine, flooding in through wall-to-wall windows and skylights. The room, which looked out on the rear garden, obviously had been added later to the original boxy house.

In contrast to the nearly antiseptic tidiness of the rest of the house, Dan's office was a mess. The sunlight illuminated books stacked six high on every flat surface, file folders spilling off the desk onto the floor, unopened mail piled up in a wire basket. Yellow lined pads, filled with Dan's tiny script, were scattered around. Yellowing newspapers littered the floor.

A tattered cushion, apparently Scoop's bed, was stuffed under the desk.

"Dan wasn't terribly neat," Patricia apologized. "I wouldn't know where to start looking for his notes on the story he was working on when he died."

Jane eyed the three-drawer file cabinet.

"The file cabinet would be the obvious place to keep files," Jane suggested.

The widow tried the top drawer. Locked. The chrome locking button was pushed in and no key was in the key slot.

"I don't know where Dan kept the key."

"A lot of people keep the key to their file cabinet in the top desk drawer," Jane pressed. "I do."

Looking uncertain, Patricia McLean slid open the top drawer of the desk. Jane peered over her shoulder. Inside was a bigger jumble than on top of the desk. The widow rummaged through the papers. No key.

"Try the side drawers," Jane urged.

One by one the widow opened the side drawers. All messy. But no key. Wait. In the bottom drawer, under a bunch of chewed-up dog toys, something glinted.

"That looks like a key," Jane said, pointing.

Patricia took the key to the file cabinet, put it in the lock, and turned. It opened.

Jane felt a rush of adrenaline. She moved toward the files.

"I don't know . . ." the widow frowned uncertainly.

"Pat, somewhere in Dan's notes there may be a clue that will lead to the person who poisoned him," Jane cajoled. "My reporter's instinct tells me Dan was killed to keep him from breaking a big story. What that story was and who didn't want it broadcast could be somewhere in his notebooks. I want to find out who killed him."

The widow looked torn, wary but not wanting to appear inhospitable or suspicious.

"Dan was a great investigative reporter." Jane delivered

her clincher. "He was my idol. This is something he would have done."

"I think you're right about that." Patricia McLean smiled, again, it seemed, with a touch of sarcasm. "All right, see what you can find."

She was *not* taking advantage of an unsophisticated woman, Jane insisted to herself.

Patricia McLean cleared a place to sit, picked a book from one of the piles, and sat down to read while Jane poked through the dead correspondent's files.

Dan McLean would be doing exactly the same thing if he were investigating a murder, Jane reassured herself.

She pulled out the top file drawer. What she found inside was not what she'd expected. Dan McLean apparently was writing an autobiography. The drawer was filled with file folders, each containing a chapter of his life. "Chapter Four: Covering the War." "Chapter Eight: Ted Turner Discovers Me." "Chapter Ten: Love & Marriage." "Chapter Fourteen: The Faxgate Story."

Not unusual, Jane thought. Lots of people in Washington assumed their lives were suitable for framing. And books about celebrities, especially TV celebrities, were big sellers.

The middle drawer was for routine household documents. The mortgage. College brochures. Receipts. Tax returns. Warranties. Jane sneaked a look at the tax returns. Jesus! No wonder every reporter yearned to be on television.

"Find anything?" Patricia inquired.

"Not yet," Jane replied.

Most of the bottom drawer was filled with Dan's scripts and clippings, going all the way back to faded copies of his first stories as a green wire service reporter in Vietnam. An entire career, and it didn't even fill one file drawer. Jane shivered involuntarily.

In the back of the bottom drawer, concealed under a CNN sweatshirt, was what Jane was looking for. Five reporter's notebooks, long and narrow to fit in a man's suit pocket or a woman's purse.

Jane's heart raced. She felt like she did as a kid one summer at camp when she found the treasure in a treasure hunt. The treasure wasn't much, a plastic bag of assorted miniature candy bars. But she'd found it before any of the other kids. She felt equally giddy now.

"I think I may have found Dan's notes on the story he was working on," Jane informed the widow.

Patricia looked up momentarily, then returned to her reading.

Jane took the notebooks to the desk, sat down, and opened the first one.

Her euphoria faded. Dan McLean's handwriting was so crimped and his notes so cryptic that Jane could not decipher them. Like most journalists, Dan had developed a private shorthand, symbols and abbreviations that only he could translate.

In a couple of places Jane could make out the capital letters HA. Could that stand for Hammond Administration? Heart Attack? Or maybe somebody's initials. But whose?

There were dollar signs and plus marks and a lot of references to VN. Jane assumed that stood for Vietnam. But she had no idea who or what the letter G signified. And there were a lot of Gs in the notebooks. Grady Hammond? Garvin Dillon, the White House press secretary? Newt Gingrich? Germany? She couldn't even guess.

She kept reading, hoping to recognize a clue. But each notebook seemed more indecipherable than the one before.

She wondered if Jerry Knight could be of help. He had been a reporter in the Vietnam War. He might be able to connect the references to VN with some of the other mysterious notes. No. She wasn't going to give him the opportunity to tease her about being too young to remember the war. Or to berate her parents for demonstrating against the war.

Besides, if there was a big story in these notebooks, she wanted to keep it for herself.

Jane focused on Dan's tiny writing and enigmatic code, trying to tease out the meaning. CC? Could that be Chuck Colson from Nixon's Watergate dirty-tricks gang? Nixon, of course, sent American boys to die in Vietnam for six years after he promised to end the war. Or maybe it was Colbert Clawson, the head of the Secret Service. Or maybe . . .

After going through all five notebooks, Jane was still unable to extract from Dan's encoded jottings and puzzling abbreviations any comprehension of the story he was investigating.

"Well?" Patricia McLean said.

"I'm afraid I can't translate his notes," Jane conceded. She sounded disappointed.

"I'm so sorry," the widow commiserated, rising.

"Pat, would it be presumptuous to ask you to let me take Dan's notebooks with me? I'd like to show them to some other people who might be able to decipher them."

Maybe she was aggressive enough to be a good reporter after all, Jane thought.

"Oh, dear," the widow replied. "I . . . I don't think so. I'd rather you didn't."

"I understand," Jane mumbled, hurriedly returning the notebooks to their hiding place in the back of the bottom file drawer.

The two women said good-bye stiffly in the foyer, promising to call each other if they discovered anything that might shed light on Dan McLean's murder.

CHAPTER NINE

WALKING THROUGH THE quiet Spring Valley neighborhood toward Massachusetts Avenue where she hoped to find a taxi, Jane was so lost in speculation about Dan's notebooks that she didn't notice the dirty white car pull to the curb next to her.

"Hey, Miss *Washington Post,"* the driver called out.

It was Detective A. L. Jones.

She opened the car door, shoved an empty root-beer can and crumpled donut wrappers onto the floor, and got in.

"Detective Jones," she greeted him blandly. He looked pugnacious and tired, as usual.

"You making a condolence call?" he asked, not showing any surprise at finding her a half block from Dan McLean's house.

"Something like that. And you? Are you going to question Patricia McLean about Dan's murder? Or are you bringing her some news about the case?"

"You're pretty nosy, aren't you?" the stumpy detective grunted.

"That's what I get paid for," she shot back.

A.L. moved his gun holster around to his hip from where the car seat was pressing it into his back.

Jane wondered whether he did it to impress her.

"I get paid to close cases," the detective growled, "not to mouth off to newsies."

"So, when are you going to close the McLean case?" she asked with mock guilelessness.

"I'm working on it," he responded defensively.

"Me, too," she said.

"What were you *really* doing at McLean's house?" he demanded. "You weren't making no condolence call."

Jane debated how much to tell him. Jones had really been responsible for unmasking Curtis Davenport's killer a year before, although she and Jerry Knight had helped. Thanks to A.L., she'd gotten a break on the biggest story of her life. Maybe they should team up again. A police detective could question suspects and test evidence in ways a reporter couldn't.

Okay, she'd give him a little bit of information and in return hoped to get a lot more information from him.

"Pat McLean let me look at the notes Dan made on the story he was pursuing when he was killed," Jane explained. "I think he was poisoned to prevent him from breaking a big scandal. If so, there might be a clue in his notebooks."

Jones looked interested. He rubbed his gray stubble with a beefy paw. "What did you find?"

"I found five notebooks in the bottom of a file cabinet in Dan's office."

"And?"

"I couldn't make them out."

"What do you mean you couldn't make them out?"

"Dan wrote in some kind of personal code. A lot of initials. A lot of abbreviations. I couldn't decipher them."

"Damn."

"That's my reaction, too," Jane agreed.

The detective picked at his gray mustache.

"What kind of initials you talking about?" he asked.

"G. CC. HA. VN. I think VN could stand for Vietnam. Dan might have been working on a story about Vietnam."

A memory of Vietnam floated into the detective's mind. He

was tramping along a muddy road with his platoon. Sprawled in the road was a black bicycle and a dead girl, maybe seven years old, in a thin cotton dress darkened with blood from the sniper's bullet that had passed through her chest. Black flies swarmed in and out of her mouth and eye sockets.

Jones shook off the memory. These flashbacks of the war were coming more and more frequently.

Jane noticed his distant expression, but didn't understand what caused it.

"Even if you could make out what McLean wrote in his notebooks, Miss Lady Reporter, what makes you think they have anything to do with his murder?"

"I don't know for sure, Mr. Detective," she answered. "But reporters have to trust their instincts. And my instincts tell me that in these books are Dan's notes about somebody who did something he shouldn't have done. And that somebody could have killed Dan to keep him from revealing it on TV."

"Lot of ifs and coulds."

"I know."

"You can't even read the damn notes."

"I know."

It would be so much easier to be chasing some drug boy over on Minnesota Avenue than to be trying to fit these puzzle pieces together, the detective thought.

"Suppose I told you there might be another motive," A.L. volunteered.

"Like what?"

"Like jealousy."

"You mean Dan's affair with Kristi Thatcher?" Jane replied smugly, to show the detective she knew more than he did. Or at least as much as he did. "I don't believe a United States Senator would knock off a television correspondent who was fooling around with his wife."

"Maybe it wasn't Thatcher," Jones rumbled. "Maybe it was another husband didn't like his wife sleeping with McLean."

Jane's smugness evaporated. "There were others?"

"Oh, yeah. Mr. Dan McLean was one busy dude with the ladies."

It wasn't fair, Jane thought. Married people having sex like rabbits. She was single and had maybe one date a month. If she was lucky. Not counting Jerry Knight, of course.

"People don't really kill each other anymore over affairs, do they, Detective Jones?" Jane asked. "Isn't that rather old-fashioned?"

"When I first started as a cop, it was one of the main reasons people killed each other. Wives busting cheating husbands. Husbands busting cheating wives. Girls cutting men done them wrong. Now, people busting people for looking at them wrong or playing the wrong music. Or for no reason at all. But sex still gets into it. You hear of Lorena Bobbitt?"

"Come on, Detective. This is Washington, D.C. All people here care about is politics."

"Politicians still got feelings," A.L. replied.

"Hmmm, I'm not sure about that." Jane laughed. "So, I can write that you're investigating a sex motive for Dan's murder?"

"No, you can't," Jones barked. "Don't quote me saying nothing."

"You're *not* investigating a sex motive?"

"I'm investigating everything," A.L. growled.

"Including Dan's notebooks?"

"If you don't know what they say, I can't investigate 'em," Jones responded with exasperation. "What am I supposed to investigate? A bunch of 'G's? A bunch of 'VN's?"

He was right about that, Jane acknowledged. "Are you going to talk to Mrs. McLean?" she asked.

"Yep."

"Will you tell me what you find out?" Jane asked.

"Nope."

"Why?"

"You'll put it in the newspaper."

She couldn't argue with that.

"Why do you hate reporters? Or is it just me?"

"Because they put what you tell 'em in the newspaper."

There seemed to be a pattern to his thinking.

"Want to make the same deal we had on the Davenport case?" she offered, opening the car door. "I'll tell you what I find out if you tell me what you find out."

"What have you found out?"
"Not much."
"Come see me when you find out something."
Well, he didn't say no, she thought hopefully.
Jane walked four blocks to Massachusetts Avenue and hailed a cab to take her back downtown. Russ would chew her out for being out of touch for so long.

CHAPTER TEN

Colbert Clawson, director of the Secret Service, presided over a meeting on Dan McLean's murder from the head of a walnut conference table in a meeting room on the eighth floor of an office building at 18th and G, the Secret Service headquarters. Around the table sat a dozen men and women involved in the case, including A. L. Jones of the D.C. Homicide Squad, who was nominally in charge of the investigation, Lawrence Frieze of the Secret Service's White House protective detail, Clifford Wolfe of the FBI, White House Press Secretary Garvin Dillon as the personal representative of President and Mrs. Hammond, and assorted technical experts and assistants.

Clawson was a lanky man in his middle sixties, with pale, unhealthy-looking skin and flaccid black hair. In dress, he was conservative and predictable, alternating between a black suit with white shirt and gray tie, and a gray suit with white shirt and black tie. For this meeting, he wore a black suit.

Grady Hammond's appearance on the *Night Talker* show had set off such a furor that Clawson had been forced to call a press conference to claim the news media had misinterpreted his remarks about not investigating the incident at the correspondents dinner.

Of course, he told the press conference the Secret Service intended to give its full support to the D.C. police, the FBI, and other law-enforcement agencies to catch McLean's murderer. However, since there was no evidence of an attempt on President Hammond's life, the Secret Service, by law, could not take over the case. But the agency would certainly be an active participant in the investigation, Clawson assured the press, and would be looking carefully for any sign that the President had been the intended target.

His double-talk had defused the furor. But Clawson knew he'd blotted his record. He'd have to keep his head down and avoid any more negative publicity. Otherwise, under Washington's hardball rules, he'd be asked to take early retirement from the job he loved, or worse, be shuttled to some boring and invisible job in the bureaucracy. No government official ever survived the enmity of a First Lady. Nancy Reagan had taken out Clawson's own boss, Don Regan. Grady Hammond obviously had assigned her friend Garvin Dillon to keep an eye on Clawson. He couldn't afford another slip.

So he scheduled the coordinating meeting to give the impression that he was vigilantly pursuing every clue that might suggest there had been a plot to kill the President.

In fact, the investigation was going nowhere. No progress had been made in finding who had poisoned McLean's food, much less whether the poison had been intended for Hammond. Clawson congratulated himself on his wisdom in ducking jurisdiction.

"I'm happy to report that press coverage of the case seems to be diminishing," Clawson announced, opening the meeting. "Detective Jones, why don't you begin by bringing us up to date on your investigation."

It was eight A.M., not the best time of day for A.L. He'd been up until almost dawn trying to catch a drug boy who'd busted a fifteen-year-old crack-addicted girl and dumped her nude body behind a carry-out on Benning Road. The detective had staked out the house of the boy's girlfriend off North Capitol Street near Children's Hospital. But the guy never showed.

A.L. had gotten two hours sleep before his clock radio

woke him with a silky, soulful Barry White ballad on WKYS. For the meeting, he put on his one good suit, a subtle blue plaid number he'd picked up on sale at Joseph A. Banks.

On the table in front of him sat a cup of weak, lukewarm coffee. The china cup and saucer were embossed with the Secret Service seal. A.L. wished it were a large cardboard container of steaming coffee from Dunkin Donuts.

"Not too much to report," Jones declared in a deep rumble. "We're reinterviewing all the waiters and waitresses, kitchen help, other hotel people who were working that night. So far, they're all coming up clean. We're working with Immigration and Naturalization"—he nodded down the table toward a stern-faced woman representing that agency—"on the two waiters carrying the fake green cards. Nothing to report yet. Rechecking the hotel kitchen for any sign of poison. Nothing there, either. I went to McLean's house yesterday and interviewed the widow again. She didn't give me anything new." A.L. flipped through his bent notebook. "And that's about all I've got."

Jones didn't like these meetings. Too many people worried about what the media was going to say about them. He sensed all kinds of political cross-currents he didn't even understand. He wasn't comfortable in a group like this. A.L. liked to work alone. He wasn't about to tell everything he knew to a bunch of uptight white dudes he didn't know or trust. That's why he didn't mention McLean's active sex life. Or the dead man's indecipherable notebooks.

"Dr. Wu, William Wu, of the D.C. Medical Examiners Office will report now," Clawson announced, "on the cause of McLean's death. I know you're busy, Doctor. Sorry to take you away from your work so early in the morning."

"No problem," the little Chinese morgue doctor replied in a high-pitched voice. "My patients aren't going anywhere. They'll be waiting for me when I get back."

He laughed maniacally.

"Your report?" Clawson prompted.

Wu consulted his papers. "McLean died from asphyxiation. He couldn't breathe. Stomach contents indicate he ingested a poison which paralyzed his breathing."

"What poison?" the FBI's Wolfe asked.

"I won't be able to identify the poison until the toxicology tests come back," the autopsy doctor explained. "It wasn't a common variety, cyanide, arsenic, strychnine, anything like that. You can't buy it over the counter at CVS."

Again, the high-pitched hysterical laugh.

"When do you expect the toxicology report?" Clawson asked.

"Ten days. Maybe two weeks."

The Secret Service director looked pained.

"It's a long time, I know," Wu said. "The lab's busy. Lot of death going around these days."

The medical examiner once more cackled crazily.

"Anything else?" Clawson asked.

"Nothing."

"The final item on today's agenda is a report from Lawrence Frieze of my staff on the Secret Service investigation of recent threats against the President. Larry?"

"In the thirty days preceding the incident at the dinner," Frieze intoned, "the Secret Service received twenty-seven threats against the President and/or Mrs. Hammond which were judged credible enough to warrant further investigation by the Service, the FBI, or local law enforcement. As a result of those investigations, two individuals were placed under surveillance."

Colbert sneaked a glance at Garvin Dillon. The press secretary had his elbows on the walnut table, his chin resting on his hands, his eyes staring steadily at Frieze. His face was blank. Would he report back to the President and First Lady that the Secret Service had been vigilant? Or sloppy? Colbert couldn't tell.

"Following the incident at the dinner," Frieze continued his report, "the Secret Service, with participation by the FBI, revisited the sources of those twenty-seven threats and has concluded that none was involved in the poisoning of Dan McLean."

"Well, just to keep the record straight on that," Clifford Wolfe interrupted, "the FBI provided investigative assistance at the request of the Secret Service. But the Bureau did not take part in the screening of the original threats, nor did we participate in the decision on which threats warranted follow-up, either before or after McLean's death."

So the game was CYA, Colbert noted. Cover Your Ass, a tradition among survival-oriented Washington bureaucrats. With the investigation getting nowhere and an angry First Lady raising hell on the radio, the participants were primarily concerned with making sure they and their agencies didn't get blamed for screwing up.

Colbert stole another glance at Dillon. His expression still told nothing about what he was thinking.

"Continue, Larry," Colbert commanded.

"Since the White House went on the Internet during the Clinton administration, a fairly steady stream of abusive and threatening messages have arrived in that manner, almost always anonymous and very difficult to trace," Frieze explained. "After the McLean episode, and to be sure his death had nothing to do with the President, we reviewed the file of hostile Internet messages received by the White House in the preceding sixty-day period."

"What do you mean 'very difficult to trace'?" A. L. Jones asked. He was way out of his depth with this computer shit. He had a computer on his desk at Homicide headquarters for storing files and writing reports. Sometimes it worked. Sometimes it didn't. Usually he wrote his reports on a beat-up typewriter.

"Ned?" Frieze nodded at a Secret Service computer expert.

"It's not unusual for people to use untraceable pseudonyms on the Internet and other on-line services," the expert advised the group. "The simplest way is to sign up for the service under a fake name. A more sophisticated method is to use a remailer. You send your message down the line to the remailer and the remailer sends it on to its destination. The recipient can't trace it back to the original sender. There are dozens of remailers on the Internet, some of them in foreign countries. And, of course, the hackers are constantly devising more elaborate methods to hide their identities."

A.L. nodded as if he understood the explanation. He didn't.

"Anyhow . . ." Garvin Dillon prodded.

"Anyhow," Frieze resumed, "by putting some heat on the remailers and by using some advanced software of our own, we've tracked down the sources of almost all the threatening Internet messages. Most of them turned out to be harmless hackers. A lot were teenagers. We asked local law-enforcement agencies to keep an eye on"—he checked his notes—"three of the senders."

"You tracked down 'almost all' the threats?" Garvin Dillon cut in.

"All but one," Frieze acknowledged.

"And that one was . . . ?" the press secretary pressed.

"Ten days before the McLean episode, a message arrived at the White House's Internet address from a group which signed itself 'The Survivors of Cam Hoa.' The message was rambling and made no specific threat against the President. But it demanded that he break off diplomatic relations with Vietnam because of the discovery of the grave of American prisoners. The group must know a lot about computers, because we've been unable to trace the sender."

"And who are 'The Survivors of Cam Hoa'?" Dillon asked.

"We have no such group in our files, nor does the FBI," Frieze answered. "Our friends at Langley"—he dipped his head toward the representative of the CIA—"have some sketchy information about an organization with that name, suggesting it might be a small group of former Green Berets."

"But," the CIA man interrupted, "that information comes from a source whose credibility we rate as Category B-3, 'unverified.' "

More CYA, Colbert noted.

The room was silent.

"Anybody else have anything to contribute?"

No one spoke.

"All right, then," the Secret Service director concluded, "I'd say the number-one priority right now is to locate 'The Survivors of Cam Hoa' and find out whether they had anything to do with McLean's death. And, if so, whether they were really aiming at the President. Agreed?"

Still no one spoke.

"Good. Let's pencil in another meeting for the day after tomorrow. Same time, same place. Sooner, of course, if anyone comes up with anything."

Colbert checked Garvin Dillon's reaction. Nothing.

A. L. Jones looked at his watch. He calculated how quickly he could drive to the nearest place to buy coffee.

CHAPTER ELEVEN

THE NEAREST COFFEE was two blocks north, across Pennsylvania, at a Starbucks.

A.L. had never been in a Starbucks. Seemed like a white yuppie thing to him. But he was desperate for coffee. Might as well try something new. He parked the white Ford in a loading zone.

The pretty young black woman behind the counter gave him a dazzling smile. A.L. noticed her hair was in fat braids, African style.

"May I help you?"

"Coffee," he growled.

"Grande?"

"No, coffee."

"Yes, sir, small or large?"

"Large."

"One grande. Latté? Espresso? Cappuccino?"

"I just want some coffee."

He should have tried to find a Dunkin' Donuts, Jones fumed. At least a 7-Eleven.

"You want the coffee of the day?" the young woman asked.

"Yeah."

"Our coffee today is Chocolate Amaretto."

"Sounds great. Let me have one."

"For here or to go?"

"To go."

He sure had to answer a lot of questions to get one cup of coffee.

Finally the woman behind the counter handed him a waxy cardboard container with a plastic dome lid.

"Can I get you anything with that?" The woman motioned to the pastry case.

A.L. smiled and rubbed his ample stomach. He shook his head no.

"You look like you could use a chocolate-chip muffin," she coaxed.

"Yeah? I could use ten pounds less around my middle, too."

"No muffin, huh? Okay, then, that's a dollar forty-three."

For one cup of coffee? Starbucks *was* a white yuppie thing. Not for working people.

"Come back again," the woman behind the counter told him, flashing another dazzling smile. "Try a latté next time."

Maybe he would. Starbucks was a hassle. But she was kind of interesting.

A.L. carried the coffee to his car. He took a sip through the narrow hole in the dome. His face scrunched up. It was sweet! Tasted more like chocolate than coffee. But it was hot. And it satisfied his craving for caffeine.

The detective sat at the curb in his white detective's car, sucking the hot liquid through the plastic lid, burning his mouth, and thinking about the case.

The inside of the Ford was a mess. The floor was littered with empty root-beer cans, McDonald's wrappers, and plastic audiocassette boxes. A wrinkled suit was wadded up on the passenger seat. Jones hadn't had time to drop it at the dry cleaners.

The puzzle pieces weren't going together in the McLean case. No suspects. Nobody saw nothing at the dinner. Still waiting to find out what kind of poison was used. The widow was a blank. He hadn't had time to talk to any of McLean's assorted girlfriends. Or to the assorted husbands of the girlfriends. McLean's notebooks might as well be written in Greek. That damned girl newsie from the *Post* was bugging him again. Captain Wheeler was on his case to come up with *something.* And the Uncles were in such a hurry to run away from the case they were tripping over their dicks.

Shit runs downhill, they say. And A.L. knew, as usual, he was at the bottom of that hill.

He checked his watch again. He was due in court. But that would be fast. The public defender would win another continuance for the crew member A.L. had arrested for popping a Korean clerk while holding up a sandwich shop. After court, Jones would spend a few hours interviewing some of McLean's girlfriends. Then he'd pick up LaTroy at school, assuming LaTroy went to school.

Ever since he was a little boy growing up in a narrow row house on 19th Street NE, A.L. had thought that nearby Eastern High School was one of the most beautiful buildings in Washington. It was imposing, a block long, constructed of warm red brick and cream-colored sandstone, four stories high, in the gothic style popular in the 1920s. The school had leaded windows, a circular driveway curving through an entrance portico, and a sundial high up on the front wall, just under the fortresslike battlements.

Jones had once written a report on Eastern for a design class at Howard, before his family's precarious finances had forced him to drop out and give up his dream of becoming an architect.

Sitting in his cluttered car in front of the school, waiting for LaTroy, A.L. was pleased to see how little Eastern had changed since his childhood, even though the surrounding neighborhood had run down. All the school's windows reachable from the ground were now covered with bars, of course. But the lines of the building were still lovely, like a gothic castle. There was no graffiti on the beautiful red brick. And the green lawns looked verdant and well cared for.

A bell sounded. The doors immediately popped open. Teenage boys and girls came out. All of them were black.

For a time, whites had moved to Capitol Hill—not this far east, but getting closer—renovated the tall Federal-style town houses, gentrified the area, attracted new restaurants, bars, and shops. They were 'sixties people, making a statement by living in an integrated neighborhood.

A.L. had watched most of them leave for the suburbs, chased away by crime and fear of crime, by high taxes and the incompetent city government, by lousy schools and hostile neighbors, by a decline in civility, by homeless alcoholics sleeping in their doorways, pissing on their sidewalks, hassling them.

It wasn't just whites leaving. Jones knew a lot of black friends who had moved to the suburbs for the same reasons. He'd thought about moving to Prince George's County himself. But it would be like giving up on his hometown. And he wasn't ready to give up. Yet.

Many of the students pouring out of the high school lit up cigarettes the instant they were out the doors. Some weren't ordinary cigarettes, A.L. noted. Some were plainly marijuana nails and some were probably marijuana and crack geek sticks. Here and there he saw youngsters with hands cupped over their noses, obviously geezing, inhaling cocaine.

The detective spotted LaTroy Williams.

He got out of the car and approached the boy. The other teenagers moved away. They knew Jones was a cop. They'd seen him at the school on police business just three weeks before, when one of LaTroy's classmates had been crittin' with a member of a rival crew, engaging in a macho staring match. The boy had been popped right there on the sidewalk, not ten feet from where A.L. was standing now.

"Whatta you want?" LaTroy asked the cop sullenly. "I ain't done nothin'."

"That's why I'm here, to make sure you don't do nothin'. Get in the car. I'm taking you home. Where you staying? Your sister's?"

"Whatta you care?" the boy mumbled, head down, worried what his friends were thinking. "You ain't my father."

"Where's your father?"

"I ain't got no father."

"I can be . . ." A.L. stopped himself. He wasn't ready to

say out loud that he was trying to save this boy. He wasn't sure what LaTroy's reaction would be if he did say it.

"You at your sister's?" Jones repeated in a gruff baritone.

"Yeah," LaTroy acknowledged, shoving aside an empty Starbucks container and getting into the car.

"You thinking you gonna pop those drug boys did your mama?" A.L. asked as they pulled away from the school.

"Maybe. You gonna stop me?"

"Man, why don't you squash that beef before you get hurt?"

"Leave me alone."

"I'm trying to help you."

"I don't need no help."

"You need a *lot* of help. You mess with them drug boys, you get slammed."

"I don't care."

"You don't care if you die?"

"No."

They rode in silence awhile, north on 15th Street. Jones knew the neighborhood well. He'd delivered the old *Washington Star* around here after school. He'd help old ladies lug their grocery bags home on Saturdays for quarter tips.

"LaTroy, that earring makes you look like a fool."

"You want me to dress white, like you? Impress whitey?"

"Who *you* impressing, dumbass? The gangbangers?" Jones gestured toward LaTroy's unlaced black Nikes and baggy shorts that reached below his knees. "You trying to get down with the bad boys?"

"At least I ain't down with whitey."

"Listen, boy. It's a white world. You want to get somewhere, you dress white, you talk white, you act white."

"Yeah? Well, I don't want to get nowhere, so I ain't gotta do all that shit."

"Man, that's real fucking smart. Listen, asshole. You gonna make something of yourself, you got to do it all yourself. Ain't nobody gonna give you nothing. Ain't nobody gonna feel sorry for you. You screw up, ain't nobody to blame but yourself. You end up with your friends painting your name on a wall."

A.L. gestured through the windshield toward a neon pink

legend sprayed on a boarded-up storefront: MISS YOU, PIGMAN. RIP. A modern urban memorial where a teenager was gunned down.

"You got one life, Troy," Jones told the boy. "Then you dead. Forever. It ain't like TV. You don't get up and walk away at the end of the show."

LaTroy didn't respond. He stared out the window at the spray-painted epitaph.

As soon as they walked into the sister's apartment, LaTroy flipped on the TV set. A cable channel featuring rap music videos came on the screen.

Jones yanked the plug out of the wall. "No TV!" he barked. "Stay off the streets! And study!"

"What I get out of studyin'?"

"You get maybe a little better chance of livin' past your sixteenth birthday."

LaTroy glared at the detective petulantly. But he obeyed. The boy was writing in his loose-leaf notebook when A.L. left.

Jones thought maybe he'd gotten through to the boy, a little.

CHAPTER TWELVE

A HUGE POPULATION of Vietnamese refugees had moved to the Washington suburbs since the war.

One stretch of Wilson Boulevard—a road that zigzagged through the older neighborhoods of Arlington on the Virginia side of the Potomac—was known as Little Saigon because so many Vietnamese had settled there and opened shops and restaurants in the aging one- and two-story buildings.

Little Saigon was only a mile or so west of Jerry Knight's apartment in Rosslyn, and he often ate dinner there before heading into Washington for his midnight talk show. He liked the spicy food and the Vietnamese beer, the unpretentiousness of the cafes and the cheerfulness of the people.

But mostly he went to Little Saigon again and again in hopes of eventually understanding the chapter of his life when he'd been a radio reporter in Vietnam.

Sometimes Jerry invited Jane Day to join him for dinner in Little Saigon. And sometimes, if she wasn't on deadline at the *Post* and if she wasn't particularly outraged by something he'd said on the *Night Talker* program, she accepted.

Their relationship was edgy. Not outright hostile, as it had been when they first met a year earlier after Curtis Davenport's murder. But edgy.

Jane—like every woman—was a challenge to Jerry. He wanted her to like him.

Jane was at once repelled and fascinated by Jerry, who stood out as a larger-than-life, eccentric, colorful, outspoken character in a city of mostly bland workaholic wimps.

The only thing they had in common was their love for lively political discussion. Jerry, the Newt Gingrich conservative, and Jane, the Ted Kennedy liberal, spent much of their time together in debate over their opposing ideological and cultural viewpoints. Real debate, based on their beliefs, not the made-for-TV sound bites put into the mouths of politicians by their hired media manipulators.

As they were now, across a table at the Cafe Dalat on Wilson Boulevard.

"The press will never give this President a fair break," Jerry opined, dipping his white porcelain spoon into a bowl of thick *pho* soup. "The first real conservative President since Reagan, and you liberals are determined to destroy him. It's like a blood sport with you. Everything he does, you put the most negative spin on it."

"Please!" Jane retorted disdainfully, lifting a piece of *cha gio* spring roll with the bright orange chopsticks. "Dale Hammond doesn't need *my* help. He's doing a great job of destroying *himself.* The American people are the ones putting the negative spin on his presidency."

"How would you know what the American people think?" Jerry asked. "When was the last time you interviewed anyone outside the Beltway?"

Jane couldn't recall the last time she talked to a source who lived more than ten miles from Connecticut and K. To hide that fact, she wisecracked, "I talked to my mother in L.A."

"Oh, yeah, now there's an unbiased source."

Jerry caught the eye of the tiny Vietnamese waitress. *"Ba Me Ba,"* he ordered. The *33* Vietnamese beer was now brewed in France, but the red, white, black, and gold label still evoked memories of his years in Saigon.

"Your mother," Jerry picked up the discussion. "Didn't you tell me once you were five weeks old when she wheeled you to your first 'Impeach Nixon' rally in your baby buggy?"

"I was eleven when that crook was forced to resign, so you must have me mixed up with one of your bimbos, of which I understand there are many," Jane fired back.

"Ah, going negative," Jerry exclaimed. "Typical liberal tactic. You're losing on the facts, so you get personal."

"What makes you think I'm losing on the facts?"

The waitress cleared the appetizer dishes and set their main courses on the plain white paper placemats, a whole fried fish for Jerry, a plate of vegetarian curry for Jane.

Jerry opened a round glass container of red *nuoc mam* and carefully dribbled a few drops of the pungent fish sauce onto his food. It wasn't as strong or as smelly as the authentic *nuoc mam* he'd tried in Vietnam. But still strong enough burn his lips and sting his eyes.

More than anything, it was the smells in the restaurant that brought back the memories of Saigon and the war. If it weren't for the glass office towers rising up nearby and the modern automobiles zipping past, he could easily imagine the Cafe Dalat was on Hai Ba Tranh, not far from his room in the Caravelle.

The owner hadn't spent much to decorate the long, narrow restaurant, or to deaden the clamor. The heating and air-conditioning ducts were exposed. Light globes encased in straw baskets hung on white wire from the ceiling. Additional light was provided by sconces attached to the rough stucco walls and decorated with tacky artifacts like conical straw hats and sandals. Above their table hung a map of Vietnam.

The tables were small, topped with wood-grain Formica. The customers sat in dark, bentwood chairs with lime-green fake leather cushions.

Jerry suspected that many of the diners, in cotton sport shirts and gray slacks, were veterans who came because they had the same unresolved feelings about the war that he did. Some of the customers were obviously too young to have been in the war. For them, the Cafe Dalat was just an inexpensive, slightly exotic neighborhood restaurant.

"You're on *my* case about the liberal media?" Jane resumed their debate after the waitress had brought Jerry another bottle of *Ba Me Ba* in its distinctive green glass bottle.

"You, the official mouthpiece of the right wing? When Grady Hammond has an announcement to make, she goes on the *Night Talker* show instead of facing real journalists in the White House briefing room."

"Of course she does. Why wouldn't she pick an objective and unbiased forum instead of subjecting herself to hostile questions, disbelief, and plain rudeness from reporters like you?"

"Objective and unbiased? You call yourself objective and unbiased? Give me a break. Next to you, Rush Limbaugh is objective and unbiased."

"That's the nicest thing you ever said," Jerry thanked her mockingly.

"Grady Hammond didn't go on your show because she thought you'd be objective and unbiased. She went on your show because she knew you'd fawn all over her and let her make all kinds of unsubstantiated charges without challenging her."

"Yeah, I read what you wrote about it in the *Post.* You gave her that special treatment the liberal press reserves for the conservative wife of a conservative President. I don't want to exaggerate, but would it be fair to say you expressed a certain amount of *skepticism* about her theory that somebody intended to poison the President and got McLean by mistake?"

"Skepticism? Her claim is total bullshit."

"In other words, you have a few gnawing doubts about its validity," Jerry teased. "Is that a fair assessment?"

Jane pinched a clump of rice between her chopsticks and popped it into her mouth. "Hammond's a flop," she proclaimed. "He came in promising lower taxes, less government, less welfare, less regulation, a balanced budget, and he hasn't delivered. People are disillusioned. So the White House figures his last chance to win reelection in two years is to whip up sympathy by spreading the story that somebody tried to poison him to stop his conservative program. And, of course, the White House knows *you'll* buy that story and shovel it out to the right-wing nutcases who listen to your show. My job as a journalist is to call it bullshit when it's bullshit."

"You can't conceive, can you, that there are *left*-wing

nutcases out there who are so angry at Dale Hammond's efforts to root out sixty years of failed liberal statism and restore basic American values that they would try to get rid of him? You won't even entertain that possibility, will you?"

"No," Jane replied tersely. "I won't entertain your ultraconservative conspiracy theories. The simple explanation is that somebody *meant* to kill Dan McLean, and *did* kill him, probably because he was digging into a story they don't want broadcast."

Jane didn't tell Jerry what she'd learned about Dan McLean's marital infidelities. She knew he'd just use it to smear a great reporter.

"*Liberal* used to mean keeping an open mind, examining all the facts, reaching your own conclusions. Now it means marching in lockstep, accepting the common wisdom of political correctness, not deviating from the approved line."

"Oh, and *conservative* means having an open mind? Don't you mean having *no* mind?"

The dinner-table debate was typical of their relationship. It was the main reason they *had* a relationship. Their conversations were intellectually stimulating, stirring their competitive and ideological juices, honing their skills for the killer put-down.

For Jane, their verbal sparring was preferable to encountering a newly minted, slick-haired lawyer at the Sequoia Bar whose idea of conversational brilliance was asking, "So, what do you do?" And for Jerry, her spirited refusal to accept his views was a refreshing provocation after a string of empty-headed chicks.

The owner of the Cafe Dalat, Nguyen Cao, approached their table.

"Mr. Jerry! How are you? You enjoy the food?"

"Mr. Nguyen! Yes, of course. Delicious, as usual."

The owner always referred to Knight as *Mister Jerry* and Jerry always referred to the owner as *Mister Nguyen,* even though Cao was his last name.

Nguyen Cao was a short, round man with shiny black hair and expressionless black eyes. He could pass for forty or seventy. Jerry could never tell. Mr. Cao had a large, dark mole on his left cheek from which grew a single gray hair at least an inch long. No matter how hard Jerry tried, he couldn't help staring at the hair when he talked to Mr. Cao. The cafe owner was dressed in a short-sleeve polyester shirt of pale green, a narrow black tie, shiny black slacks, white socks, and sandals.

"Join us," Jerry invited. "You know Jane Day."

"Yes. How are you, Miss Day?"

"Sit down," Jerry invited again.

"No. No. Can't sit. Too busy."

Mr. Cao spoke the English words in the high-pitched whine and staccato cadence of his native language.

"How's your family?" Jerry asked the roly-poly restaurant owner. "Your daughter . . . ?"

"Crystal. She graduates high school in one month. She's val . . . valley . . ."

"Valedictorian?" Jane prompted.

"Yes! She's valedictorian. Very smart."

"And your son?" Jerry asked, lapsing into his interview mode, as he did often, even off the air.

"Jeffrey. He's studying at MIT. Very smart also. He got a job this summer at Microsoft." His round face beamed with pride.

"You must be proud of them," Jane commented.

Mr. Cao nodded enthusiastically. "My children are number-one children."

Jerry put his hand on Mr. Cao's arm in a gesture of admiration. "America is still the land of opportunity. You came here with no money. Strange country, strange city. You didn't speak the language. Now you own your own restaurant, you bought a house, you bought a car, your children are thriving. Maybe our own poor could succeed, too, if they weren't so dependent on a government handout and if they weren't told constantly that they're helpless victims."

"Oh, come on, Jerry!" Jane snapped. "Want me to give you a dozen reasons why there's no comparison between the two groups? Let's start with slavery."

Mr. Cao giggled uncomfortably. "You two always fighting. I overhear you fighting about Mr. Dan McLean."

Jane and Jerry stopped arguing. They both sensed that Mr. Cao had something to tell them.

"I overhear Miss Day say Mr. Dan McLean was working on big story. Some people maybe don't want big story on TV. Maybe they kill Mr. Dan McLean to keep his story off TV. Mr. Jerry disagree. But Miss Day is right."

Jane and Jerry exchanged looks.

"How do you know that?" Jane asked Mr. Cao.

"I hear things."

"What things? From whom?"

"I hear things," Mr. Cao repeated. "Around here." He waved his hand vaguely. He could have meant in the restaurant, or he could have meant in the surrounding Little Saigon community.

"What story was Dan working on? Who wanted to stop him from getting it on the air?" Jane fired a barrage of questions. "Who told you about it? Can you arrange for me to interview them? Do you know who poisoned Dan?"

Mr. Cao smiled apologetically. His flat black eyes flicked back and forth between Jane and Jerry.

Jane remembered the cryptic initials VN that showed up repeatedly in Dan's notebooks. They must have stood for Vietnam.

"Did the story Dan was working on have something to do with the war?" Jane asked the owner.

"Miss Day, I survive the war. I survive the Communists' camp, reeducation camp. I become a boat person. I survive that. I survive refugee camp. I survive your Immigration Service." He smiled apologetically at his dig. "Every day I survive the gangs out there." He nodded toward the street. "You know how I survive all that?"

Nervously twisting a tangled orange curl around her finger, Jane expectantly waited for him to answer his own question.

"I survive all that by not talking to reporters."

Mr. Cao giggled, as Vietnamese often do after they've said something impolite to an American.

A customer was waiting at the register to pay his bill. Mr. Cao hurried off.

"Come back soon, Mr. Jerry, Miss Day."

Jerry saw Jane's irked expression and burst out laughing. He loved it whenever anyone put down the news media.

CHAPTER THIRTEEN

K. T. ZORN, JERRY'S diminutive producer, was already at the All Talk Network studios on the top floor of an office building at 23rd and M when Jerry arrived from Little Saigon for his show.

Jerry found her in the control room, studying her ever-present clipboard. K.T. wore black slacks tucked into black boots, a bulky black sweater over a black turtleneck, and a black beret pulled raffishly over her gray crew cut.

"Any friend of Zorro's is a friend of mine," Jerry kidded her about her outfit.

She held up two fingers, her sarcastic reminder that he'd used the line before. She'd heard *all* his lines before. Maybe ten times before.

Jerry's first task when he arrived at the studio each night was to open his hate mail. It arrived daily by the hundreds. He relished the vituperation. It got his juices flowing for the show and validated his impact on the audience.

"Listen to this one," he commanded K.T. " 'I'd like to call you an asshole, but that would be an insult to all the billions of anal orifices in the world.' "

K.T. and Sammy, the Vietnamese engineer fiddling at his control panel, both laughed.

"I didn't think your listeners knew big words like 'orifice,' " the producer teased. "I picture them as mostly preliterate white guys in bowling shirts."

After working for Donahue, Gumbel, and Limbaugh, K.T. was not intimidated by stars. She'd learned that their colossal egos were just masks to hide their little-boy insecurities.

Jerry, ignoring her jibe, lifted another letter from the pile and read it aloud in outraged tones.

" 'I guess you conservatives will be happy when poor children are starving in the streets. You are so far to the right you make Newt Gingrich look like a moderate.' Well, that one's not so bad. Newt Gingrich *is* a moderate."

K.T. hopped up on the stool at her producer's console. Her feet didn't reach the floor. Sammy went into the studio to check the microphones.

The next item on Jerry's stack of hate mail was an unsigned postcard.

" 'I hope you die of a lingering and excruciatingly painful disease affecting your private parts,' " Jerry read.

"Why do they hate me, K.T.?" he asked plaintively. "I'm just trying to bring enlightenment into their lives, trying to lead them out of the darkness of dependency on big government into the sunshine of personal responsibility. Besides, I'm lovable."

Maybe it was time to move on, K.T. thought. Jerry's conservative rap was getting tiresome. Maybe she'd try working for Jenny this time. Or Oprah. No, not Oprah.

After a few more letters, Jerry grew tired of the ritual and dumped all the hate letters into the trash can. He never wrote replies.

He wandered into his office and dialed the number of a young woman he'd met two nights earlier at a Heritage Foundation reception. No answer. He called Jane's apartment. No answer. She'd probably gone back to the newsroom. She'd forbidden him to phone her there. A social call from Jerry Knight could ruin her standing with her liberal colleagues at the *Post.*

The exhilaration he'd gotten from reading the denunciatory letters was wearing off. He felt down, and lonely. He looked at his watch. Eleven-thirty. Thirty minutes to airtime. That would pick up his mood. It always did. He felt most alive when the microphone light went on. Jerry wandered back to the control room.

"Who's the guest tonight?" he asked K.T. He looked over her shoulder at the jottings on the producer's clipboard.

"No!" Jerry shouted. "Not her!"

K.T. had booked a hugely popular singer who was spending less and less time singing and more and more time crusading against the wearing of fur.

"You know I hate that kind of guest!" Jerry exclaimed. "They're so self-righteous. They're so damn sure they know what's good and what's bad for the rest of us. They're like national nannies, making us take our castor oil."

K.T. ignored his outburst. She'd heard this tirade before.

"If she didn't contribute millions of bucks to liberal causes, nobody would pay any attention to her. But those mental midgets on Capitol Hill invite her to testify about animal rights issues, as if she were an expert, because they know she'll attract the TV cameras."

Jerry's juices were flowing again.

"I think you book these airheads because you know how much I hate them," Jerry told K.T. "You do it deliberately to get me riled up, don't you?"

Of course she did. A riled-up Jerry Knight was great radio.

"Fifteen minutes to airtime," Sammy alerted them.

Jerry began his preshow ritual, sipping hot tea from a mug that said JERRY DOES IT ALL NIGHT and humming up and down the scale to warm up his vocal cords.

"Where'd you have dinner?" K.T. asked, sniffing the air in the control room in an exaggerated manner. "You ate at that Vietnamese place, didn't you?"

"How'd you know?" Jerry replied.

"I can smell it. What is that stuff? It smells like rotten fish."

"It *is* rotten fish, or a sauce made from rotten fish. *Nuoc mam.* Is it strong?"

"Is it *strong*? Phew!"

Jerry self-consciously swished the tea around in his mouth to kill the smell.

"Who'd you go with?" K.T. asked teasingly. "Miss Liberal Media?" She waggled her eyebrows lasciviously.

"Why? Are you jealous?"

"You're not my type, honey."

"I know. But maybe *she* is."

K.T. aimed a mock karate chop at his neck.

"Want to hear something interesting that happened at dinner?"

K.T. shrugged. Jerry's idea of interesting was often her idea of boring.

"Mr. Nguyen, the owner, came over to our table. Jane and I had been talking about Dan McLean's death, and Mr. Nguyen said he heard—apparently in the Vietnamese community—he heard that the murder might have had something to do with a story McLean was working on. He didn't say so specifically, but the implication was that the story had something to do with the war."

"Really?" For once, Jerry's idea of interesting really was interesting.

"I have a friend who's a producer at CNN," K.T. offered. "Maybe she knows what McLean was working on. Or can find out."

"Will you ask her?"

"Sure."

"Maybe I can find out something, too," Sammy interjected. "If somebody in the Vietnamese community knows what happened to Dan McLean and why, I will try to learn of it."

Jerry had never heard Sammy string together so many words. But, of course, he was the perfect one to explore Mr. Nguyen's nebulous comment about Dan McLean's death.

"Great, Sammy." Jerry welcomed the offer. "Let me know what you find out."

Jerry's instincts told him they were embarking on a quest far more complicated and surprising than they could imagine.

"Five minutes to airtime," K.T. warned. "Better get in the studio. I'll bring your guest from the Green Room. I know you're eager to meet her."

Jerry carried his mug of tea into the studio, humming up and down the scale one last time.

The star swept in, with her retinue—a bodyguard, a PR woman, and a *much* younger stud in tight leather pants.

"Quiet, please," Sammy requested over a speaker from the control room.

Jerry waited until ten seconds before the opening theme. Then he leaned across the baize-covered table and whispered to the star, "So, you don't believe in killing animals for clothing?"

"I certainly don't," she affirmed.

"Then how come you're wearing leather shoes?" Jerry snapped.

She opened her mouth. But before she could reply, the theme music blared from the speakers and the announcer began his introduction. They were on the air.

Jerry had her on the defensive before the show was five seconds old! This was going to be fun! The host no longer felt depressed. He and his loyal followers were going to demolish this Beverly Hills limousine liberal.

CHAPTER FOURTEEN

KAVANAUGH'S WAS SUCH a quintessentially typical suburban workingman's tavern that FBI special agent Michael Tagliaferro thought it could have been the creation of some Hollywood set designer. Dark and dank with a long wooden bar down one side. Chrome bar stools with seats covered in pastel Naugahyde. Lots of illuminated Budweiser and Miller signs. A jukebox heavy on country and seventies rock. In the back, varnished wooden booths and Formica tables for those brave enough, or hungry enough, to order from the plastic-covered microwave menu.

Kavanaugh's was the designated location for Tagliaferro's periodic meetings with Del Bloch, a salesman at the Lincoln-Mercury dealership in the nearby Montgomery Auto Park. Bloch was a freelance FBI informant who phoned Tagliaferro three or four times a year with tips, usually about suspicious customers trying to sell a car in a hurry or to buy a car for all cash. They'd arrange to meet at Kavanaugh's, usually at three P.M., between the lunch crowd and the after-work crowd, when the bar was nearly empty.

Bloch had phoned Tagliaferro that morning and suggested they meet.

The FBI agent drove out Canal Road and Clara Barton Parkway, along the Maryland bank of the Potomac, and around the Beltway, instead of driving through the city. It was longer, but faster.

He turned off the Beltway at the second Colesville Road exit. A half-mile north and he was at Four Corners, the heavily commercialized intersection of Colesville Road and University Boulevard. They were two of the oldest roads in Washington's Maryland suburbs. What had once been winding country lanes had long since been widened into four-lane divided highways.

Tagliaferro knew the area well. He'd grown up nearby, in Silver Spring, one of Washington's first suburbs, and had attended the University of Maryland, termination point of University Boulevard.

The Four Corners neighborhood of modest homes, mostly built before and during World War II, was struggling to resist decay and to retain its character. Many white workers and retirees, who had lived there for decades, were staying. But the houses of those who left or died were mostly bought or rented by immigrants from Asia and Latin America.

Tagliaferro noticed that the red brick Methodist church built in the wide median of University Boulevard had a sign on its lawn announcing services in Korean characters as well as one in English.

He drove through the congested Four Corners intersection and turned right into the aging Woodmoor strip shopping center. He parked his car between two fading white lines painted on the crumbling asphalt. The agent removed the gun in its clip-on holster from his belt and slid it under the seat. He took off his suit coat and tie and locked them in the trunk.

He looked like an insurance estimator or an aluminum-window salesman stopping off for a couple of cold beers after a day's work, not like an FBI agent meeting an informant.

Bloch was already in a booth, his back to the door, a half-empty Miller Light bottle in front of him, when Tagliaferro entered Kavanaugh's.

They shook hands formally. The agent slipped into the bench facing the front, so he could see who came in. Bloch always left that seat for him.

"Tag. How you doing."

"Great, Del. You?"

"Not too bad."

An ancient waitress, thin as a stick, wearing a pink nylon uniform the color of Pepto-Bismol, appeared.

"Get you something to drink, hon?" she asked Tagliaferro.

"Iced tea, please." He was on duty.

"Get you gentlemen something to eat?"

"Yeah, how about a plate of nachos," Bloch ordered. "Big plate."

"Coming up." The waitress shuffled away.

Bloch was a fat man with straggly gray hairs combed over his sweating scalp. His white shirt gapped at the buttons. Several chins piled up above the tight collar. His paisley tie was unfashionably narrow. His paunch pressed against the table.

Jesus. He'd let himself go, Tagliaferro thought. It was hard to connect this pile of blubber with the Del Bloch he'd first met half a lifetime ago in a dusty compound in Vietnam, a twenty-three-year-old Special Forces trooper, 155 pounds, hard, muscled, wearing only black shorts, holding the severed head of a Vietcong in one hand and a bloody bayonet in the other, and laughing joyously.

"So, you have something for me?" Tagliaferro asked after the skinny waitress had delivered his iced tea and departed. "Drug dealer trying to buy a Continental with a duffel bag full of ten-dollar bills?"

"This is something different, Tag." Bloch sounded out of breath when he spoke, like fat men do, even when they're sitting still.

"Yeah?"

"You ever hear of a group called the Survivors of Cam Hoa?"

Tagliaferro showed no reaction.

In fact, a memo had circulated in his division a few days earlier directing the agents to squeeze their sources for information about a group with that name.

"I'm not a member myself," Bloch assured Tagliaferro. "But I know a couple of guys who are. Ex-Berets, not too happy about the way the war turned out. You know what I mean?"

The agent nodded.

"They still gripe a lot about the media coverage of the war and the antiwar demonstrations. Pulling out and leaving a lot of loyal Vietnamese at the embassy. That shit. Some of them think there's American prisoners still alive in Nam. A lot of them think the prisoners they found in that grave in Hanoi died a long time after the war ended. But, you know, they're harmless. The most they do anymore is put on fatigues and crawl around in the woods, firing paint pellets at each other. You know, those war games? I never go with them."

How could you, you fat slug? Tagliaferro thought. You couldn't crawl two feet if your life depended on it.

The waitress arrived with a huge plate of burned nachos, a second bottle of Miller Light for Bloch, and a refill on the iced tea for Tagliaferro.

"So?" the agent prompted his informant when she left.

"So, anyhow," Bloch panted, "one of the members who's a friend of mine got word through the grapevine that the FBI thinks the Survivors had something to do with killing that TV guy, McLean."

"Uh-huh," Tagliaferro grunted encouragingly but noncommittally.

"My friend hears that the FBI thinks maybe the Survivors were really trying to knock off the President."

"Yeah?"

"This guy knows I know you, so he asked me to give you a message."

"Which is?"

"Which is, no way they had anything to do with it, Tag. Some of them are pissed that the President didn't react more to the discovery of the prisoners' grave. But they're not pissed enough to, you know, try to kill him." Bloch was having trouble catching his breath.

"You believe your friend?"

"Sure." Bloch stuffed nachos into his mouth nervously.

"Maybe he wants you to tell the Bureau this to throw us off the trail."

"I don't think so."

"Where'd your friend hear that the Bureau is interested in the Survivors of Cam Hoa?"

Bloch shrugged. "I don't know. The grapevine. You know."

"What's your friend's name?"

"Come on, Tag. I promised him I wouldn't tell." Bloch swallowed half a glass of beer.

Tagliaferro remained silent, sipping his iced tea, waiting to see if Bloch would volunteer more. He didn't.

"Okay, I'll pass on your friend's message," the agent said.

He pulled out his wallet, removed two $100 bills, and passed them to Bloch under the table.

"Call me if you have any more information."

Tagliaferro slid out of the booth. Kavanaugh's was filling up with the after-work crowd.

The agent called his superior from the pay phone outside the men's room. He arranged a twenty-four-hour-a-day tail on Bloch, as well as taps on the informant's office, home, and cellular phones.

CHAPTER FIFTEEN

TIMOTHY COLLINS, ONE of Jane Day's senior colleagues on the presidential beat, answered the phone in the *Post*'s cubicle situated on the lower level of the White House press room.

"It's for you," he advised Jane, giving her a funny look. "He says he's Jerry Knight."

"Tell him I'm on deadline," she instructed, staring at her computer screen. "I'll call him when I get time."

Collins relayed her message.

"He says he's at home," Jane's colleague reported, sounding like he was stifling a snicker. "He says you know the number."

Jane would have welcomed a break from the story she was writing, a short piece about an obscure presidential directive on farm price supports, a subject she barely understood and found boring. She was sure the *Post*'s inside-the-Beltway urbanite readers would find it equally boring. But she couldn't talk to Jerry in front of Timothy.

She knew that most of her liberal peers in the news media looked askance at the fact that she occasionally went out with the most famous conservative talk-show host in

America. She tried to keep their relationship quiet. But she was aware of the head-shakings and the cluckings.

And those reactions were getting very old very fast! Okay, she disagreed with his politics, too. But why did everything in Washington have to be based on politics, including the correctness or noncorrectness of pairings? Matalin and Carville had gotten married, hadn't they? And their politic differences were at least as great as hers and Jerry's.

Wait a minute. Nobody was talking about getting married here. She and Jerry were an occasional couple. Very occasional. What was wrong with that? Even with all of Jerry's drawbacks, spending time with him was better than being alone. Not a ringing endorsement, but the truth.

Lately, more and more of her friends were pairing off. Jamie in the *Post* Sports department had announced at lunch recently that she had fallen in love with a Brazilian soccer player and was chucking the news business to marry him and follow him all over Europe on the World Cup circuit.

Jane's role model was her friend Angela. Angela had been swept off her feet by a Wall Street financier who had come to Washington to give the Clinton administration economic advice. They now lived in a big house in Greenwich Village, had two darling kids, a nanny, and a patio.

Jane's mother Mavis, of course, kept Jane apprised of the marriages and birth announcements among her friends and cousins in California, along with not-so-subtle hints that Jane was being left behind.

"There is a lid until nine A.M.," a disembodied voice announced over the public-address system in the White House press room, meaning no more news was expected until the next morning.

Timothy Collins stuffed his papers into his briefcase and squeezed out of the cubicle.

"See you tomorrow," he said to Jane. "Say hello to Jerry for me. Tell him I think his show is *much* better than Rush's."

He cackled derisively.

Jane finished her farm price support story, hit the SEND button on her computer, and zapped it back to the newsroom at the *Post.* She was certain it would end up chopped to three graphs and buried on about A27.

She phoned Jerry Knight at his apartment.

"I asked you not to call me at work," she blurted out as soon as he answered.

"Why? You don't want your liberal friends to know you know me?"

"Exactly."

"I appreciate your candor. It just proves once again that angry white male conservatives are the last minority group which it's still socially acceptable to insult."

He sounded like his feelings were really hurt. She hadn't meant to do that.

"Sorry. I've had a shitty day. Are we still going to the reception at the Canadian embassy?"

"That's why I called," Jerry explained. "I can't make it."

"What happened, did you get a better offer?" she flared.

"Yeah, I did."

She was stunned that he would confess so readily to preferring another woman. One of his bimbos, no doubt.

"I got a better offer from the president of the network," Jerry elaborated. "He says I've got to have dinner with a potential big sponsor, the head of an insurance company that's interested in buying five commercials a night, five nights a week, for fifty-two weeks."

"Sounds terrific," Jane said without enthusiasm.

"It is!" Jerry insisted.

"I said it was."

"You don't believe me, do you, that I've got to go to dinner with a client?"

"Sure I do," she replied with even less enthusiasm. Why should she, with his reputation?

"Come by the Palm, if you don't believe me. You'll see us there."

"I've got to go. Have fun." She hung up before he could say anything else.

The phone rang almost immediately. She let it ring until he gave up.

Why was she so upset about being stood up for an overcrowded and noisy embassy reception by a man about whom she had such ambivalent feelings?

Good question. Jane didn't know the answer.

"Dorothy! Get a life!" she shouted to the overweight and gaudily dressed Dorothy Swisher of Knight-Ridder, the only other reporter still at work in the White House press room. "Come on, let's walk up to the Mayflower bar and hit on visiting moguls."

CHAPTER SIXTEEN

A.L. JONES ARRIVED at the apartment of LaTroy Williams's sister at seven-thirty A.M. and rapped on the door. The detective figured he'd drive the boy to school, make sure he'd done his homework, warn him again to stay away from bad company, guns, and thoughts of revenge. But no one answered the door.

Jones drove his dirty white Ford to Eastern High School and parked in the circular driveway. He got out and jived with the kids he knew, waiting for LaTroy to show up. But when the bell rang for the start of classes, the boy had not arrived. A.L. went to LaTroy's homeroom in case he'd come in another door. But he wasn't there.

Fool, A.L. thought, steering his Ford west on East Capitol Street, away from Eastern. Maybe LaTroy was dead. Nah. Jones would have heard of it. But the boy was probably in trouble. Or about to get himself in trouble.

A.L. parked in a bus zone across the street from the Congressional Market at 5th and East Capitol. The store's glass windows had been replaced with shatterproof Plexiglas. Security detectors were suction-cupped to the inside. Good protection in that neighborhood, A.L. thought. But the white shades pulled down inside the windows were a bad idea. People passing by couldn't see a robbery in progress. Not that they were likely to stop and help.

Jones squeezed down the narrow aisle to the cooler and removed a can of root beer.

The Asian woman at the cash register waved away his money.

"You no pay. Please. For you, free."

She knew he was a policeman and welcomed the momentary protection from the hostility, threats, and petty thievery she encountered daily.

To repay her, Jones stood conspicuously just inside the front door, drinking his soda and sternly eyeing every customer who entered.

Through the window he could see the Capitol dome gleaming white in the spring sunshine at the end of the street.

A.L. acknowledged to himself that the stops at Eastern and at the market had been stalling tactics. He was avoiding his appointment at the Capitol. Actually, he had mixed emotions about the appointment.

Jones thought the Capitol was the most beautiful building in the world. He took delight in the fact that the winner of the eighteenth-century competition to design the Capitol, Dr. William Thornton, was an amateur with no formal architectural training. A.L. could relate to that. Although his own architectural studies at Howard had been aborted, he still considered himself an amateur architect, or at least an amateur architectural historian.

So normally he loved to visit the Capitol.

But the detective dreaded this impending visit. He had an appointment to interrogate Senator Norton Thatcher about his wife Kristi's affair with Dan McLean and what bearing it might have on the murder of the CNN correspondent, if any.

A.L. helped himself to another root beer, putting off his departure as long as possible. Finally he nodded good-bye to the Asian cashier. She bowed. He went out, got into his car, and drove toward the white dome at the end of the street.

The Capitol had been a work in progress ever since George Washington, wearing his Mason's apron, had laid the cornerstone in 1793. Almost continually since then, it had been under construction, renovation, or expansion. Like a cathedral, never finished. A cathedral of democracy. Yeah. A.L. had read that somewhere.

Jones had phoned his friend Terry Pritchard of the Capitol Police the day before to get some background on Senator Thatcher. The senator was in his third term, a Democrat from Tennessee, who had worked his way up to chairman of the Commerce Committee before the Republicans took control of Congress.

One fact in Terry's report stuck with A.L. Thatcher was a pharmacist by training. His family owned a chain of drugstores in Tennessee. Could be important, since McLean had died of a mysterious poison not yet identified.

Pritchard also advised A.L. that the senator had a short temper and an abundance of self-importance.

Jones hated this kind of interrogation. Thatcher was a big-time white dude. *Real* big-time, a type A.L. rarely encountered and avoided whenever he could. And A.L. was going to ask him questions about his wife screwing around with another guy. The detective anticipated his meeting with the senator would be as unpleasant, or more so, as his exasperating confrontation with the lobbyist Pat Howell and her fat K Street lawyer during the Davenport murder investigation a year earlier.

Thatcher's suite of offices was in the Hart Office Building. It was the newest of the three buildings lined up on Constitution Avenue north and east of the Capitol grounds to house senators and their ever-growing staffs. The three buildings—all named for fairly recent, admired senators—had been built in different eras and their architectural styles were badly mismatched. The only thing the three block-square fortresses had in common was their construction material—Washington's inescapable white marble.

The oldest, Dirksen, was neo-Roman with ornate carved columns, balustrades, and cornices. The middle building, Russell, was vaguely 1930s modern and had no character at all. Hart had a sleek, suburban office park look with eighteen-foot-high windows. A.L. chuckled as he remembered the controversy that attended the opening of Hart. Some senators had been outraged that ordinary tourists on the street could look through the glass walls and see them working—or *not* working.

Jones parked on First Street in a spot reserved for the handicapped. He was an aging, harassed, overworked black cop suffering depression because he was losing the battle to the bad guys. Yeah. He qualified for handicapped parking.

Thatcher received Jones in his high-ceilinged inner office with a view south through the wide windows toward the Supreme Court building. The office was enormous, with the desk and working area at one end, a meeting area with a conference table at the far end, and a sofa and easy chairs in between.

The senator led A.L. to the sofa and easy chairs. The detective figured the entire Homicide headquarters, all the cubicles and interrogation rooms, could practically fit into this one office.

The walls were covered with dozens of "grip and grin" photographs—black-and-white eight-by-tens of the senator smiling and shaking hands with all the Democratic luminaries of his era. Clinton. Carter. Cuomo. Fellow-Tennessean Al Gore. The father, Albert Senior, who had once occupied the Senate seat Thatcher now held. And the son, Clinton's VP. George Mitchell. Ted Kennedy. A scattering of movie stars and country-music singers. Even one with the Republican Reagan.

Displayed on the end table next to the sofa was a silver frame holding a color photograph of a beautiful woman. Kristi Thatcher, Jones guessed.

"Coffee?" the senator offered.

"Sure," the detective grunted.

Thatcher was much shorter than Jones expected. Not more than five-four, five-five. Not just shorter, but small in every dimension, actually dainty. Filling a television screen with his face made him appear bigger than he really was. Thatcher was fastidious in his dress. A well-fitting sport jacket of nubby gray silk, sharply creased charcoal gray flannel slacks, highly polished black loafers, a crisp white shirt, and a black-and-white tie in the newest bold pattern.

A blond secretary in a tight skirt and tight sweater, a smile fixed on her face, delivered the coffee. She teetered out on high heels, closing the door noiselessly behind her.

"So, I gather you're here on Homicide business?" Thatcher asked in a surprising gentle voice. "It's about the McLean case, I believe you told my appointments secretary?"

"Yes, sir, it is." A.L. removed a slightly smudged business card from his wallet and handed it to the senator.

"A. L. Jones," the senator read through his rimless half-glasses. "Would A.L. stand for 'Abraham Lincoln'?"

Jones looked surprised.

"We have quite a few 'Abraham Lincolns' among the African-American citizens of my state," Thatcher explained softly. "At least among the older ones. Not so many among the young people, of course. They tend to be 'Jamals' and 'LaShawns.' I don't think Abraham Lincoln would be very happy about the people who have taken over his Republican party."

"Yeah, well," Jones replied, tugging a notebook from the pocket of his jacket.

"Shall I call you Abe?" Thatcher asked.

A.L. frowned.

"How about Detective Jones, then?"

They each took a sip of coffee before beginning.

"You know about Dan McLean and Kristi?" Thatcher offered, almost in a whisper. "Of course you do. That's why you're here."

The detective was confounded by the senator's ready admission of his wife's relationship. He hadn't expected that.

"I'm sixty-four years old, Detective Jones," Thatcher continued unprompted. "Kristi's my second wife. When Marianne died of cancer, I was thrown for a loop. I was lost. I didn't know how I was going to get on with my life. Kristi was my legislative assistant in those days. I'd known her family for years. Smart girl. And pretty. She was runner-up in the Miss Tennessee contest. She helped me get through Marianne's death, and . . . I was sure I was in love with her."

Thatcher took a sip of coffee from his china cup.

A. L. Jones didn't speak.

"Kristi's thirty years younger than I am, Detective Jones," the senator explained in his soft voice. "And you know women."

Unexpectedly, he laughed. "Ah, women!" Thatcher's tiny eyes crinkled. "Are you married, Detective Jones?"

"I was."

"And?"

"She told me I was 'difficult to live with.' She's a nursing supervisor up in New Jersey. Married to a doctor."

"So you know women."

"Uh-huh," A. L. Jones growled.

"I have my work," the senator said dryly, not laughing anymore. "You have your work. And modern women do what they do."

Jones stared at his notebook. He hadn't written a thing.

"McLean wasn't Kristi's first . . . boyfriend. She's young, and lively. I'm so much older than she is. And my work often keeps me here late into the evening. I travel. Speeches. Trips to the state. So I can understand her seeking . . . her own social life. She never lets it interfere with her official duties. And she is companionable, for when I need companionship. Don't you ever get lonely? Don't you just want someone there?"

He was rambling, in his whispery voice. A.L. listened, turning the senator's words over in his mind. Thatcher sounded so reasonable, so understanding.

But maybe it was bullshit. Maybe Thatcher was pretending to accept his wife playing around so A.L. wouldn't think he was mad enough to kill McLean.

"You don't care if your wife—"

"Of course I care," Thatcher cut off the question. "What are my alternatives? Throw her out? Create a public scandal? That surely would interfere with my agenda here of stopping the Republicans from undoing a half-century of progress. A public scandal, even if I'm the innocent party, would not sit well with the voters of Tennessee. It might result in my defeat in the next election. Besides, creating a public scandal is not in my nature, Detective Jones, no matter how much pain I feel because of Kristi's . . . lifestyle. Divorcing her is not an alternative. My generation believes in suffering in silence. Accepting life as it is."

"One alternative is getting rid of her boyfriend," A.L. suggested.

The senator laughed again. "Thank you, Detective Jones,

for believing me capable of such passion," Thatcher said, speaking so softly Jones had to lean forward on the sofa to catch the words. "I'm not. I'm perfectly suited to serve in 'the world's greatest deliberative body.' I have a deliberative nature. I'm a man of contemplation, not of action. The Senate does not welcome men who make grand gestures, who take drastic actions on their own. Rather, it is the perfect home for men like me, who live by compromise. We must all make compromises in life, must we not? Without compromise, life would be unending conflict."

The detective was not fully persuaded. "Were you at the dinner where McLean was killed?" he asked.

Thatcher laughed again, almost silently. "I was in Chattanooga that night, speaking to the annual spring meeting of the Chamber of Commerce. You can check that. What do you call it? I have an *alibi.*"

"You could have paid someone to do it," Jones said. Why should he treat Thatcher any different from any other suspect? The senator sounded so sincere. But still, he had a motive.

"I didn't," Thatcher replied. "I wouldn't. I couldn't."

The senator stared out the window toward the white temple of the Supreme Court a block away. "I wish I could have," he whispered.

The senator stood up. A. L. Jones rose, too.

"Are you wondering why I told you all this so readily?" Thatcher asked, leading the detective toward the door.

"I guess so."

"I have nothing to hide. I lead an exemplary life. And I'm not responsible for Kristi's conduct. You knew about Kristi and McLean, anyhow. If I'd tried to deny it, it would merely have aroused your suspicions toward me. So I volunteered the truth. The truth is the perfect defense. Isn't that what they say?"

Senator Thatcher placed his tiny hand in A.L.'s paw, shook once, and turned toward his desk.

The detective went out, pulling the door shut behind him. White people. They had the damnedest morals.

CHAPTER SEVENTEEN

"LISTEN TO THIS one," Jerry Knight commanded. An hour before airtime, the *Night Talker* host was reading his hate mail.

" 'You and the rest of the ultra-right-wingers will only be satisfied when you put the National Endowment for the Arts out of business, so all the promising young artists in this country and their children will be starving in the streets. Your idea of great art is the *Playboy* centerfold.' "

"Right on, sister!" Jerry's producer, K. T. Zorn, clapped her hands in mock support for the letter writer.

"How can you applaud that trash?" Jerry demanded. "You want your tax money going to some jerk who puts a crucifix in a jar of piss and calls it art?"

"Better than my taxpayer's money going to some fat-cat white male tobacco-company executive."

"K.T., you're fired!"

"Really? I wish you'd told me before I schlepped in tonight." The diminutive producer hopped off the stool at her control-room console and began gathering up her things.

"Only kidding!" Jerry reassured her. "Really, K.T., I was just fooling. Where's your sense of humor?"

"And I was looking forward to going to work for Jenny Jones," K.T. said, returning to her stool. They'd played out this scene before.

K.T. exchanged a silent look with Jane Day that said, *How do we put up with him?*

Jane had come to the studio with Jerry after one of their usual argumentative dinners at Asia Nora two blocks away. She'd come because the guest on the *Night Talker* show that night was a Democratic state governor who was considering running for his party's nomination to face Hammond in two years. Jane wanted to meet him early, in case he won. It would give her an advantage over other Washington reporters.

"Oh, now here's an intelligent one," Jerry proclaimed, taking another letter from his stack of abusive mail. " 'The real agenda of you neofascists is to put all African-Americans into concentration camps.' Neofascists? I'm out here on the frontier of freedom every night fighting to preserve the American system of opportunity and free enterprise which the Founding Fathers established, and they call me a neofascist? Unbelievable! That's what you liberals have been reduced to. Name-calling to cover up the absence of ideas."

K.T. returned to the preprogram checklist on her clipboard, ignoring Jerry's rantings. Jane sat in the technician's chair, listening on the telephone while Russ Williamson read her the edits he'd made in her story for the next morning's *Post.* Sammy the technician was in the studio performing minor repairs to the guest's microphone.

It was quiet in the control room except for the continuous low hum of the broadcast equipment and Jerry's periodic exclamations of outrage.

"By the way," K.T. broke the silence. "I spoke to my friend at CNN about what stories Dan McLean was working on."

That got the attention of Jerry and Jane.

"And?" Jane prompted.

"My friend wasn't working with Dan herself," the crewcut producer explained, "but she has a friend who was preparing the graphics for one of his stories. And that friend thinks McLean was gathering evidence that the government is involved in some kind of computer espionage or computer surveillance, something about computers."

Jane pulled her notebook from her shoulder bag.

"What kind of surveillance?" she asked. "Like monitoring what people send on the Internet?"

"Dan never told anybody exactly what he was doing," K.T. replied. "Or at least my friend's friend never heard. Dan was secretive about his investigations."

"And that's all your friend's friend knows?"

"That's it," K.T. replied.

Jane was disappointed. Computer surveillance didn't sound like a blockbuster scandal. It didn't sound big enough to get the correspondent killed. She tried to recall Dan's crimped and cryptic notes. The initials CC showed up a couple of times. Could that stand for computer—computer, what?

"I heard something different about Dan McLean," said Sammy.

The other three focused on the Vietnamese technician. He spoke so seldom.

"What did you hear?" Jerry asked.

"I know a man, he's in a—not exactly a gang—a club of Vietnamese men. Friends from the old days in Saigon," Sammy explained in staccato English. "This man heard that Dan McLean was asking questions about the end of the war."

"What kind of questions?" Jane asked, scribbling in her pad.

"He was asking about somebody in the government who screwed up something at the end of the war."

"What's the name of the person in the government?" Jane pressed, writing fast.

"The man I talked to didn't know," the technician reported. "Or, if he knows, he didn't tell me. With this man, it's not good to ask too many questions."

A scandal about somebody in Dale Hammond's administration making a big mistake at the end of the Vietnam War. That was more like the kind of story Jane would expect Dan McLean to be digging into. And the kind of story that might drive the official involved to take drastic measures to keep it secret. But Sammy's information was skimpy.

Jane tried to remember if anything she'd seen in Dan's notebooks tied in with this angle. The frequent VN notations could have stood for Vietnam, she concluded. But she couldn't recall any other recognizable names in the coded notes. CC? G? Could those initials stand for the name of the Hammond administration official Dan was investigating? She'd have to dig out news stories from the early 'seventies and see if anyone connected with the end of the war had those initials.

"Remember that night we had dinner in Little Saigon?" Jane reminded Jerry. "The owner said he'd heard that Dan was working on a story that someone was anxious to keep off TV."

"No, that's not what he said," Jerry replied, dumping the rest of his hate mail into the trash can. "He said he'd heard us arguing over whether Dale Hammond or Dan McLean was the real target, and he said you were right that McLean was."

"Yes, and he went on to say he'd heard that someone might have killed Dan to prevent him from broadcasting the story he was working on. Now Sammy confirms that Dan was investigating a high official of Hammond's administration."

"No, not a 'high official,' " Jerry corrected. Someone 'in' the government."

"All right, 'in' the government," Jane conceded. "It's still starting to add up."

"Add up? To *what*?" Jerry demanded. "Thirdhand innuendo? No confirmation. No name. No details. No *nothing*. You're going to take a whack at Dale Hammond in your paper with no evidence at all?"

He was right, Jane admitted to herself. She had nothing that Russ would allow in the paper. But now she knew where to start looking.

"I don't have any evidence *yet*," Jane told Jerry heatedly. "But I'm going to *get* the evidence."

"You liberals," Jerry reported. "You'd do anything to embarrass a conservative President, wouldn't you? Even if what Sammy heard is right, it was twenty-five years ago. The guy must have been a low-level nobody then."

"Right," Jane said. "Maybe now he's a high-level *somebody*, and he doesn't want the world to know what he did then."

"What did he do?" Jerry demanded.

"I don't know!" Jane shouted. "I'm going to try to dig it up."

"And if you can't dig it up, you'll *make* it up!" Jerry shot back.

Jane stormed out of the control room, heading for the Green Room to ingratiate herself with the possible future Democratic presidential candidate.

Midnight. The hands of the studio clock aligned at twelve.

"It's midnight, and ATN, the All Talk Network, presents radio's most popular all-night talkmeister, Jerry Knight and the *Night Talker* show, live from Washington, D.C.," the announcer proclaimed. "For the next five hours, sit back and listen while Jerry entertains, informs, and sometimes enrages you. If you're working, studying, or just having trouble sleeping, you are not alone. Ladies and gentlemen, here to keep you company all night is Jerry Knight, the Night Talker!"

The theme music blared, then faded. On the other side of the glass wall, Sammy jabbed his finger at the host. The red ON AIR light came on.

Yes! It was the moment Jerry lived for. No matter how he felt before airtime, the opening of the show always energized him.

Millions of people out there listening. He couldn't see them and they couldn't see him. That's why he loved radio. The audience adored him only for his voice and his ideas. It was a pure form of communication. Not like TV. Appearance and staging and pictures counted for too much on television. Besides, viewers would bug him in airports and on the street if they became familiar with what he looked like.

Radio was his medium.

"Hello! Hello, you lucky night people! I am back among you. The Night Talker, certified, guaranteed, and warranteed to be the greatest living radio talk-show host, once more taking to the battlements to restore our way of life from the fine mess made these past sixty years by the liberals. Go ahead, feel free to boo and jeer when I say the word *liberals.* It's not really a dirty word, but it should be."

In the control room, K.T. turned to Jane. "He's on a roll tonight."

Jane pantomimed throwing up her dinner.

"Of course, the liberals launched another attack on our President, Dale Hammond, today," Jerry rolled on. "The liberals can't stand to see a conservative President succeed in shutting down the political-correctness police, can't stand to see a conservative President cutting the greedy off welfare, can't stand to see a conservative President whacking away at the bureaucrats, who have been sitting on their fat butts for too many years making *your* life miserable. If you like what President Hammond's doing, stand up right now wherever you are—go ahead, stand up—stand up and yell out loud, 'Keep it up, President Hammond! Keep it up!' Go ahead, just yell it out!"

It was going to be another wild night, K.T. thought. All the phone lines on her console were flashing already.

Jane held her head in her hands. This was the man she had dinner with? This was the man she halfway liked? She hoped her parents never found out, her California-liberal parents. Still, something attracted her to him. Jerry was outrageous. He was spunky. He was entertaining. And he had convictions.

In a town of bland white-bread men, Jerry Knight was seven-grain stone-ground organic with olives.

"Now, if you *like* political correctness, welfare cheats, arrogant bureaucrats, and high taxes, our guest tonight is just the man for you," Jerry raved on. "Right now he's upholding the liberal big-government big-spending big-taxes ideology of Walter Mondale, Michael Dukakis, and Bill Clinton in just one state. But if his dreams come true, he'll be imposing that ideology on the whole country!"

The guest smiled uneasily. What had he gotten himself into? He looked around with apprehensive eyes for his press secretary to rescue him.

CHAPTER EIGHTEEN

A.L. JONES THOUGHT he was making headway with LaTroy Williams.

The detective was waiting in the driveway of Eastern High School when classes let out. The boy got into his dirty white car with a minimum of complaint.

But to all A.L.'s questions about how he was doing in school, his elusive sister, and his beef with the crew that shot his mother, LaTroy answered in monosyllables, defensive grunts, or hostile silence.

Jones drove to a clothing store in the H Street Connection. The modern, suburban-style strip mall looked out of place on the bedraggled street. It was one of the few new structures built since rioters torched many H Street stores following Martin Luther King's assassination. The places that survived were now mostly liquor stores, one-chair beauty shops, and storefront churches.

When he saw where they were going, LaTroy muttered, "Oh, man . . ." He left unsaid the rest of the sentence, *I ain't wearing that cracker shit.*

Nevertheless, the boy grudgingly let Jones buy him a pair

of blue jeans to replace his oversized below-the-knees shorts. But he insisted on the equally baggy cargo jeans with multiple pockets and multiple pleats.

Well, it was a little progress, Jones thought.

Next, the detective drove to his apartment. The LeDroit Park neighborhood near Howard University was better than the drug-infested Kingman area where LaTroy lived with his sister, and A.L.'s apartment was better than the sister's rundown place. But not a lot better.

Jones's plan was to get the boy settled down with his homework, away from the lure of crews, drugs, and guns at least for a while. A.L. would leave LaTroy with his schoolbooks and loose-leaf binder for two hours, while he drove to the morgue to interview his friend Willie Wu about the Dan McLean poisoning. Then the detective would take the boy out for pizza, a real sit-down meal, before reluctantly returning him to the jungle.

As A.L. opened the door of his apartment for LaTroy, the phone was ringing.

It was Lawrence Frieze, the Secret Service agent.

"Did you see it?" the agent asked with no preamble.

"See what?" A.L. replied.

"You watching CNN? Turn it on."

A.L. cradled the phone on his shoulder and zapped the TV set with the remote. Channel 42 faded in slowly on his aging set, like a photograph emerging in the developing tray.

A spiky-haired blond anchorwoman was talking about the murder of "our colleague," Dan McLean.

"Keep watching," Frieze instructed. "They're showing it over and over again."

And sure enough, in a moment the anchorwoman cued a fuzzy black-and-white video clip playing in slow motion. A legend across the top of the screen in yellow said "Amateur video—CNN exclusive."

"Recognize it?" the Secret Service agent asked.

A.L. squinted at the grayish scene. Before he could identify the indistinct images, the anchor explained that the video was tape of the headtable at the White House Correspondents Association dinner, taken by a guest with a handheld camcorder.

"Now watch this," Frieze said.

On the screen, a portion of the picture was highlighted in a circle. In the circle, a blurry figure in a waiter's uniform bent over one of the headtable guests.

"The videotape shows the waiter serving Dan McLean right here," the anchor narrated. "But Dan is not paying attention because he's talking to the person next to him, National Security Adviser Gregor Novasky."

A.L. stared at the screen intently. The slow-motion video was hypnotic.

"Pay attention, now," the Secret Service agent on the phone commanded.

"Right here, you can see the waiter reach into his pocket," the anchor continued. The picture was so hazy, A.L. would not have picked up that detail without her prompting.

"And—we'll stop the tape—here the waiter takes something out of his pocket and drops it into Dan's soup bowl. We don't know what he put in the soup," the anchor concluded, "but there's a very good chance it was the poison that killed our colleague. Police have no immediate comment on this dramatic video."

Jones killed the sound with his zapper. "Where'd they get the tape?" he said into the phone.

"Apparently the wife of some out-of-town editor was so ga-ga about attending the dinner she taped everything in sight with her camcorder," Frieze said. "She didn't realize she had a shot of McLean's murderer until she got back to Kansas or wherever she's from. She sold the tape to CNN for fifty thousand dollars."

"Sold it to CNN?" A.L. rumbled in his weary baritone. "How come she didn't bring it to Homicide, or to you?"

"Jones, have you been living on another planet?" the Secret Service agent asked. "You never heard about free enterprise in the age of tabloid television?"

"I heard about it," the detective said bitterly. "It means selling evidence instead of bringing it to the cops, don't it?"

"CNN will play the tape again shortly," Frieze advised. "Record it on your VCR and you'll have a picture of the murderer to go on."

"Ain't got no VCR," Jones replied.

"You don't have a VCR?" the Secret Service agent repeated incredulously. "Everybody's got a VCR. How do you watch movies?"

"I *had* a VCR till somebody stole it."

"Stole it out of a cop's apartment?" Frieze sounded even more incredulous.

"Cop's apartment or not a cop's apartment, don't make no difference to these street boys. They steal from their own mothers if they need money for crunch, or for sneakers."

"Jesus, what kind of neighborhood do you live in?"

"I live in one of the *better* neighborhoods," the detective told him.

"Okay, listen," the Secret Service agent instructed. "Go to CNN. I'm sure they'll make you a copy."

"Okay, man, but that thing's so out of focus, nobody can make out who it is."

"Computer-enhance it," Frieze told him.

"Yeah," A.L. said flatly. "Computer-enhance it."

Frieze was silent.

"The Secret Service—" Jones started.

"—is out of it," the agent finished the sentence. "The video clearly shows that McLean was the target of a deliberate poisoning. That waiter never went near the President. We were right all along. It was not an attempt on the President's life."

"Yeah, well . . ."

"Good luck," Frieze concluded, and hung up.

"Man!" LaTroy commented.

A.L. had been so engrossed in the videotape he'd forgotten the boy was there.

"You stay here and study, hear?" the detective instructed. "No TV! There's food in the refrigerator. I'll be back soon as I can."

"Can I go with you?" the boy asked. The detective noted a spark of interest in LaTroy's eyes that he'd never seen before.

"Not this time, LaTroy," he responded in a kindly tone, not wanting to discourage the teenager's curiosity. "But another time. Okay?"

The boy nodded and lapsed back into his usual sullen silence.

Through the apartment's dusty window, LaTroy watched the detective drive away in his white Ford. When the car was out of sight, the boy threw his books into his backpack and left, taking off for the streets.

CHAPTER NINETEEN

A.L. DROVE EAST on Florida Avenue. The deteriorating neighborhood of once-sturdy two- and three-story red brick row houses grew worse with each passing block. The doors and windows of many buildings were sealed with plywood sheets or cinder blocks. Groups of furtive, hopeless black men clustered on corners and in doorways. Youngsters with the eyes of animals watched his car pass, tensed, ready to pounce or flee.

Trees still grew here, their leaves greening in the spring sun, another reminder of the neighborhood's more genteel past. But nearly every tree was banded by neon-colored posters advertising nightclubs and hip-hop shows.

From his amateur studies of Washington's architectural history, the detective knew that until the middle of the eighteenth century, Florida Avenue had been the northernmost boundary of the city's residential and commercial development. Beyond was rural. And now, once again, the avenue was like a wild frontier.

What a change, Jones thought, since he'd accompanied his father on Saturday visits to this neighborhood in the decade after World War II. Come to see friends, people newly arrived from the Carolinas, Pullman porters and white people's maids, laborers, barbers, post-office workers, the first generation of Negro file clerks and typists in the government.

The people were mostly poor then, too, he recalled. But to a little boy the place seemed lively and exciting, with the sound of raucous laughter and the smell of frying fat in the air. He remembered the crowds, heading for Griffith Stadium to see the Homestead Grays play a Negro League game when the Washington Nats of the still-segregated major leagues were on the road. Or to the Howard Theater to see Billy Eckstine or Lena Horne or Bojangles Robinson.

Griffith Stadium was long gone, replaced by a hospital, and the Howard was a mustard-colored ruin defaced with graffiti.

And now there was menace in the air, not laughter.

A.L. turned right on North Capitol Street and then left a couple of blocks before Union Station. The nondescript CNN office building rose up from a vast parking lot. It looked like a sea of car roofs was lapping at the building's sides. A gigantic sculpture composed of jumbled metal panels squatted in the plaza in front.

In the lobby, Jones showed his badge to the security guard, who waved him toward the elevators. "Newsroom's on eleven," the guard instructed.

A.L. wandered the narrow corridors of tan walls and turquoise doors on the eleventh floor until he encountered a young woman with three gold rings piercing her left ear.

"Who's in charge here?" A.L. asked her.

"Can I help you?" she replied warily.

"Yeah. You can take me to whoever's in charge."

"If this is about something we had on the air, sir, you should write a letter." She took his arm and tried to steer him back toward the elevator.

Jones wrested his arm away and showed her his badge. "Who's in charge here?" he repeated.

"Oh m'God. I'm sorry. Come on. I'll show you."

She led him to an office looking out on the great parking lot.

Behind the desk sat a thin man with curly red hair and a

pinched face, wearing a plaid cotton sport shirt.

"Len? This guy's a detective. He wants to talk to you."

Introduction done, she ducked away.

"Yeah?" Len challenged.

Jones showed his badge again. He tugged a smudged business card from his wallet and handed it across the desk. It was his last one. Len studied it. A.L. looked around the office.

Eight TV sets glowed mutely in a cabinet facing the desk. Each set was labeled with a black and white card: CNN, CNN HEADLINE, C-SPAN, C-SPAN II, NBC, CBS, ABC, and INCOMING. A.L. figured that one was not going out over the air, since part of the time it showed bands in rainbow colors and part of the time it showed reporters fiddling with their earplugs.

"Detective Jones?" Len said, waving him toward a chair. "I'm Len Albertson. I'm the assistant bureau chief. What can I do for you? I'm guessing it's about the McLean tape, right?"

"Right," the detective replied. "I need a copy of that videotape."

"Oh." Albertson's face became even more pinched. "I don't think I can do that. At least, not without talking to Atlanta. I don't think they'll approve it. We never give tapes to the police. You know, it's a First Amendment thing."

"First Amendment, bullshit!" Jones exploded. His stumpy body popped out of the chair. He leaned across the desk. "I'm conducting a murder investigation and that tape shows the murderer. I need it! Now!"

"Well, I can't give it to you now," Albertson protested shakily, pushing back from the detective's glowering countenance. "It's our policy, no tapes to the authorities."

"Can you believe this shit?" Jones asked the ceiling.

"Didn't McLean work here?" he shouted at Albertson. Jones often lost control of his temper when he was tired. "Don't you *want* us to catch whoever busted him?"

"Of course I do," the assistant bureau chief replied weakly. "Dan was my colleague. But it's not my decision. I've got to call Atlanta. I'll call now, okay? Just wait outside. Just a few minutes, okay? Maybe they'll change the policy."

"Fuck the policy!" A.L. shouted, and stomped out of the office.

Goddamn newsies, Jones raged to himself. Always writing that the cops are incompetent or lazy or crooked, can't stop crime. But when it comes to helping the cops, they give you that First Amendment bullshit.

Jones needed coffee.

"Hey, bro'." An athletic black man in jeans and a MILLION MAN MARCH T-shirt called to him from a small, dark room filled with monitors and electronic equipment. "Remember me, man?" he asked Jones, motioning the detective into the room.

The detective didn't.

"Remember that drive-by shooting near the Navy Yard?" the man prompted. "You know, got those people at the bus stop? I was the sound man on the camera crew. Tried to interview you, remember? But you wouldn't say nothin'."

Jones recalled the encounter vaguely. There were so many killings, so many TV lights in his eyes, so many shouted questions. He couldn't remember the specific episode.

A.L. grunted noncommittally.

"I'm Charles Jackson," the man introduced himself. "I'm working as a tape editor now. I heard you and Len going at it. What's the beef? He won't give you the tape of that guy poisoning Dan?"

"He won't give it to me *yet,*" A.L. replied. "He's got to call *Atlanta.* See if it's okay to change the *policy."* The detective mimicked Albertson's timorous voice.

"Shit, Len's scared to take a leak without calling Atlanta." The editor laughed. "They just gonna jerk you around. I'll give you a tape."

"Yeah?" A.L. was surprised.

"Yeah. I dubbed an extra copy for myself. I'll give it to you and make myself another one." He removed an oblong gray plastic box from his canvas briefcase and handed it to the detective.

"Thanks," A.L. said in a deep rumble.

"Hey, man, I liked Dan," Jackson said. "He was a tough dude. I wanna help you catch the guy who did it."

"If I can tell what he looks like," Jones replied. "I saw the tape on TV. It's so fuzzy I don't know if I can make an ID."

"You gotta get the tape enhanced," the editor instructed.

"Yeah? How do I do that?"

Jackson flipped through an alphabetical file of name-and-address cards. He copied the information from one of the cards and handed it to A.L.

"Go see this guy. He lives over in Alexandria somewhere. He's a computer freak. He does work for CNN sometimes. Tell him I sent you. He can do so much shit with tape you won't believe it. When he's finished working on that tape, you'll be able to count the fillings in that waiter's teeth."

"Thanks," Jones rumbled again.

"Hey, man. Forget it."

CHAPTER TWENTY

COLBERT CLAWSON, THE Secret Service director, arrived at the family quarters on the third floor of the White House at eight P.M. by prearrangement. The President's press secretary, Garvin Dillon, met him in the marble-floored elevator vestibule and escorted him up a narrow staircase to the solarium, where the President and his wife were waiting.

The solarium was a favorite spot for Dale and Grady Hammond, as it had been for previous White House occupants. Susan Ford and her school chums had listened to rock-and-roll records there. Richard Nixon had brooded there as his presidency collapsed. Dale and Grady often ate dinner from trays in the solarium, talking about the events of the day, and then working on the papers they'd brought home from their offices.

The wall of glass, following the curve of the Truman balcony below, presented a spectacular view across the South Lawn and the round greensward of the Ellipse beyond the fence to the white obelisk of the Washington Monument gleaming in its circle of spotlights.

Behind the monument was the round dome of the Jefferson Memorial, then a glistening swath of the Potomac River, and, on the far shore, Virginia, lined with trees greening in the spring warmth. A continuous string of jetliners on their final approach to National Airport gracefully skimmed low from right to left, their strobe lights flashing, their landing gear already down.

But the four people gathered in the solarium were not there for the scenery.

The pale Clawson, in gray suit and black tie, had requested the meeting to report on CNN's videotape of a waiter apparently dropping something into Dan McLean's food at the White House Correspondents dinner. The director was eager to demonstrate to the President that the videotape vindicated his original decision to avoid Secret Service jurisdiction in the case.

The Secret Service chief had brought a copy of the tape, recorded off the air. He inserted the black plastic cassette into a VCR player and pressed the start button.

They watched in silence, listening to the anchorwoman's description.

"So," Clawson summarized, stopping the tape, "it's apparent from this video that McLean was the intended victim, not you, sir"—he nodded toward Dale Hammond—"and we're closing out our involvement."

"Thank you so much, Colbert," the President said, "for your diligence in—"

"I can't see a damn thing on that tape," Grady interrupted.

"We're having the tape electronically enhanced, ma'am," Clawson explained in a patronizing tone. "But even without the enhancement, it's obvious that a waiter deliberately dropped something into McLean's soup, presumably the poison that killed him."

" 'Presumably?' " Grady pressed sarcastically. " 'Presumably?' Since when was 'presumably' good enough for the Secret Service?"

"Ma'am—"

"Who *was* the waiter?" the First Lady cut him off. "Why would he want to poison Dan McLean? You're not even sure the tape shows the waiter dropping something into McLean's soup, are you?"

Clawson had been in the Secret Service since Lyndon

Johnson. All the wives had been a pain in the neck. But this one was a special pain in the neck. This one and Hillary.

"Ma'am, we *are* sure the video shows the waiter dropping something into McLean's soup," the Secret Service director explained with elaborate patience, as if talking to a child. "We don't know the waiter's identity, or why he did it. Since it's obvious now that the incident did not involve an attempt on the President's life, those questions are not the responsibility of the Secret Service. They are the responsibility of the Metropolitan Police. And we've already notified the D.C. Homicide Squad."

"The D.C. Homicide Squad?" the First Lady snorted. "How about the Keystone Kops? They're more efficient."

Clawson did not respond. In some ways, he thought, this one was worse than Hillary.

"Why don't you *do* something?" Grady now addressed her husband. "The Secret Service is obviously running away from this case. Why? What are they trying to hide? Why don't you *order* them to find out what the hell happened at that dinner? You *are* the President, remember?"

"Now, hon," Dale Hammond responded soothingly. "The Secret Service knows what it's doing. And besides, the videotape shows that waiter wasn't—"

"Oh, Dale, you are so trusting sometimes," the First Lady interrupted him. "Sometimes you are too trusting for your own good."

She flounced out of the solarium. The three men remaining could hear her denouncing them as she hurried down the stairway.

"Mr. Colbert, I'm very sorry," the President apologized. "Grady means well."

"That's all right, Mr. President, I understand," the Secret Service director replied magnanimously. He was glad she was Hammond's wife and not his.

They stood and shook hands formally in front of the stunning night view.

Garvin Dillon escorted Clawson back to the elevator.

"You're going to announce that the Secret Service is out of the case?" the press secretary asked.

"Yes," Clawson relied, looking at his watch. "I'm scheduled to appear on *Larry King Live* at nine o'clock."

"Of course," Dillon commented sardonically. "New definition of news: If it doesn't happen on CNN, it doesn't happen."

"Grady Hammond wants you to call her right away," K. T. Zorn informed Jerry as soon as he arrived at the ATN studios shortly before eleven P.M. "She says it's important."

The talk-show host went into his office, closed the door, and called the private number the First Lady had given him. She answered on the first ring. Grady wanted him to put her on the air that night so she could denounce the Secret Service.

Jerry agreed immediately. But he was sorry she would be on a phone hookup from the White House rather than in the studio with him.

As soon as Jerry hung up from Grady, he called Jane Day's apartment. No answer. Where was she at that hour? She never had a date. He dialed her number at the *Post,* even though she had given him instructions never to call her there.

"Who's calling?" asked the newsroom assistant who answered.

"Tell her it's Ted Kennedy," Jerry replied, mimicking a Boston accent.

Jane came on the line immediately. "Senator?"

"No. It's me."

"Goddamn it, Jerry!"

"I was just trying to boost your reputation at the paper."

"What do want? I'm busy."

"Are you still mad at me for canceling out on the Canadian embassy thing?"

"Actually, I'm very grateful to you, Jerry. I ran into Harrison Ford after your call, and we ended up spending a wild night together."

"Really?"

"What do you want? I'm on deadline."

"Are you writing about the videotape and the Secret Service announcement?"

"Yes."

He heard the keys clicking on her computer.

"I guess you think the tape proves your theory that Dale Hammond was not the real target of the poisoner," Jerry said.

"I'm hanging up, Jerry. I haven't got time for this."

"Listen to my show tonight, Jane," Jerry said hurriedly before she could break the connection. "Grady Hammond's going to be on."

"Oh, no! Not again!"

"Yep. Listen in. You'll get the real story."

"Another dynamite show tonight, friends!" the host proclaimed as soon as Sammy cued him. "We've got Grady Hammond, the First Lady, standing by on the phone. The First Lady, and a *great* lady. A great *conservative* lady. She's got something she wants to say to the people of America, and she decided to say it *here,* on *my* show. Grady Hammond didn't ask to go on Rush's show. And she certainly didn't ask to go on Larry King's show, that liberal creep. She asked to go on Jerry Knight's show, the *Night Talker* show. Why? Because I am the world's greatest radio talk-show host. Certifiably the greatest. She knows I'm fair. She knows *her* enemies are *my* enemies. And she knows you people out there are the world's greatest audience. So, without further ado, direct from the White House, here is the very outspoken, the very smart, and—if I may say so—the very beautiful First Lady of the United States, Ms. Grady Hammond!"

"Jerry's in heat." K.T. muttered in the control room. "Why doesn't he buy her a corsage and invite her to the prom?"

Sammy snickered.

For the next thirty minutes, in response to Jerry's fawning questions, Grady elaborated on her complaint that the Secret Service was unjustified in dropping out of the investigation of the McLean poisoning on the basis of a blurry and inconclusive amateur video.

She reiterated her suspicion that the President may have been the intended target of enemies of his conservative policies. And she spun out her theory that the Secret Service might be ducking the case because it was afraid of uncovering some terrible secret it didn't want revealed.

"I've been telling you for years that funny things are going on in Washington, folks," Jerry pontificated. "*Real* funny. And I mean funny peculiar, not funny hah hah."

• • •

Jane Day was writing furiously at her computer in the nearly empty *Washington Post* newsroom. And she wasn't happy.

First she'd written a story based on the CNN broadcast of the camcorder videotape. Jane hated it when television scooped her.

No sooner had she finished that story for the first edition than she had to rewrite it to include Colbert Clawson's comments on *Larry King Live.* Another damn TV scoop. She felt like she was nothing but a transcript service.

And here it was after midnight and she was rewriting again for the final editions to include Grady Hammond's allegations to Jerry Knight on the *Night Talker* show.

"You two deserve each other," she told the radio on her cluttered desk.

To top things off, her editor, Russ Williamson, was giving her a hard time about including in her story a hint that Dan McLean was killed because he was about to break a story involving a Hammond administration official who wanted to hide an embarrassing episode dating back to the end of the Vietnam War.

"You've got no sources for that," Russ scolded her, leaning over her shoulder so that his cheek brushed her cheek. "No sources, no facts, no confirmation."

"The Vietnamese technician on Jerry Knight's show heard that McLean was asking questions about an administration official who committed some kind of screwup at the end of the war," Jane responded. She twisted a curl of orange hair nervously around her finger.

"That's a joke, right?" Russ asked. "That's an April Fool's joke a couple of weeks late, right?"

"McLean's notes on the story he was investigating are full of the initials 'VN,' " Jane argued weakly. "That must stand for 'Vietnam.' The story is starting to come together, Russ."

"I don't believe this," the editor sputtered. "*What* story? What's the name of the government official McLean was about to expose? What was the embarrassing Vietnam episode this official was trying to cover up?"

"I don't know," Jane replied defensively.

"Come on, Jane. You know better than this. We can't put vague, unsubstantiated, third-hand allegations about some anonymous official in the paper. Scoffield would demote me to obits and fire you."

"I'm going to prove it," Jane said defiantly.

"Okay, look," Russ said more sympathetically, straightening up. "You've got enough in this story already. You work on that other angle tomorrow, and when you nail it down, we'll run it big."

"All right," she surrendered.

"I think you should move this higher." He tapped a paragraph on the screen with his finger.

"Get out of here," Jane snapped. "If you want me to finish this piece for the final, leave me alone."

Russ started back toward his editor's station. "How about a drink when you're finished?" he asked. "You've had a rough night. You deserve a drink."

"Oh, yeah," Jane shot back. "I deserve a drink. With *Brad Pitt.*"

Immediately following his interview on *Larry King Live,* Secret Service Director Colbert Clawson returned to his office. The building was quiet and nearly deserted at that hour.

Waiting in Colbert's office by prearrangement were Clifford Wolfe, assistant director of the FBI, and G. Belmon Christianson, special assistant to the director of Central Intelligence. Christianson had been a legendary operative. Now he looked ancient, his legs stiffened and his spine bent with arthritis. But his mind was sharp as ever.

When Clawson arrived, Wolfe and Christianson were swapping tales of past adventures.

The men shook hands.

"Did you bring it?" Clawson asked Wolfe.

"Right here." The FBI official withdrew a plastic box from his black leather briefcase, opened it, and removed a VHS videocassette.

"Enhanced?" Christianson rasped.

"Enhanced," Wolfe assured him.

Clawson swung open the doors of an enormous, ornately carved cherrywood cabinet. Inside was a television set with a dark metal case and a large screen. On a shelf beneath the TV set was a VCR player.

The three men stood on the deep Oriental carpet in front of the cabinet and watched the video. It was the amateur's tape from the White House Correspondents Dinner, the original fuzzy image now resolved into a crisp, clear picture by computer magic.

The tape was cued to the place where the camera caught a waiter placing a soup bowl in front of Dan McLean. When the correspondent looked away, the waiter quickly removed something from his pocket and dropped it into the bowl.

Clawson rewound the tape and they watched the scene again.

The computer enhancement made it possible to discern that the waiter had Asian features.

Wolfe recognized him.

"One of yours, isn't he, Bell?" the FBI official asked Christianson.

"Used to be," the CIA man replied. He hobbled on two canes to Clawson's cherrywood desk and leaned against it to rest his crippled legs.

"Why'd you have him kill McLean?" the Secret Service chief asked.

"We didn't, Cliff," Christianson croaked. "We booted him three years ago. Unreliable."

"If he wasn't working for you, who was he working for?" Clawson asked.

"Somebody told me he did some jobs for the Bureau after we bagged him," Christianson said.

"He did one job for us two years ago," Wolfe conceded. "We didn't trust him, either."

"So who was he working for when he took out McLean?" Clawson repeated.

The three looked at each other. None acknowledged responsibility.

"Have you checked the Magnum Project intercepts?" Belmon Christianson asked Clifford Wolfe. "You could screen for any mentions of the gook on computer traffic."

"I've never heard of a Magnum Project," the FBI official replied blandly.

CHAPTER TWENTY-ONE

THE PHONE WOKE A. L. Jones.

"Shit," he groaned.

The clock's red digital numbers on the bedside table read five-thirty.

The detective had been up until three A.M., investigating the killing of a Jordanian cab driver, shot and robbed of $13 in the parking lot of an apartment building near Logan Circle, apparently by a passenger.

"Whattaya want?" Jones mumbled into the phone.

"I got your video."

"My what?"

"Your video. From that dinner? Somebody putting something in that CNN guy's food? You asked me to enhance it. Remember? You can see the waiter clearly now."

"Yeah?" A.L. sat up in bed.

The sheets and blanket were twisted around his waist. The apartment was cold and quiet. And lonely.

"I'll be there in thirty minutes," the detective told the caller.

A.L. needed coffee. Oh, thank heaven for 7-Eleven.

Jones drove his white detective's car across the Potomac

River on the 14th Street Bridge, swung around the tight cloverleaf onto the George Washington Parkway, past National Airport, to Alexandria. He picked up the videotape at the computer hacker's nondescript apartment, then reversed course in the thickening morning traffic and pulled up to the white marble hulk of the Municipal Center on Indiana Avenue at six-thirty A.M.

In the messy cluster of Homicide offices on the third floor, A.L. wove through the tightly packed desks, past the sullen suspects waiting to be questioned, around the trash cans overflowing with McDonald's wrappers and pizza boxes, to the coffeemaker. The clouded pot contained only a half-inch of cold coffee. He poured it into a Styrofoam cup anyhow. He needed it.

The only VCR that worked worth a damn was in Captain Wheeler's office. The captain wouldn't be in until ten. At the earliest. Probably out late again, in his skinny suit and pencil mustache, at some soiree, sucking up to the mayor.

A.L. was surprised at what the computer geek had been able to do. The previously blurry tape was clear as a movie. The detective watched the waiter on the video place a bowl in front of McLean. The correspondent's head was turned toward the man sitting next to him. The waiter swiftly but unmistakably removed something from his pocket and dropped it into the bowl.

The detective rewound the tape and watched it again.

Jones could see that the waiter had Asian features. Korean, maybe. Or Vietnamese or Chinese. The police interviews with the waiters after McLean's murder had turned up all those nationalities. And a lot more.

"Hey, Michelle," A.L. shouted.

"Yeah?" the woman shouted back from the dispatcher's desk. "What you want, honey?"

"Mai Ling here?"

"She just left. She was working all night on that Chinese gang thing."

"Well, tell her to come on back."

It took Detective Mai Ling Fung-Berrigan a half-hour to get back to the Homicide offices. Jones used the time to go out for a fresh container of coffee.

She was a small, neat woman in her mid-forties, with black hair cropped in bangs. She wore a shiny blue gabardine suit, plain white cotton blouse, and sensible black shoes. She did not look like she'd been up all night, Jones thought.

He'd worked with her on a couple of cases. She was good.

Detective Fung-Berrigan, a former probation officer in San Jose, California, had joined the D.C. Homicide squad seven years earlier when her husband, a scientist, transferred to the National Institutes of Health in Bethesda.

Her knowledge of Asian languages and customs was in demand as Washington's large Oriental population expanded. Asian shopkeepers seemed to be particular targets of the street boys. And in some parts of the city, the street boys were Asian.

"What's up?" Fung-Berrigan asked Jones.

"I want you to look at a videotape with me."

"Yeah?"

"Did you see that tape on CNN, some amateur shot it, the dinner where McLean was poisoned?"

"I saw it," the woman detective replied, "but I couldn't make out much. It was out of focus."

"It was, but it ain't now."

She looked quizzical.

"Some computer dude 'enhanced' it. Yeah, that's what they call it. Means he made it clear."

"And?"

"The waiter who served McLean looks like he's Asian on the tape."

"Ah! And all Asians look alike to you." Fung-Berrigan's black eyes smiled mischievously. "So you want me to ID him for you."

"Yeah," A.L. mumbled.

A.L. and Fung-Berrigan looked at the tape several times on Captain Wheeler's VCR. On the fourth replay, she pressed the PAUSE button when the closest, clearest view of the waiter appeared on the screen.

"Wait here," the woman instructed Jones.

She returned in a moment with a black loose-leaf binder. Inside were mug shots of dozens of Asian men under sheets of clear plastic.

"Gang members," she explained.

A.L. nodded. All the men in the photos looked to him like the waiter frozen on the TV screen. But he didn't say that to Mai Ling Fung-Berrigan.

She flipped through the mug shots, looking back and forth between the binder and the TV screen.

"Here," she said at last, tapping one of the photos with a flaming red fingernail. "This is him."

She removed the photo from the binder and held it next to the image on the TV set.

"That's the guy," Fung-Berrigan concluded. "He's Vietnamese."

"How can you tell?"

Fung-Berrigan shrugged. "I can tell."

A. L. Jones's normally dour demeanor brightened. For the first time, some puzzle pieces might be fitting together in the McLean murder.

"Whatta you doing now?" Jones asked Fung-Berrigan.

"Going home, fixing my husband breakfast, and going to sleep."

Jones looked disappointed.

"You want me to help you find this guy?"

A.L. nodded.

"Let me make a phone call."

She went into a narrow cubicle, cupped her manicured fingers around the mouthpiece, and told her husband he'd have to make his own breakfast and drop their daughter at day care.

Jones and the woman detective drove first to the Washington Hilton.

It was still early, but the hotel's banquet manager was already in his office next to the mammoth kitchen. The enormously fat, bald man in white shirt, white pants, and white apron, was supervising preparations for serving breakfast to two thousand attendees at the annual convention of a chiropractors association.

The detectives spread the photos of a half dozen Asian men removed from Fung-Berrigan's black binder on the banquet manager's messy desk. Jones asked him to identify any men he recognized as waiters hired for the correspondents dinner the night McLean was poisoned.

The banquet manager shuffled through the photos. He picked the same one Fung-Berrigan had.

"This one was working that night," the banquet manager advised them.

A.L. was getting excited. Jigsaw pieces were starting to fit together.

"What's his name?" the detective asked.

"Duc? Fuc? Yeah, Duc, I think."

Fung-Berrigan gave Jones a self-satisfied nudge. It was a Vietnamese name.

"You got an address?" A.L. pressed.

The banquet manager flipped through a file box of three-by-five cards on his desk.

"Here," he said, withdrawing a card.

On the card was stapled a tiny photo. It looked like the same man on the videotape.

Under the photo was typed a name, Duc Phu Vo, and an address in the Columbia Heights section. The card contained a listing, written in different colored inks, of dates and events, apparently indicating those occasions when Duc had been hired as a waiter. The correspondents dinner was on the list.

Duc's address was on Euclid Street between 14th and 15th near the northern edge of Malcolm X Park.

Jones knew from his architectural studies that in the late nineteenth and early twentieth centuries, a senator's wife named Mary Henderson had championed the area as a fashionable neighborhood of posh apartment buildings, stately town houses, and even mansions. She and the senator had maintained the most elaborate mansion of all, known for decades as the Henderson Castle. But their castle and that era were long gone.

The block where Duc lived was a line of run-down row houses, the windows on the ground floors protected with black iron bars. Some of the houses were boarded up and abandoned. Only the abundant trees flourishing in the grass strip along the curb recalled an earlier gentility.

Detectives Jones and Fung-Berrigan scaled the steep cement stairs from the street to the tan stone building where the waiter lived. A red motorcycle was parked in the overgrown front yard. Once a family's three-story town house, the building had been divided into apartments. The lock on the front door was broken, so Jones and Fung-Berrigan entered without buzzing.

They found Duc's name on one of the pried-open mailboxes. His apartment was on the top floor.

The detectives climbed the three flights of steps, slogging through trash. On the second landing, their feet crunched syringes in the stairwell. A.L. opened his coat so he could reach the gun in his waist holster quickly if necessary. Even a cop wasn't safe in the city these days, he thought. Especially a cop.

The door to Duc's apartment was ajar. Fung-Berrigan knocked. No answer. She knocked again. Only silence from within.

A.L. pushed open the door warily. Cheap paper shades were pulled down over the dirty windows, letting in a dim yellow light. The place was sparsely furnished: a card table, two folding aluminum lawn chairs, a sagging sofa, a tilting metal floor lamp with a rip in the shade.

A tiny kitchen was dark and empty.

The detectives moved down a narrow hall to the bedroom. A.L. now had his hand on his gun. The bedroom, too, was sparsely furnished: cardboard boxes overflowing with clothes, a plaster lamp sitting on a chipped white end table, two mattresses on the floor.

And, in the murk, A.L. made out a man sprawled on one of the mattresses, a small, dark-haired man dressed only in a T-shirt and undershorts. The T-shirt was blotched with dark stains. He laid still. Jones had no doubt he was dead.

Fung-Berrigan reached into her shoulder purse, withdrew a flashlight, and shined it on the man's face.

The mouth was wide open and the eyes were closed. But A.L. recognized the face as the waiter in the videotape, the man on the Hilton's file card.

Duc Phu Vo.

Dead.

Jones looked at his watch. A little after eight. He had intended to drive LaTroy to school, to make sure the boy didn't cut classes. No time now.

After radioing for crime-scene investigators and a morgue wagon, Jones and Fung-Berrigan canvassed Duc's neighbors about the waiter's death. For a frustrating hour, they roamed the apartment building's littered and stinking hallways. They learned nothing.

Some of the tenants pretended not to be home, even when Jones shouted "Police!" Those who did open their doors—some terrified, some defiant—insisted they'd heard nothing, seen nothing, known nothing.

"Shit!" A.L. bellowed, kicking at a plastic syringe on the cracked tile floor of the dark second-floor landing.

He couldn't really blame them for clamming up. Seemed like half the people busted in D.C. by the bad boys were popped to keep them from identifying the shooters in some earlier bust.

Twice in the last month, Jones had watched boys he'd arrested walk out of court laughing and free because intimidated witnesses, fearing retaliation, refused to testify. Threats by the judge and promises of protection by the police hadn't persuaded them to risk their lives.

Hell, you can't make witnesses put their own heads in the noose.

"A.L."

"Yeah, I know, Mai Ling. We ain't gonna get nothing out of these people. Go on home. Fix your husband his breakfast."

It was too late for that. But Detective Fung-Berrigan appreciated the thought.

CHAPTER TWENTY-TWO

Back from her morning jog on the black asphalt bicycle path in Rock Creek Park, Jane stood under the shower and pondered how to pursue the story of Dan McLean's murder. She was stuck.

Based on the CNN correspondent's notebooks and on what Mr. Cao and Jerry Knight's technician Sammy had heard in the Vietnamese community, she believed that McLean was working on an investigative story about some cover-up involving the Vietnam War, and that he had been poisoned to stop him from exposing it. But she didn't have anywhere near enough evidence to get that story in the paper.

And maybe she never would. Jane was in one of her self-doubting moods. Maybe she'd never confirm her hunch. Maybe her hunch was wrong.

The friend of K.T.'s friend at CNN said Dan was working on a story about government computer surveillance when he was killed, not a story about Vietnam. She needed to follow up on that. But how?

Maybe Dan's active sex life had provoked a vengeful husband. Or a vengeful wife. Jane didn't think people killed for jealousy anymore. But Detective Jones thought they did, so she couldn't completely dismiss the idea.

Jane stepped out of the shower and wrapped herself in a luxuriously thick white terry towel big as a sheet, a gift sent by her mother, Mavis, from Neiman Marcus in Beverly Hills.

"You must never settle for anything except the finest quality," Mavis had instructed her daughter since childhood. "Better to do without than to accept second-rate."

When Jane had to do without the finest quality because of her middling reporter's salary, her mother often sent her what Mavis thought she should have—like the towel—over the daughter's protests of independence.

A husband for her daughter was the one area where Mavis Day seemed willing to lower her standards, Jane thought, rubbing her stringy orange hair between the folds of the giant towel. Ever since Jane celebrated her thirtieth birthday five years earlier, her mother had ever more urgently pressured her to find a husband.

Mavis, who had prodded her since she was a teenager to strive for success in a career, now implored her with equal persistence to get married.

The next time her mother asked "So, honey, are you seeing anyone?" Jane was going to tell her about Jerry Knight.

Probably not. Unless she wanted to give her mother a heart attack. And her father, too. Her parents were Rosenberg-defending, Nixon-hating, war-protesting sixties liberals, the offspring of Hoover-hating, Roosevelt-loving, Hiss-defending forties liberals.

Jane couldn't even imagine the conversation.

"Hey, Mom, guess what? I'm going out with a conservative talk-show host who makes Rush Limbaugh look like a moderate."

The next sound would be the thud of her mother collapsing on the floor.

But if her relationship with Jerry got serious, she'd have to tell her parents.

Big "if."

Jane dropped the towel to the floor and stared at herself in the mirror.

She felt ugly.

For two weeks she'd been following, more or less religiously, a new diet she'd read about in *Cosmopolitan,* the rice-and-orange-slice diet. And she hadn't lost a pound. In fact, she'd gained a pound. Well, really two pounds.

Jane looked down at her naked body, still damp from the shower. Big thighs. Overabundant ass. Skimpy breasts.

And her face. Jane leaned toward the mirror. The eyes were okay. Big. Green. Her best feature. But her nose! Her hair!

"Agggggh."

Jane let out a mock scream.

Bloomsbury, her cat, looked up from his tuna fish. She must be in one of those moods.

While Jane dressed, she had an idea about where to seek fresh information for her story of Dan McLean's murder.

She'd visit Detective A. L. Jones.

"A.L.?" Jonetta, the uniformed policewoman assigned to help in Homicide, shouted from her desk at the entrance to the warren of offices. "You here?"

"Yeah?" his weary baritone shouted back from amid the chaos. "Whatta you want?"

"That girl reporter here to see you. You going to be famous again, A.L.? Can I have your autograph?"

The detective appeared.

"Miss Day," A.L. growled. "Lemme guess. You're here about Dan McLean. Right?"

"Right." She extracted a reporter's spiral notepad from her oversized tapestry shoulder bag.

"I ain't got but a couple of minutes," Jones grunted. "And I ain't going to tell you nothing. But might as well tell you nothing where it ain't so noisy."

He led her to a sparsely furnished office that was, for the moment, not being used.

"Well, at least it's not the interrogation room, where you took me the first time we met," she commented. "Remember?"

"Yeah," he responded laconically.

Jane thought he looked like he'd been up all night. Probably had. If not, he'd slept in his clothes.

By contrast, she looked like she'd stepped out of a fashion advertisement. She wore a hunter green pant suit with a criss-cross cream silk blouse and a pair of Bruno Magli pumps she'd bought on sale at Saks. They actually made her legs look sexy.

It was the killer outfit she wore whenever she was having an ugly day.

"You want coffee?" A.L. asked.

"No, thanks."

"Good. It's awful today."

Jane flipped open her notepad. "So, are you getting anywhere on the case?"

"Yeah," A.L. replied vaguely. "I'm getting somewhere."

The detective was distrustful of newsies in general and this weird orange-haired girl in particular. She'd tried to hustle him on the Davenport case, thinking he was a dumb cop who would fall for her sweet talk. She and the Night Talker dude, playing amateur detectives. They could have gotten themselves slammed if he hadn't saved their asses. And this one tried the sweet-talk bit on him again when he encountered her leaving McLean's house. Newsies. They never got it right.

Captain Wheeler poked his head into the office where they were talking.

"A.L., where's that report on the waiter?"

"Coming, Captain. Fifteen minutes."

"What waiter?" Jane demanded. "The waiter on the videotape?"

"Yeah," A.L. conceded.

Shit. Why'd the captain have to come in when he did? Now she'd want to know all about it.

"You know who the waiter was?" Jane asked in an excited voice.

"Vietnamese guy named Duc. Duc Po Vu. Pho Vo Duc. Something like that."

Jane's ballpoint went into overdrive. She scribbled frantically in her notepad without taking her eyes off the detective's furrowed mahogany face.

"Do you know where he is?"

"Yeah."

"Where?"

"In the morgue. Dead."

A.L. smiled at her smugly. Got her that time.

"Dead?" Jane confirmed. "How?"

"Found him in his apartment couple of hours ago. Somebody popped him twice in the chest."

Jane's pen flew over the paper. Her eyes remained riveted on A.L.

"Who did it?"

"Dunno."

"You don't have any idea?"

"Some pipehead, probably. Popped him and took his stuff to sell for drugs."

"What's the pipehead's name?"

"Interview's over," A.L. declared. "I gotta finish the report for the captain." The stumpy detective started toward the door.

"Can I write this?" the reporter asked.

"I can't stop you. The guy got popped. It's a fact."

"And you know he was the waiter who served Dan?"

"He's the dude on the videotape. The hotel says it's him—Duc, or whatever his name is."

"Wow!" Jane enthused. "I've got my story for tomorrow."

"Don't write that the cops don't have any idea who busted him," A.L. ordered.

"But you said—"

"Don't write it!" the detective ordered more firmly.

"If you said it, I can write it," Jane bristled. "You never said it was off the record."

"My job description don't require me to talk to you no more," A.L. rumbled in a threatening baritone.

"All right," Jane surrendered, figuring it was more important to keep A.L. as a future source than to burn him with one minor quote now. "I'll leave out what you said. You didn't understand the ground rules."

The cacophony of the Homicide offices penetrated their quiet enclave. A woman's wailing lament. A detective berating a suspect. An angry string of expletives. A TV set. Phones ringing. Jonetta shouting.

Jane flipped through her pad, reviewing her notes. "The waiter was Vietnamese, right?" she asked A.L.

"Right," the detective said.

"Remember what I told you about Dan's notebooks?" Jane recalled their encounter outside McLean's house. "They had a lot of references to 'VN.' Must have stood for 'Vietnam.' Jerry Knight's technician says he heard in the Vietnamese community that Dan was investigating a blunder at the end of the war by someone who's an official in the Hammond administration now. And the owner of a restaurant in Little Saigon heard something similar."

"So?" A.L. asked, eager to get rid of her.

"So now the waiter who poisoned Dan turns out to have been Vietnamese. It's beginning to add up."

"To what?"

"To what I've been saying all along. Dan was killed to keep him from broadcasting a story that would be embarrassing to some big shot. And the story had something to do with the war."

A.L. had another flashback to his time as a soldier in Vietnam. He was flying in a Huey, sitting on a pile of green rubber body bags containing the shredded pieces of his buddies. Blood oozed through the zippers. He tried to stand up. The crew chief waved him down. In his head A.L. could hear the *whomp whomp* of the rotors.

Jones shook the scene from his mind.

"I have a plan," Jane Day offered.

"Yeah?"

"Let's you and me and Jerry Knight go to dinner in Little Saigon and see if we can persuade the restaurant owner to tell us more about what he heard in the Vietnamese community about Dan's murder. Maybe he has some leads you can investigate—"

"—and you can write about."

"And I can write about," Jane conceded.

"Maybe there's a simpler explanation," the detective suggested. "Maybe it didn't have anything to do with Vietnam. Maybe McLean's wife is the jealous type and she hired that waiter to drop her old man because he was running around on her."

"I don't see it," Jane protested.

"Or maybe Senator Thatcher hired that waiter because

McLean was sleeping with his wife. Could have been a lot of husbands hired that waiter. McLean messed around with a *lot* of women weren't his wife."

"I know you think Dan's murder was a sex thing. But being unfaithful is not exactly a rare affliction among married men."

Jane thought of Russ and about two dozen other husbands who'd come on to her. "If irate wives and irate husbands had all the cheating men in Washington knocked off, you'd have a murder epidemic on your hands."

"I've *got* a murder epidemic on my hands," A. L. Jones rumbled.

"Will you at least *talk* to the Vietnamese restaurant owner?" Jane persisted. "What have you got to lose?"

What did he have to lose? He wasn't getting anywhere with what he had.

"When?" A.L. asked.

"I'll set it up and let you know," Jane promised.

"Bye, honey," Jonetta said as Jane left the Homicide offices.

That girl sure did like to dress herself up, the policewoman thought.

CHAPTER TWENTY-THREE

THE DETECTIVE'S REMARKS about McLean's dalliances gave Jane an idea.

She still didn't believe Dan was the victim of jealousy. But the mention of Kristi Thatcher suggested to the reporter that the girlfriend might know more details about the story the CNN correspondent was investigating than the widow Patricia McLean did.

Standing outside the Municipal Center, Jane looked at her watch. She had to hurry to make the daily White House briefing. Afterward, she'd try to talk to Kristi Thatcher.

The briefing was dull. Jane offered the paper a few paragraphs. To her disgust, the desk informed her they'd be wrapped into the congressional correspondent's story on the battle over Hammond's legislative program.

The White House used to be the premier beat in Washington, and Jane was ecstatic when she won the assignment. But with a weakling like Hammond in the Oval Office, all the action had shifted to the Hill. Jane felt like she was in a backwater. If she hadn't grabbed the McLean story the night of his murder, she'd never get a byline at all.

After a quick and unhealthy lunch from the vending machines at the rear of the briefing room, Jane phoned Norton Thatcher's house.

"Jes?" a heavily accented voice answered.

"Mrs. Thatcher, please."

"Not here."

"What time will she be back?"

This produced a burst of what might have been Spanish.

"Donde esta la Señora Thatcher?" Jane tried out one of the few phrases she remembered from high school.

Her rudimentary Spanish must have been awful because the housekeeper tried to answer in English.

"She go hair. Getting hair. Jes."

Hair? Like getting her hair styled?

"She went to have her hair done?" Jane asked into the phone. "She went to George's Hair Salon?"

"Jes. Getting hair."

"Gracias," Jane thanked her. *"Hasta . . . hasta . . ."* something.

George's was a guess on Jane's part and received a less than firm confirmation from the housekeeper. But it was worth a try.

Jane phoned the hair salon. She knew the number by memory. Muriel, the receptionist, answered.

"It's Jane Day."

"Miss Day, I'm sorry. It's so busy today I don't think we can fit you in. There's a White House state dinner tonight, you know. We're packed."

"I don't need an appointment, Muriel," Jane explained. "I'm calling to find out if Kristi Thatcher is there."

"Mrs. Thatcher? Yes, she arrived about ten minutes ago. You want to talk to her?"

"No, thanks. I'll catch up with her later. She should be there, what, another hour?"

"Oh, yes, at least." Muriel laughed. "She's getting the full treatment."

Jane was sure that Dan McLean's mistress would not willingly agree to see her. So she would ambush Mrs. Thatcher when she left George's.

Meanwhile, Jane had time to contact the other woman in Dan's life—*one* of the other women—his wife.

"Hello?" the widow answered the phone warily.

"Mrs. McLean, it's Jane Day from the *Washington Post.* Do you remember me?"

"Yes," the woman answered in a guarded tone. "You were here a while back looking through Dan's notebooks."

"Right," Jane rushed on. Mrs. McLean did not sound like she wanted to continue the conversation. "The notebooks indicate Dan was working on a story about Vietnam before he died. I have a couple of other sources who have heard he was investigating a member of the Hammond administration who made some kind of blunder at the end of the Vietnam War."

"Yes?"

"Did he ever tell you any details of that story?"

"I told you when you were here, Jane, that Dan never discussed his work with me," Patricia McLean stated crisply. "I don't think I can help you."

Jane sensed the widow was about to hang up.

"I don't want to be a pest, Mrs. McLean, especially at a time like this. But if I can find out the details of the story Dan was working on, it might point to who killed him. Would you let me look at his notebooks one more time?"

Jane held her breath. Say yes, she prayed.

"I have no objection to your looking at his notebooks again," Mrs. McLean replied. "But they're no longer here. A man from CNN came and picked them up a few days ago. He said the network wanted to continue pursuing the story and needed the notebooks for background information."

Jane was disappointed. She doubted CNN would let her see the notebooks.

"Do you know the name of the man who picked them up?"

"I'm sorry, I don't remember. My memory, since Dan's death . . ." She trailed off.

"If you think of anything that might help, please call," Jane urged.

"I will," Patricia McLean promised unconvincingly. "I hope you get your story."

"I want to find out who killed Dan, and why," Jane declared.

"Yes." The widow hung up.

One last call before Jane headed for George's. She left a message on K. T. Zorn's voice mail asking her to find out from her friend at CNN the name of the person at the network who had retrieved Dan McLean's notebooks.

Jane waited for Kristi Thatcher at the bottom of the steps leading down from the hair salon to 29th Street.

After about ten minutes, the senator's wife appeared. She wore white tights, a white peasant blouse cinched with a thin silver belt, a necklace of white beads, and white fashion sneakers. A tiny silver lamé purse hung from a long white cord looped over her neck. Her blond hair was sprayed into immobility. Her lips and nails were startlingly red.

Jane guessed they were about the same age. But not in the same league, lookswise. This was a seriously stunning woman. She inflamed Jane's feelings of inadequacy. No wonder Dan McLean had cheated on his wife.

"Mrs. Thatcher?" Jane approached her as she came down the steps from George's.

"Yes?" Her pale gray eyes showed a slight touch of fear.

"I'm Jane Day of the *Washington Post,"* she introduced herself quickly.

"Jane Day of the *Washington Post,"* Kristi Thatcher repeated. "I've seen your byline. You're covering Dan McLean's murder. And this is what they call an ambush interview."

Kristi's forthright manner surprised Jane. Well, forthright answers deserved forthright questions.

"I understand you were a close friend of Dan's."

"I really don't want to talk about my private life on a Georgetown streetcorner, Jane," the senator's wife said dismissively, but with a soft Southern burr in her voice. "I really don't want to talk about my private life with you at all. Am I going to be the *Style* section's bimbo of the week?"

"I don't write for *Style,"* Jane replied, "and I don't write bimbo stories."

"Good!" Kristi laughed. "Because I'm not a bimbo. Oh, I'll bet you've heard that one a lot in Washington, haven't you? 'I am not a bimbo.' But, really, I'm not. I know I *look* like a bimbo. But do these sound like a bimbo's statistics? Vanderbilt University, bachelor's degree in political science, cum laude. Master's degree in history from Yale. A few credits and one dissertation short of a doctorate in public administration from Georgetown. I suppose there are well-educated bimbos. Or, by definition, does bimbo mean dumb?"

"Look, Mrs. Thatcher—"

"Of course, isn't the secret of success for women in Washington to look like Donna Rice, talk like Pat Schroeder, think like Ruth Bader Ginsburg—"

"—and marry like Kristi Thatcher," Jane finished the aphorism.

Mrs. Thatcher tossed back her blond head and laughed unabashedly. "I like you, Jane Day!"

"Mrs. Thatcher—"

"Kristi."

"Kristi, I don't know if you're a bimbo and I don't care if you're a bimbo," Jane told her. "I don't want to know about your relationship with Dan McLean. All I want to ask you is whether you know anything about the story Dan was working on when he was killed."

Mrs. Thatcher shaded her pale eyes and scrutinized Jane. "Honestly?"

"Honestly," the reporter assured her. "I believe Dan was killed to prevent him from broadcasting the story he was investigating. It might have had something to do with Vietnam."

Kristi's face grew somber. It made her look older. "Maybe I can tell you something that will help. But it's got to be off the record."

"I can't do that," Jane informed her. "I want to print the story."

Kristi shrugged. "No off the record, no information."

"Kristi, you may know something that will unravel the mystery of Dan's murder. You owe it to his memory—"

"Jane, please, save it." Kristi Thatcher held up her hand to stop Jane's pitch. "I'm not one of those unsophisticated Senate wives just arrived from the sticks who fall for that speech. I've been around this town awhile. Don't insult my intelligence. I'll talk to you about Dan's work off the record or not at all."

"How about 'not for attribution'?" Jane countered. "I can use the information in the paper, but I won't attribute it to you."

Kristi looked dubious.

"You can trust me," Jane urged.

The senator's wife threw her head back and laughed again. "Can I trust you as much as Newt's mother trusted Connie Chung? Shall I whisper it to you, 'just between the two of us'?"

Jane reddened. She hated it when people thought she was even in the same business as the TV tabloid stars. "I'm not Connie Chung!" she said heatedly. "If I promise no attribution, I keep my word!"

"What about your editors? Will they keep your word?"

"I won't tell them you're my source."

"Can you do that?"

"Yes," Jane answered, even though she wasn't sure she could.

Kristi stood on the sidewalk next to George's, deciding.

"All right," she said at last. "I'll talk to you. But only about Dan's work, nothing else. And you will not use my name in print or even tell your editors where you got the information. Deal?"

Kristi stuck out her manicured hand. Jane took it and shook.

"Deal."

"Come on, we'll walk down to Sequoia and have a drink while we talk," Kristi proposed.

Elated, Jane followed her down the red-brick sidewalk toward the Potomac River at the foot of the street. They crossed a small viaduct over the C&O canal. The muddy ditch and the dowdy row houses lining its bank looked like a postcard scene from the English countryside rather than trendy Georgetown.

Twenty-ninth Street dead-ended at K Street, in the gloom under the ugly green steel superstructure of the Whitehurst Freeway. The Whitehurst—a mile-long four-lane road elevated on steel legs forty feet above K Street—slashed through

Georgetown from one end to the other, blocking one of the best views in the city from some of the highest-priced real estate in the city at the fourth-floor level.

Proposals to tear down the eyesore were regularly defeated by an unlikely coalition of Georgetown residents who didn't want the tens of thousands of cars that traversed the bypass daily to be dumped onto their narrow neighborhood streets, and the commuters in the cars who didn't want to be forced onto the surface streets, either.

Jane and Kristi crossed K Street and emerged from the perpetual shade of the Whitehurst at Washington Harbor, a six-story tan brick complex of offices, apartments, restaurants, and shops occupying a block-long esplanade directly on the river. The jumble of lumberyards, cement plants, sand and gravel pits, rendering factories, and flour mills which had formerly defaced the prized Georgetown riverfront had mostly been cleared away.

The two women walked through the fountained courtyard dividing the two semicircular wings of Washington Harbor and down a flight of brick and granite steps to a much larger fountain surrounded by flowers and tall grasses. A white pylon rose from the fountain, higher than the tops of the buildings.

On the far side of the fountain, terraces rose, sprouting with a forest of blue umbrellas shading round cafe tables and white plastic chairs.

Jane and Kristi pulled open heavy bronze doors and entered the turretlike building which housed the restaurant Sequoia.

"Stairs or elevator?" Jane asked.

"Stairs," Kristi replied. "Good for the calf muscles."

Sequoia's main dining room was an enormous white cavern with thirty-foot windows opening on the river. The high ceiling was dotted with hundreds of tiny lights strung on wires like stars.

Jane started toward the bar on a balcony above the dining room, a favorite evening hangout for many of her twentysomething and thirtysomething friends.

"Let's sit on the terrace," Kristi suggested.

It was a perfect Washington spring day, sunny, pleasantly

warm, with a cooling breeze blowing from the river. The sodden humidity of Washington's summer had not yet descended.

They wove through the tables toward the outdoor bar. A few couples lingered in wicker chairs over the remains of late lunches.

The bar was covered with a blue awning. Ceiling fans turned under the awning's peak. The bartender, wearing a high-neck white tunic, took their orders. Stoli on the rocks for Kristi, glass of white wine for Jane. Jane rarely drank during the day. But she'd written her paragraphs for the next day's paper. It would be fun to get a slight buzz in the afternoon warmth.

They dragged their wicker stools away from the bar and sat side by side under a tree for privacy. They placed their drinks on a gray shelf attached to the terrace's railing. The Potomac was no more than twenty feet away.

No wonder Sequoia was one of the hottest spots in town. The view was spectacular. To the left, the round, balconied lines of the Watergate complex, the stark white box of the Kennedy Center, and two low-lying bridges across the river, the Memorial and the Teddy Roosevelt. Directly across the river from Sequoia, the green sanctuary of Roosevelt Island. And to the right, the six high, soaring spans of the old yellow stone Key Bridge between Georgetown and Rosslyn.

A line of powerboats and cabin cruisers was tied up along the cement quay, their passengers in shorts and bikinis, sunning themselves and drinking beer.

"They sure have cleaned up the river," Kristi offered, taking a tiny sip of her icy vodka. "When I first came to Washington, it was just about an open sewer. Now I see people sailing Sunfish, people waterskiing."

"A friend of mine tipped over in a sailboat once near Haines Point," Jane recalled, "and her doctor made her get shots against—I don't know—typhoid, hepatitis."

Nevertheless, they savored the idyllic river scene, not speaking for a time.

"So," Kristi broke the silence. "You want to know about Dan's story."

"I do," Jane said, turning on her stool toward her companion. "Do you mind if I take notes?"

Kristi shrugged.

"Did Dan tell you what he was working on?" the reporter asked, extracting a pad and ballpoint from her shoulder bag.

"Not for attribution?" Kristi asked.

"Not for attribution," Jane confirmed.

"He was working on a couple of things," Kristi related, dabbing her upper lip with a paper napkin. "One was about the government using computers to spy on people, reading their Internet messages, logging their phone calls, things like that."

"Yes," Jane responded encouragingly. That must have been the story the friend of K.T.'s friend at CNN was doing the graphics for.

"But you seem to be more interested in his Vietnam story," Kristi continued.

"He *was* working on a story about Vietnam," Jane said excitedly, her hunch confirmed. "Did he tell you any details?"

"Some," Kristi replied. "I know he stumbled on a memo written at the time of the peace treaty, when Nixon pulled out the American troops and the prisoners were returned. When was that? Seventy-three? Seventy-five?"

"Seventy-three."

"Right. The memo said North Vietnam was not holding any more Americans. But Dan found out there *were* still Americans being held. And he thinks the memo writer knew it but said there weren't so the peace treaty wouldn't be wrecked."

Jane scribbled furiously in her notebook, her eyes riveted on Kristi's face.

"Who was it?" she asked. "Who wrote the memo?"

"Dan told me it was someone who's now an official in Hammond's administration," Kristi replied, taking another sip of vodka. "That's why he thought it was such a big story. Whoever wrote that memo is still around and high up in the government."

"It *is* a big story," Jane blurted. "Who is it? Who's the official?"

"Dan would never tell me," Kristi, answered. "He was

afraid I'd tell Norton. My husband is a member of the Intelligence Committee, you know. Dan wanted to break the story first."

Jane sagged in disappointment. "He never told you the name?"

"No. Sorry."

Jane drank her wine and studied her notes. The river scene spread out before her was forgotten. Was Kristi Thatcher holding out? Did Dan's girlfriend really know the name? At times like this, she wished she could force people to answer her questions, like a real detective. Like A. L. Jones.

They ordered another vodka and another wine.

"Did his story get Dan killed?" Kristi asked. Jane turned toward her again. Her gray eyes were sad.

"I don't know. Maybe. Probably."

"You're trying to find out who did it?"

"Yes. If I can. It would help if you knew the name of the Hammond official Dan was going to expose."

Jane needed that name!

"I know," Kristi said. "But he wouldn't tell me."

"He told you so much else. . . ."

"Yes," Kristi agreed. "Pillow talk."

"What?"

"Pillow talk," Kristi repeated with a melancholy smile on her crimson lips. "You know, whispering things to each other in bed after sex."

Jane took a gulp of wine to hide her discomfort at the blunt revelation.

"Dan loved to talk about his work in bed. And I loved to listen. Apparently his wife didn't. . . ."

Her voice trailed off. She sipped the vodka. "What's the proper demeanor for the mistress when her lover dies?" Kristi asked softly into her glass.

Jane had no answer for that one.

"So, what about *your* pillow talk?" Kristi asked the reporter, suddenly ebullient again.

"I don't have nearly enough of it!" Jane replied.

"Been there!" Kristi laughed, putting her arm around Jane's shoulder. "Come on, who's the man in your life? You know all about *my* romances. Now I'm turning the tables. Tell me about *yours.*"

"Not much to tell," replied Jane, wishing there were more. "I've always had mixed feelings about men. I enjoy their company. I enjoy looking at their bodies . . ."

"Just *looking*?"

". . . but I'm turned off by their jock humor and their emotional immaturity."

"You and every other woman I know," Kristi commiserated. "So you've never had a serious relationship?"

"Oh, yeah. I had a long fling in college and afterward with the campus radical. Sean."

Jane was swept by recollections.

"He was so outdated, a sixties radical in the Reagan eighties. I think that's one of the things I found endearing about him. Sean was so intense about his politics. And, of course, I was a flaming liberal, so being with him made me feel like I hadn't missed the whole antiwar, antiestablishment thing of the sixties."

"What happened?" Kristi prodded.

"After his first year in law school, Sean changed. I don't know. I guess he got into the yuppie career thing too much for me. We started fighting a lot and getting on each other's nerves. I finally moved out."

"Ever see him?"

"Nah. I heard a couple of years ago he had become a Los Angeles deputy district attorney. Now he's prosecuting the same people he once wanted to lead in a rebellion against the system." Jane laughed ruefully and took a sip of wine.

It was a shock to Jane when she and Sean broke up. She had imagined what their children would look like. Together, they had even picked out names. She could hardly remember now, but she thought the girl's name was going to be Erin and a boy would be Dylan.

"And that's *it*?" Kristi said. "One romance in your life?"

"I guess I've steered clear of serious involvements with men since Sean. I seem to have a talent for dating guys who are destined not to work out. Six months with one. Three dates with another. Married men." Oops, she hadn't meant that as a shot at Kristi. "Mostly the men I've dated have just been somebody to hang out with for a while. No one to bring home to mother. Of course, my job is not exactly conducive to long, candle-lit dinners."

"You seem pretty career-oriented," Kristi commented, apparently not offended by Jane's comment about dating married men.

"I *am* ambitious," Jane conceded. "It's a trait my mother taught me. 'Don't let a man get in the way of your career.' I've heard her say it a thousand times. Of course, now she wants to know when I'm going to settle down."

"Typical mother." Kristi laughed. "Have you introduced her to Jerry Knight?"

"How'd *you* know about Jerry?" Jane demanded.

" 'All the beautiful women tell Turgot their secrets.' " Kristi imitated the Turkish hairdresser's accent. "And Turgot tells their secrets to all the other beautiful women."

"I'm never going to George's again," Jane fumed.

"In which case you'd miss a lot of the juiciest gossip," Kristi reminded her. "Sean and Jerry. You've covered both ends of the political spectrum. Maybe you should try for a middle-of-the-roader next time."

"Jerry reminds me of Sean, in some ways," Jane mused. She felt relaxed and muzzy from the wine and the warmth. "They're complete opposites in their political beliefs. But they're both outspoken. They're both passionate advocates for their views. They both hate hypocrisy. They both hold firm principles. At least Sean did before he turned into a yuppie lawyer!"

"So, are you serious about Jerry Knight?" Kristi asked.

"I don't know," Jane replied simply.

Kristi didn't press her.

The two women drank and giggled and told tales about the men in their lives until the after-work crowd started filling up Sequoia's terrace and Kristi had to leave to get ready for the state dinner.

CHAPTER TWENTY-FOUR

FOR THE DINNER in Little Saigon, Jerry Knight picked up Jane Day in his new black Cadillac, a replacement for his old black Cadillac, which had been blown up by Drake Dennis, the environmental guerrilla who was eventually charged with Curtis Davies Davenport's murder. Jerry's ex-wife Lila had been driving the car when it was blown up, but suffered only minor injuries, to Jerry's disappointment.

Although Jane's feelings for Jerry were warming, she still felt uncomfortable about letting her liberal colleagues at the *Post* see her with the conservative talk-show host. So she asked him to park around the corner from the paper, on M Street, and wait for her there.

Affronted, he ignored her request. Jane found the big Cadillac parked directly in front of the main entrance of the *Post* on 15th Street.

"I asked you to wait for me on the side street," she grumped, slipping quickly into the passenger seat and slamming the door.

"Maybe you'd like me to wear a mask so your liberal friends won't recognize me," Jerry suggested.

"Good idea," Jane retorted. "Maybe you should wear a costume, too. The brown plaid sport jacket's a dead give-away."

"Hey, give it a rest," Jerry flared, sounding genuinely offended. "Men have feelings, too, you know."

"Really?" Jane said in mock surprise. "First I've heard of it."

Jerry steered the mammoth vehicle straight west on M Street. It was seven P.M. but the wide one-way street was still crowded with homeward-bound motorists. Washington wonks worked late. The route was especially jammed at the five-way intersection at Connecticut Avenue and again where M Street narrowed and doglegged into Georgetown.

A light spring drizzle fell, wetting the street and further slowing the traffic. Jerry never understood why a few drops of rain panicked Washington drivers. He theorized that many came to work in the capital from places where it rarely rained and they had no experience in wet-weather driving.

"This car is like a tank," Jane whined as the Cadillac crept through the traffic. "What's it get, two miles a gallon?"

"What do you care? I'm buying the gas."

"I care because driving a car this size in a time of diminishing resources, when thirty percent of the children in America go to bed hungry every night, is unconscionable."

"So, if I trade in my car for a smaller one, all those children will get something to eat?"

"You know what I mean," Jane fumed.

"Yeah, I know what you mean," Jerry said, giving the finger to a driver who cut in front of him. "You mean you hate the Caddy because it's an *American* car and you liberals hate anything to do with America. You'd be happy, wouldn't you, if I drove one of those Japanese tin cans?"

Jerry gestured through the windshield at the sea of more politically correct Hondas and Toyotas stalled around them.

"At least Japanese workers take pride in their work," Jane argued earnestly. "Their cars hold up. They're not shoddy. They don't fall apart like cars built by American workers, who don't give a damn."

"Really? Really?" Jerry was agitated now. "Well, for your

information, most of the Japanese cars you love so much are made in Ohio and Kentucky by *American* workers! What do you say to that?"

It was about normal for one of their discussions.

The Cadillac was stuck in an interminable line of cars waiting to turn left from M Street onto Key Bridge. Jerry always guessed wrong driving through Georgetown. When he took the center lane, some driver in front of him invariably wanted to turn left through the unbroken line of traffic coming the other way. And when he got in the right lane, some clod invariably blocked it by double parking.

"You were done early tonight," Jerry reopened the conversation once he'd finally accelerated through the turn onto Key Bridge on a yellow light. "You didn't have a story to write for the morning?"

"About Hammond?" Jane snorted. "Are you kidding? He's a nothingburger. All the action's in Congress. I thought the White House was going to be a great beat. But I can't get in the paper with him. He doesn't *do* anything. Hammond's irrelevant."

"Sure, that liberal paper of yours thinks a President's not doing anything unless he's starting a dozen new government programs and raising taxes to pay for them. If he's zeroing out programs and cutting taxes, he's 'irrelevant.' "

"If Hammond was leading that fight, at least I'd have a story about giving his rich supporters a tax break at the expense of the hardworking middle class," Jane said. "But the Speaker is doing all the cutting. The President just goes along with him. Hammond is such a cipher!"

"Maybe Grady will run for President when Dale's term is up," Jerry teased. "You wouldn't call her a cipher."

"Please!" Jane made a motion like she was gagging herself with her finger. "That's when I move to Canada."

"Yeah, I think you'd love it there," Jerry said with exaggerated solicitude. "Socialized medicine, high taxes, and dislike for Americans. You'd fit right in."

On the Virginia end of the bridge, Jerry steered the car through Rossyln, a cluster of glass towers bustling with thousands of office workers during the day but deserted now. His penthouse apartment was on the edge of Rosslyn with a spectacular panoramic view of Washington across the Potomac.

After dinner, maybe he'd suggest that Jane come up and see his view. He'd known her a year and never even kissed her. Inviting her to his apartment now wouldn't exactly be rushing it. Normally, he invited women up on the first date. Sometimes *before* the first date.

Jerry turned right onto Wilson Boulevard.

"What's the deal on dinner with A. L. Jones?" Jerry asked as he negotiated the twisting boulevard. "He doesn't have a clue who poisoned McLean, does he? He wants us to give him some ideas, right? No wonder there's so much crime in Washington. The D.C. cops are such incompetents! What do they catch, ten percent of the murderers? And the ones they catch, what's the sentence? Two years? Three years? I can think of people I'd kill if I was sure that's all the time I'd serve."

He thought of Lila.

"Did you forget that A.L. figured out who killed Curtis?" Jane asked. "And arrested Drake Dennis while you were cowering under the table in your studio?"

"I was not cowering! I was broadcasting the whole thing live!"

"Besides, this dinner was my idea, not A.L.'s. He thinks Dan was killed by his wife or by a cheated husband. You know, Dan wasn't exactly faithful to his marriage vows."

"And you don't agree with that scenario."

"I certainly don't."

"You people with the liberal morals can't understand how someone could feel betrayed by the sexual infidelity of a spouse, can you?"

"You mean someone like your ex-wife?" Jane laughed. "Ex-*wives?"*

Jerry had no comeback for once.

"I think Dan was killed because he was digging into a story that the murderer wanted to keep hidden," Jane continued. "I'm pretty sure the story had something to do with Vietnam."

She didn't reveal what Kristi Thatcher had divulged on Sequoia's terrace the previous week. If she told Jerry that Dan was investigating a high official of the Hammond administration, he would go into one of his the-media-is-out-to-get-conservatives tirades. Besides, she didn't want anyone else to get a whiff of what she was on to.

"I've seen Dan's notebooks," Jane confided. "They show he was working on a Vietnam investigation. Sammy says he heard the same thing. The waiter who put the poison in Dan's food was Vietnamese. And Mr. Cao at the restaurant told us he'd heard in the Vietnamese community that Dan was killed because he was getting too close to a big story. So I invited A.L. to join us to see if he can persuade Mr. Cao to talk more about what he's heard."

"If I remember right, you didn't used to think much of A.L. as a detective," Jerry recalled.

"I've changed my mind."

"I thought K.T.'s friend at CNN said McLean was working on a story about computer surveillance by the government," Jerry reminded her. "If some rogue bureaucrat was running that kind of spying operation, he probably had a big incentive to get rid of the TV correspondent who was about to blow the whistle on him."

"Another source confirmed that Dan was investigating the government's computer spying," Jane said, careful not to reveal that Kristi Thatcher was her source. "But my gut tells me it was the Vietnam story that got him killed."

"What about Grady Hammond's theory that the President was the real target and that McLean got the poison by mistake?"

"White House spin," Jane scorned the idea. "Not even the Secret Service believes it."

"The Secret Service doesn't exactly have a great batting average," Jerry countered. "Oswald. Sirhan. Bremer. Squeaky Fromme. Sara Jane Moore. Hinckley. Planes crashing into the White House. Bullets fired at the White House. People climbing the White House fence. Shall I go on?"

"I take your point," Jane said. "But this time, the Secret Service is right."

"You liberals can't accept the idea that someone would try to kill the President to stop him from returning conservative values to America."

"If you start one more sentence with 'you liberals,' I'm getting out of this car and taking a cab." Jane reached for the door handle.

Jerry had developed a keen sense of when he was about to cross the line between mildly irritating her and thoroughly pissing her off.

He changed the subject.

"The restaurant owner's name is Mr. Nguyen, not Mr. Cao."

"No, it's not," Jane insisted. "Nguyen is his first name. Cao is his last name."

"You don't know what you're talking about."

"With Asian names, the last name's first and the first name's last," Jane insisted. "His name is Cao Nguyen. So, it's Mr. Cao."

"Then why doesn't he correct me when I call him Mr. Nguyen?" Jerry demanded.

"Asians are uncomfortable telling Westerners they're wrong. It's a cultural thing. So he lets you know you're mangling his name by calling you 'Mr. Jerry.' It's subtle. Obviously, subtlety is lost on you."

CHAPTER TWENTY-FIVE

A.L. WAS WAITING at the Cafe Dalat when Jerry and Jane arrived. The restaurant owner had consigned him to a tiny table at the very back of the restaurant, among the stacks of extra chairs and cases of *Ba Me Ba* beer.

When Jerry spotted Jones, he motioned the detective to join him and Jane at their choice table in the large bay window to the left of the front door, directly under a green neon OPEN sign.

Jerry knew Vietnamese were prejudiced against blacks. More prejudiced than American whites. Seating A. L. Jones at the undesirable table had been a deliberate slight. Apparently the restaurant owner saw no need to be subtle in this matter. Jerry decided not to protest.

The owner himself took their order. Jerry ostentatiously addressed him as "Mr. Nguyen." At every opportunity, Jane called him "Mr. Cao."

Jerry ordered his usual: crispy spring rolls to start, and a whole fish, head and all, for his main course. Jane picked a spicy vegetable-and-tofu dish from the vegetarian list on the back of the menu. A.L., who'd eaten nothing but C rations during his stint as a soldier in Vietnam and therefore knew nothing about its native cuisine, really wanted a McDonald's cheeseburger. He settled for wonton soup and grilled shrimp.

Jerry drank *Ba Me Ba* beer, Jane white wine, A.L. root beer.

During dinner they debated their conflicting theories of who killed Dan McLean. No converts were made.

When the waiter had cleared the dishes and set heavy teacups on the now-stained paper place mats, Jerry waved at the owner to join them. Mr. Cao sat in the vacant chair at their table. Jerry couldn't stop himself from staring at the single gray hair growing out of the mole on the owner's cheek.

"Remember the last time we were here?" Jane began. "You said you'd heard something in the Vietnamese community about Dan McLean working on a story that somebody didn't want on TV. Can you tell us more about what you heard? It might help Detective Jones catch the person who poisoned Dan."

A.L. extracted a bent notebook from his coat pocket.

"No, no," the owner protested. "I heard nothing. You make mistake."

"But you told us 'I hear things,' " Jane insisted. "Those were your exact words. I remember them clearly."

"I heard nothing," the owner repeated. His flat black eyes stared straight at Jane's face, revealing nothing.

"You got information on this case, let's hear it," A.L. rumbled. "I can get a warrant to make you talk."

"I know nothing about case," the owner replied in his staccato, high-pitched pidgin English. He kept his round face turned toward Jane, refusing to look or talk directly to the black man.

"Look, Mr. Cao, the last time we were here, you said you'd heard something about Dan's murder," Jane persisted. "*Please* tell Detective Jones what you heard. I'm sure the murder had something to do with Vietnam. If you tell us what you heard, it could help us catch the person who killed Dan. *Please.*"

"Stay out of this," Mr. Cao instructed, rising from his chair. His oiled black hair almost touched a hanging plant in the bay window. "We handle ourselves. We not need police."

The owner bowed slightly toward Jerry, then hurried away. He disappeared into the kitchen at the back of the narrow cafe.

"I'm getting the warrant," A.L. growled. "He knows something, we'll make him spill it."

"You think so?" Jerry asked. "Mr. Nguyen has survived the war, a reeducation camp, a rickety boat in the South China Sea, a refugee camp, and a neighborhood full of gangs. And he's going to talk to you about a murder because you've got a piece of paper that says he has to? Not likely."

"Yeah, well . . ."

Jane sipped her tepid tea and stared out the front window at the attractive triangular park planted across the street above the Clarendon Metro stop. She decided she had to tell A.L. and Jerry what she'd learned from Kristi Thatcher. It was the only way she could enlist their help in the next phase of her pursuit.

"I have an idea," she said, twisting an orange curl around her finger and peering into the darkening twilight.

"Which is?" Jerry prompted.

"Dan's—someone who knew Dan well told me he was about to expose an official in Hammond's administration who covered up the fact that American prisoners were left behind in Vietnam at the end of the war."

"That's garbage!" Jerry exploded. "Don't you ever get tired of bashing the President?"

Jane ignored him. "If we find out who that administration official is, we've probably found out who hired the Vietnamese waiter to kill Dan," Jane concluded.

Shit, A.L. thought. More jigsaw pieces that don't fit together. More uptown white dudes to question.

"Why would someone bust McLean to keep him from revealing a piece of paper written more than twenty years ago?" A.L. asked.

"This is political dynamite," Jane explained. "Knowingly leaving American prisoners in Vietnam? Coming on top of the discovery of the grave site near Hanoi? The public will go bonkers when they find out. And the families. Can you imagine the emotion they're going to pour out on TV? It'll destroy the reputation of whoever wrote that memo. It'll probably destroy Hammond for hiring him."

"Is that why you're going after this story so hard?" Jerry asked. "To destroy Hammond?"

"No!" Jane retorted. "You're a damn broken record, Jerry. Stop running your mouth and listen, for a change. I'm trying to find out the truth about Dan McLean's death. We'll never find out who killed him until we find out who wrote that memo."

"Hey, piece of cake," Jerry needled. "Even if there was such a memo—*if*—what are there, like a couple of thousand administration officials? How do you propose to find the one who McLean *may* have been investigating?"

"Gertrude Hammond."

"Pardon?"

"The First Lady. She's a computer whiz, right? And she must have the highest security clearance. So, she searches the White House computer files until she finds the false report on Vietnam prisoners. Then we'll know the name of the official who wrote it."

"Be serious!"

"I *am* serious! A.L.'s not getting anywhere with his jealous-husband or jealous-wife angle—"

"I'm working on it," the detective interjected defensively.

"—and the videotape has shot down your Hammond-was-the-target theory. The computer surveillance thing doesn't seem important enough to make Dan a target for murder. So, my idea that Dan was killed to stop him from broadcasting the Vietnam prisoners story is the only one that makes sense. At least let's check it out."

"How do you propose to get Grady Hammond involved in your nutso plan?" Jerry asked Jane.

"That's your job," she replied. "You know her. She's a guest on your show like every other week. And from the way you drool over her, I'd say you have a crush on her. You have her private phone number, don't you?"

Jerry nodded.

"So, call her. Talk her into doing a computer search."

"That's *my* job? Talk her into it?"

"That's your job. She gets the name. A.L. checks it out. We find the murderer."

The detective didn't want to be there, getting pulled into this newsie's crazy plot. He wished he were in a public housing project on Naylor Road trying to find some drive-by shooter.

What did he have to lose, Jerry ruminated, recruiting Grady for Jane's scheme? He was sure he could talk her into it. And if they really did unmask McLean's killer, it would be more great publicity for him and the *Night Talker* show.

"I still think it's nutso, but I'll talk to Grady," Jerry agreed.

"Great!" Jane exclaimed, reaching over and tousling Jerry's sparse graying hair.

"Don't you two go playing amateur detective on me again," Detective Jones ordered in his deep baritone. "You find out who McLean was investigating, you tell me. *I'll* check 'em out. Got it?"

Jerry and Jane nodded.

Leaving the Cafe Dalat, they looked around for Mr. Cao. But he stayed in the kitchen.

When Jane got home, there was a message from K.T. on her answering machine.

As far as her friend at CNN could determine, nobody at the network had retrieved Dan McLean's notebooks from his house.

CHAPTER TWENTY-SIX

STEERING HIS WHITE detective's cruiser along Wilson Boulevard, heading back to Washington, A. L. Jones was called on the radio by Homicide headquarters.

"Hey, A.L., you on the bubble tonight, right?"

"Yeah, I guess so."

"Got a nasty one for you."

It took the detective fifteen minutes to reach the scene, a studio apartment in an ugly urban renewal high-rise three blocks from the Southwest riverfront.

Uniformed police and evidence-gatherers scurried about, careful not to disturb the body sprawled on the green carpet.

She was about twenty-five, a light-skinned black woman, her face placid and beautiful in death, her glossy black hair barely mussed. She was nude. A pair of white panty hose was knotted tightly around her slender neck.

An old woman keened an indecipherable lament in the narrow hallway outside the apartment. Jones decided he might as well start his interviews with her.

"Why they do that child like that?" the old woman wept. Her fat, shapeless body was wrapped in a worn chenille robe that must have been pink once. "That child was making it. She was making it. And somebody do her like that. Why? Why?"

The old woman wailed inconsolably. Her dark face glistened with tears and sweat.

She was a neighbor, A.L. learned. He managed to extract from her the information that the dead woman had come to Washington two years earlier from Alabama. She'd found employment in a beauty shop. She was saving her money to open her own shop. She was a regular attendee at a Baptist church in the neighborhood. As far as the neighbor knew, the dead woman didn't do drugs or drink to excess. The neighbor had seen men visiting the dead woman occasionally. But they seemed well-dressed, respectable.

"Why somebody do her that way?" the old woman wailed again.

"I don't know," A.L. muttered, guiding the neighbor back to her apartment. He'd try to find out.

It was one A.M. when Jones completed his investigation at the scene. None of the neighbors acknowledged hearing or seeing anything. Naturally. There was no sign of forced entry or a struggle. The killer was probably someone she knew.

Jones had the dead woman's address book in a plastic bag in his jacket pocket. Somewhere in its pages, almost certainly, was the name and phone number of whoever wrapped those white panty hose around her slender neck and choked the life out of a beautiful young woman who'd managed to hoist herself up to the first rung on the ladder.

A.L. leaned against his car, breathing in the cool night air. The drizzle had ceased.

"She was making it," he said quietly to himself. "Why somebody do her that way?"

He had to phone her family in Alabama. He wasn't up to that. He'd do it in the morning.

The detective was weary.

But he didn't want to go back to his empty apartment in LeDroit Park.

He went to Homicide headquarters instead.

Even at that hour the place was bustling with chaotic activity. A couple of complaining suspects handcuffed to chairs.

A detective talking threateningly into a phone. Shouts from behind the closed door of an interrogation room.

So much paper was piled on A.L.'s desk he couldn't see the wood. On top of the pile was a stack of message slips and envelopes paper-clipped together with a note from Jonetta written in pencil on a High's napkin.

"These are the new ones," the note advised.

One of the envelopes was addressed to A.L. in Captain Wheeler's handwriting. He opened that one first. Inside was a memo to all Homicide detectives. Because the memo was written in dense bureaucratic jargon and copied on a malfunctioning Xerox machine, Jones had to read it twice before he understood it was a notification that the district government's precarious financial status required the cancellation of all overtime pay, effective with the next pay period. Detectives working beyond normal shift hours because of caseloads or court appearances would not be additionally compensated.

A.L. got up and went to the coffee machine. The coffee was hot for a change, but weak.

He flipped through his phone messages. Witnesses who declined to be questioned. CWs, cooperating witnesses, who suddenly had to be out of town on their court dates. Snitches reporting cryptically that they had information, but leaving no phone numbers. William Wu with a terse message, "Call me."

Jones dialed the D.C. Medical Examiner's office. Willie's familiar high-pitched voice answered.

"Hey, Willie. Whatta you doing working at this hour?"

"Working the graveyard shift." The morgue doctor cackled maniacally.

A.L. was so tired he laughed at Willie's familiar joke.

"Busy tonight?" the detective asked.

"Busy? You kidding? We got standing room only here." Another crazed laugh.

A.L. laughed at that one, too. But he knew the little Chinese doctor wasn't kidding. There were so many murders in D.C. that all fifty-five shelves in the morgue's cooler were often full and Wu had to store bodies on the floor.

"You left a message to call you," Jones reminded Willie.

"Yeah, I got some information for you."

A.L. could hear Willie shuffling through papers.

"On that poison case. That TV guy."

"Dan McLean."

"Yeah, McLean. I finally got the toxicology report back on the poison."

"Yeah?"

A.L. cleared a space in the jumble on his desk and began making notes on the back of Captain Wheeler's no-overtime memo.

"It's a very rare poison, A.L. That's why the lab took so long to identify it. Goes by a couple of different names. Ryzotin. Or Belex. Comes from the root of some kind of plant in tropical climates. Africa. India. Southeast Asia. Places like that."

"What else?" Jones prodded.

"It's a very powerful toxin, A.L. Kills fast by paralyzing the victim's breathing. Just a few minutes after ingesting, dead."

That tied in with McLean's death, A.L. recalled. The videotape showed the waiter putting something in McLean's soup, and within minutes the correspondent was dead.

"Where would somebody buy it?" the detective asked.

"You *don't* buy it," Wu cackled. "As far as I can find out it's not for sale in the States. In those places, Africa, so forth, the farmers make it from roots and use it to poison predators."

"Predators?"

"I don't know. Tigers, wild animals, maybe. Stop them from eating the pigs and chickens, I guess."

"And you can't buy it here?"

"That's what I'm told."

"So where would somebody get the poison that killed McLean?"

"Beats me. You're the detective. I just cut up bodies." Again the high-pitched laugh, right at the edge of hysteria.

"That's all you know about it?"

"That's it."

"Thanks, Willie. See you soon."

"Yeah, come and visit sometime, A.L. It's real quiet around here. *Dead* quiet."

Jones hung up on Willie's crazed laugh.

The detective stared at his notes, trying to see if this new information made any jigsaw pieces fit together. The poison wasn't for sale in the U.S. So how did the murderer get it? It's made from roots by farmers in tropical climates, like Africa, Willie had said.

Something. Something stirred a memory.

A.L. tugged at the bottom drawer of his desk. It had been off its tracks for a year. Jones yanked at the drawer hard and it squealed open.

He fished a notebook from the disorderly mess in the drawer.

He flipped through the notebook's pages, searching for the notes on his interview with McLean's widow. Something connected. There. He had written down that she was a professor of tropical medicine at Georgetown University. *Tropical* medicine. He read the next page of notes. And the next. After scanning a half-dozen pages of his scribbles, he found what he thought he remembered. Mrs. McLean had told him she'd been a Peace Corps worker in Nigeria.

Nigeria. In Africa. In the tropics. Where farmers made the kind of rare poison that killed her husband. Where she could have obtained a supply and brought it home with her.

A.L. needed more coffee.

But there was nothing left but gray scum in the bottom of the pot.

He'd never believed the newsie's complicated theories about somebody busting McLean to keep him from broadcasting an exposé about American prisoners left behind in Vietnam.

Looked like the motive was much simpler. The jealous wife. A.L. had leaned that way all along.

Over the years he'd found that the simplest explanation for a murder was usually the right one.

Still. He had a lot of puzzle pieces to put together before he could make the widow. Uptown white bitch. Connected. He better have it cold before he boxed her.

Three A.M.

He'd get back to it in the morning. He needed sleep. And he had to get up early. Make sure LaTroy made it to school. A.L. hadn't talked to LaTroy in days. He needed to make sure the boy was staying out of trouble.

CHAPTER TWENTY-SEVEN

SOME OF GRADY Hammond's predecessors as First Lady, who wished to demonstrate that their interests ran to serious matters of state, had insisted on office space in the West Wing of the White House, where the President and his mostly male aides tended to important matters of foreign and domestic policy, economics, and politics.

Grady had rejected a West Wing office.

She had also rejected an office in the East Wing, where, traditionally, the First Lady's mostly female aides planned state dinners, social teas, and genteel charity events.

Grady didn't want a make-believe White House office. She had her own office on the twelfth floor of a glass tower near Dulles Airport, where she presided as CEO of H-Drive Computer Services Corp., which helped individuals and companies solve their computer problems.

Grady did have a tiny cubicle in the third-floor family quarters of the White House, where she kept a computer to perform work she brought home from her office, and to cruise the Internet when she was bored. She had created her own Home Page on the World Wide Web to receive and respond to posted messages, most of which were hostile.

Occasionally, she lurked in the Internet's chat rooms, monitoring the funny, pathetic, outrageous, and just plain stupid exchanges. The American voters, in all their varieties! Grady used an anonymous, androgynous pseudonym, HANDLER—a shortened version of her Secret Service code name—to disguise her identity during her forays on the Internet.

A couple of nights after Jerry and Jane's Cafe Dalat dinner, the First Lady was in her computer cubicle, searching databases and archives for the name of the administration official Dan McLean had been investigating.

It had been surprisingly easy for Jerry Knight to convince Grady to take part in Jane Day's scheme. The First Lady relished a challenge and welcomed almost any adventure which allowed her to break out of the stuffy confines of her life as a President's spouse. Even if the adventure could hurt her husband.

If Jane Day's theory was right and someone in Dale's administration had concealed the existence of American prisoners in Vietnam at the end of the war, the President would certainly be tarnished by the scandal.

Grady hoped her computer search would disprove Jane's conjecture and support her own theory that Dale had been the intended target of a conservative-hating assassin.

It was quiet on the third floor of the White House, except for the clack of her keyboard. The President was away making a speech. Louisville? Indianapolis? Somewhere like that. Grady had sent her attendant home and notified the Secret Service agent in charge of the night detail that she was in for the evening.

She sat in front of her computer screen wearing green satiny warm-up pants and a white T-shirt emblazoned A WOMAN'S PLACE IS IN THE CORNER OFFICE. She was barefoot, her scarlet toenails unconsciously scratching at the carpet.

Her search went quickly at first. Using her security code and her expert knowledge of computers, she called up the names of all the officials in Dale's administration above the rank of deputy assistant secretary, 4,378 names. Then she assembled a similar list from Richard Nixon's administration in 1973, when the United States withdrew its combat troops from Vietnam and the North Vietnamese supposedly repatriated all the U.S. prisoners they were holding.

Next, she tapped a few keys, instructing the computer to find names which appeared on both lists.

The machine found more than 250 matches. That said something about the longevity of government bureaucrats, she thought. Too many names to screen.

On the assumption that only an official of the Pentagon, State Department, Central Intelligence Agency, or White House staff would have written a memo about prisoners in Vietnam, Grady instructed her computer to ignore all the government agencies except those four in 1973 and to match that limited list against the list of current Hammond administration officials.

The computer whirred, then displayed the list of matches. Down to forty-three names. Still too many, though. She had to narrow it further.

Grady decided to play a hunch, that someone who dealt with foreign policy and intelligence matters in 1973 was not likely to be serving in the Agriculture Department or Interstate Commerce Commission twenty-five years later.

She reprogrammed the computer to compare a list of officials in the Pentagon, State Department, CIA, and White House in 1973 with a list of officials in those same agencies in Dale's administration, and to display the matches.

In a few seconds, the machine printed a list of ten names on the screen.

Two of the names drew her attention immediately.

One was Gregor Novasky, Dale's national security adviser. He had been with the CIA in 1973, assigned to Henry Kissinger's negotiating team at the Paris Peace Talks.

The other name that drew her attention was Dale's. He had been a deputy assistant secretary of State for International Organization Affairs in the Nixon administration.

Grady got up and walked across the long, deserted central hallway of the third floor to the kitchen. She removed a Samuel Adams beer from the refrigerator, popped the top with a silver opener engraved with the presidential seal, and returned to her computer cubicle, her bare feet making no sound on the carpet.

She drank the beer straight from the bottle.

Could Dale have written a memo avowing that all the American prisoners had been returned, when, in fact, they hadn't been?

She didn't want to believe it. Dale was a Korean War hero. He never would have betrayed American soldiers. But the worm of doubt gnawed at her conviction.

He was so accommodating. She could imagine Dale writing such a memo under pressure from his superiors, who didn't want anything to interfere with Nixon's plan to withdraw American troops from Vietnam, even the inconvenient matter of unaccounted-for MIAs. With Watergate already unraveling, Nixon's need to bolster his popularity depended on ending America's participation in the unpopular war. The issue of missing Americans had to be resolved. Or covered up.

The pressure for such a memo would have been intense.

Dale was so accommodating.

Maybe his opposition to Clinton extending diplomatic recognition to Vietnam had been an effort to assuage his guilt for what he did in the seventies.

"No!" Grady said out loud. The word reverberated in the empty family quarters.

Dale was accommodating, not tough enough by her standards. But he would never sell out American prisoners, no matter how much pressure he was under from the Nixon people.

The Hammonds had been principled Connecticut Yankees for nearly three centuries, following a stringent code of honorable conduct, performing selfless service in public office, fighting in their country's wars back to the Revolution. Dale had been a decorated Marine in Korea, a young captain leading his frightened and freezing company through a gauntlet of Chinese attackers in the retreat from the Yalu River.

No. He could not have written such a memo. It must have been Novasky or one of the other eight. If there had been any memo at all. Grady moved the mouse to clear the fish aquarium screen saver.

She studied the list that reappeared on the screen. Aside from Dale and Novasky, she recognized most of the other names. She'd met some of them. But she had no idea whether any of them had written a memo that McLean was investigating when he was poisoned.

She had to find out if such a memo was in the government's databases. If she found it, she would know for certain who wrote it. And who might have arranged Dan McLean's death in order to keep it from being revealed.

She padded silently to the kitchen and returned to her computer cubicle with another beer.

For a half-hour, Grady clicked and scrolled through menus and databases. At last, she arrived at the place where she was sure the memo was stored. The screen spelled out *National Security Archives, Special Files Section, Limited Access, Password Required, Key Code Certified Only.*

She clicked to open.

A box appeared on the screen. It read:

ACCESS DENIED
Not Key Code Certified

"Damn," the First Lady said aloud.

She tried again. Same response.

Grady retrieved from her wallet a laminated card the President's military aide had given her on Inauguration Day. It contained a list of code words and passwords, along with instructions on where she would be taken in the event of a nuclear attack, terrorist act, or other emergency. The card did not contain a "Key Code."

She tried some of the other codes on the card, but they didn't work. The computer refused to grant her access to the National Security Archives.

A skilled hacker, Grady considered trying some of the tricks she knew to tease the key code out of the machine. But she suspected the system was programmed to alert a security officer when someone tried to break in. In a few minutes, the Secret Service or FBI or one of those agencies would be banging on her door.

She didn't want that hassle.

In fact, within moments after Grady started her computer search, an Army private in a cubicle at the unmarked offices of the Magnum Project in Crystal City, Virginia, was monitoring her every keystroke and mouse click.

Grady's other choice to gain access to the National Security Archives was to try to sweet-talk Dale's military aide into giving her the key code. She was sure she could do it. She'd caught him eyeing her a couple of times.

But he might report her to Dale. Or the Secretary of Defense. It would leak to the press and they'd have a field day.

She'd better try to figure it out herself without risking a security alarm or a media frenzy.

She recalled the ten names to the screen, nine men and one woman who'd been relatively junior officials at the end of the Vietnam War in 1973 and were now senior officials in Dale's administration.

According to Jerry Knight, Dan McLean may have been about to reveal that one of them wrote a memo at the end of the war falsely reporting that all the American prisoners had been released. And that person may have hired a Vietnamese waiter to poison McLean at the correspondents dinner to keep him from revealing that secret.

The First Lady looked down the list of names again.

Dale?

If he wrote the memo, exposure would mean impeachment, the destruction of his presidency, unbearable shame. For what? For being a junior State Department officer who wasn't strong enough to resist the pressure from Kissinger and the thugs around Nixon? Not many people were able to resist that bunch in those days.

Why hadn't Dale told her what he'd done? It was such an awful burden to keep locked inside all those years, fearing exposure and ruin at any moment. And if he'd shared his secret with her, what would she have done? She would have helped him carry the burden. Made sure the episode stayed covered up. Maybe used her computer skills to erase any trace of the memo from government files. Killed anyone who threatened exposure.

My God! What was she thinking?

Could the President have arranged McLean's murder to

prevent the correspondent from broadcasting his terrible secret?

"No!" she protested aloud. "One of the others wrote that memo!"

Grady printed out the list of ten names and shut down the computer.

She retrieved a third beer from the refrigerator. She took it to bed with her, still dressed in the green warm-up pants and T-shirt.

CHAPTER TWENTY-EIGHT

FBI SPECIAL AGENT Michael Tagliaferro headed out Colesville Road toward Kavanaugh's Tavern at Four Corners in the Maryland suburbs in response to a phone call from Del Bloch requesting a meeting. The car salesman, a freelance FBI informant, had sounded nervous.

Something unusual had come up, Tagliaferro guessed, steering into a parking space in the old Woodmoor Shopping Center. Second meeting in less than a month. Normally, Bloch had information to pass on only a couple of times a year.

The FBI agent sat at their usual booth in the back, facing the door. They arranged their meetings for midafternoon, when the place was nearly empty. The lunch crowd had gone back to their jobs. The after-work drinkers hadn't arrived yet.

The ancient waitress in the Pepto-Bismol-colored nylon uniform appeared.

"Iced tea," he ordered.

A half-hour passed. The iced tea was gone. No Bloch. Tagliaferro wondered if he had the right day. He was sure he did.

He ordered another iced tea. Another twenty minutes passed. Still no Bloch. The after-work drinkers started to drift in.

"Dock of the Bay" played from the jukebox.

Bloch had never been late for their meetings. In fact, he usually arrived early. Tagliaferro was trained to be alert for changes in people's normal patterns of behavior. This was definitely a change in Bloch's pattern.

The agent had just about decided to drive to the Lincoln-Mercury dealership in the Montgomery Auto Park, where the informant worked, when Bloch sidled into the bar. He looked scared.

He hurried over and squeezed his bulk into the booth.

The skinny waitress came to take his order. Bloch waved her away.

"So, what's up?" Tagliaferro prompted.

The informant leaned across the Formica table. His chins quivered. "Saturday. Hammond's going to make a speech at the Vietnam Wall. Something's going down."

Bloch spoke so fast and in such a low whisper, the agent wasn't sure he'd heard correctly.

"Whoa. Slow it down, Del. What's going to happen Saturday?"

"I don't know exactly, Tag. Something. That's all I know."

Bloch looked around the tavern furtively. Sweat glistened among the gray strands plastered to his scalp.

He was definitely scared.

"Does it involve the President?"

The question made Bloch more agitated. "Tag, I told you everything I know. Something's going down Saturday at the Wall. That's all I know. Don't ask me no more."

"Are your friends in the Survivors of Cam Hoa involved?" Tagliaferro needed to keep Bloch talking, to milk every drop of information he had.

"Why do you ask me that?" the fat man sputtered. "Who said anything about the Survivors of Cam Hoa? Who said they were involved?"

"Well, who is involved?" Tagliaferro affected a relaxed, nonchalant tone. He hoped it would calm down Bloch, keep him talking.

But it didn't work.

"Tag, I gotta go. I told you everything I know. You gotta protect me on this. Totally. Okay? Promise you'll protect me?"

"Of course I'll protect you," the agent reassured him. "I always protect you. Come on, relax. I'll buy you a beer."

But Bloch hauled himself out of the booth and scurried for the door.

Now, that's definitely one frightened informant, Tagliaferro concluded. He didn't even wait to be paid.

The agent needed to get back downtown and report the conversation. Nebulous as it was, Bloch's tip required higher-level attention than his usual information about drug dealers paying cash for Lincoln Town Cars.

Tagliaferro paid for his iced tea and left.

Aretha was crying "Respect" from the jukebox.

The next morning, while President Dale Hammond was shaving, the telephone rang in his bathroom. It was Secret Service Director Colbert Clawson requesting a meeting as soon as possible.

"Well, come on over now, Colbert," the President suggested. "We'll have breakfast together in the family quarters."

When Dale told Grady Hammond about the call, she notified her office she'd be late and invited herself to the meeting. She didn't trust Clawson. And she didn't trust Dale to stand up to the Secret Service chief.

Clawson, back to black suit and gray tie, was surprised to find Grady at the round mahogany table set for three in the family dining room overlooking Pennsylvania Avenue.

He affected a chilly courtesy toward her. *Don't piss off First Ladies* was one of Clawson's rules for bureaucratic survival. They always won.

The three made small talk while the white-jacketed butlers poured coffee into the china cups and fresh-squeezed orange juice into the crystal goblets, and delivered their food—grapefruit slices for Grady, two bran muffins for Dale, scrambled eggs, bacon, and toast for Clawson.

As soon as the butlers withdrew, Grady asked Clawson, "So, why the hurry-up meeting?"

She was eager to hear what prompted the Secret Service chief's early-morning call. And she knew Dale would tell interminable anecdotes from his recent trip to Louisville if she didn't move things along.

Clawson put down his fork. *No one conveyed authority with a mouth full of food.* Another of the director's rules.

"We've received intelligence, which we deem reliable, that there's going to be an incident at the Vietnam Wall during the memorial ceremony on Saturday," Clawson explained. "In light of that warning, I'm recommending that you cancel your appearance there, Mr. President."

As he spoke, Clawson turned his pasty face back and forth between the President and the First Lady. Clawson never knew which one to look at. He had the title. But she had the influence.

"What kind of incident?" Grady challenged him before Dale could speak.

"We don't know for sure," the director replied. "The warning was not specific."

"Is it supposed to be directed at Dale?" she pressed.

"That's not clear."

"Is it some kind of demonstration? Or disrupting the ceremony? Or what?"

"We just don't know."

"You don't know?" Grady placed her coffee cup on the saucer with a disapproving clang. "If you don't know how serious the 'incident' is supposed to be, or *what* it's supposed to be, how can you recommend that Dale cancel a very important speech?"

"We have reason to believe the incident will be serious." Clawson addressed his response to Dale, hoping the President would take control of the conversation.

But Grady persisted.

"You have 'reason to believe' it will be a serious incident. What's the source of your information?"

"An informant."

"Who?"

"I can't tell you."

Clawson knew he'd said the wrong thing to the wrong person as soon as the words were out of his mouth.

"Can't tell me?" The First Lady jumped up and started pacing angrily. "This is the President of the United States. And I'm his wife. And you can't tell us your source?"

"Mrs. Hammond—*Ms.* Hammond, of course I can tell you. But the name wouldn't mean anything to you. The information comes from a freelance FBI informant who has provided reliable intelligence in the past. He's believed to have contacts with veterans groups which are unhappy about the discovery of the grave site of American prisoners in North Vietnam."

"So, based on a *vague* tip from a *freelance* informant—whatever that means—Dale is supposed to cancel his speech at the beginning of the Memorial Day weekend and cower inside the White House?"

Grady stood directly behind the Secret Service director so he had to twist around awkwardly to look at her. It was a tactic she often used to seize the advantage at corporate meetings.

"Is that your case?"

"Now, hon," the President spoke for the first time. "If Colbert didn't have what he considered good reasons to be concerned about my safety, he wouldn't recommend that I skip the Vietnam speech, would he?"

"Did your informant tell you the 'incident' will endanger the President's safety, Mr. Clawson?" Grady inquired.

"No," the Secret Service director conceded. "The informant warned only that an incident, a serious incident, may occur at the memorial ceremony."

"I don't get it, Mr. Clawson," Grady said. "A couple of weeks ago, a TV correspondent was murdered ten feet from where Dale was sitting and you couldn't wait to tell the world it had nothing to do with the President. Now you get an ambiguous tip from a third-string informant about an 'incident,' nothing specific, and you rush over here to tell Dale he should cancel his speech. Why the sudden excess of caution?"

"I get paid to be excessively cautious," the Secret Service director replied pompously. "On occasion, some of my predecessors did not exercise excessive caution in performing their duties, with tragic consequences. The day I fail to conduct my office with excessive caution is the day I should be fired."

"And I'm personally grateful you *do* exercise excessive caution." Dale Hammond chuckled, trying to lighten the mood in the dining room. He didn't like conflict.

Grady resumed her seat and addressed the President. "You can't cancel out of the Vietnam ceremony because of a vague tip from a part-time FBI informant," she lectured. "If the Secret Service had its way, you'd *never* leave the safety of the White House. Or, if you did, you'd go in a tank."

Clawson bristled, but did not contradict her.

"The wounds of the Vietnam War are still festering in this country, Dale," the First Lady said. "The people who served there, and the families of the ones who died there, feel their sacrifices aren't appreciated. The ones who avoided serving are feeling guilty that they stuck others, mostly the lower classes, with the burden of fighting and dying. Some think it's time to forget the whole thing so American companies can go after that market. A lot of wives and parents and buddies want to know what happened to their loved ones and friends who never came back. They want to know if the prisoners buried in that grave in Hanoi died *after* the war. There's no closure to their grief. A lot of veterans are wrestling with what that war did to them, not just physically but mentally, too. You've *got* to give that speech Saturday, Dale. That speech is going to be the start of the healing."

The dining room was still. The only sound was the muffled noise of a power mower on the North Lawn.

Dale Hammond stirred his coffee slowly with a silver spoon. He hadn't made a joke and he hadn't said "Now, hon," so Grady knew he was considering her words carefully.

"Everywhere you go, you encounter angry demonstrators demanding that you make Vietnam explain that grave and account for the missing," the First Lady reminded him, adding one more argument to her case. "Mr. Clawson says the disruption planned for Saturday may involve disgruntled veterans groups. Doesn't all that tell you a lot of people are still walking around in a lot of pain from the war? Doesn't that tell you this country is still deeply divided over Vietnam? History has given you the mission to reconcile those divisions once and for all. You can't let him scare you away from giving that speech Saturday."

Dale Hammond continued to stir his coffee in slow circles.

"Grady's right," the President said at last. "Unless you turn up more conclusive evidence of a serious threat to my safety, Colbert, I don't think I should cancel my speech. I assume the Secret Service and the police can cope with whatever demonstration or 'incident' your informant says is planned. Am I correct?"

"As always, my people will do whatever is required to protect the President," the Secret Service director replied stiffly. "We have three days, and we will be ready."

"Good, good," the President said, rising from his chair. "There are some things I need to say about Vietnam, Colbert, and Saturday at the Wall, on Memorial Day weekend, is the right time and the right place to say them."

"Yes, sir." Clawson scrambled to his feet. "Mr. President."

They shook hands.

"Ms. Hammond." He shook her hand with cool civility.

The First Lady had won. As always.

That evening, being driven in her white Mercedes on the Dulles toll road from her office at H-Drive Computer Services to the White House, Grady Hammond called Jerry Knight at his apartment on her car phone.

Jerry, just getting up from his day's sleep, sounded flustered, as he usually did when she called.

The First Lady invited him to attend the ceremony at the Vietnam Wall on Saturday.

"Dale's giving a major speech," Grady told him. "Major. About how the nation should think about Vietnam, and what course we should follow now. I know you were a correspondent there, Jerry, and you talk about it a lot on your show. I think you'll want to attend the speech. Come as my guest. I'll make sure you have a seat."

He accepted immediately, of course.

Egotist that he was, Jerry was likely to blab endlessly on the *Night Talker* show about Dale's forthcoming major speech, Grady knew, telling listeners how he had been invited personally by the First Lady to attend as her guest.

Men! She smiled to herself. The invitation was part of her plan to generate public interest in the Vietnam speech.

Jerry asked the First Lady about her computer search for the alleged Vietnam memo McLean was investigating.

"I didn't find it," she told him. Her tone of finality told him not to pursue it further.

Before the uniformed guards waved the Mercedes through the black iron gate at the Southwest Entrance to the White House grounds, Grady called another half-dozen media celebrities and encouraged them to spread the word that Dale's speech Saturday would be a blockbuster.

As soon as he hung up from the First Lady, Jerry dialed Jane Day's extension in the *Post's* cubicle at the White House.

When she heard his voice, she gave an exaggerated moan of disapproval. Jane had given up trying to dissuade him from calling her at work.

"What's up, Jerry?" she asked impatiently. "I've got five hundred words to write and I'm getting tight for deadline."

"I just got off the phone with Grady Hammond."

"I'm so happy for both of you," Jane responded sarcastically.

"She did the computer search for that memo about the American prisoners in Vietnam at the end of the war."

"Yeah?" Jane's interest perked up.

"She couldn't find it."

Jane was crushed. It had been her best chance to learn the identity of the memo's author. If the President's wife couldn't ferret out the name, Jane couldn't think of anyone else who could. She'd hit a dead end in unraveling Dan McLean's murder.

"I'm sorry," Jerry said. He sounded like he meant it. "But listen, I have some news that will cheer you up."

"Yeah?"

"Dale Hammond is giving a big Vietnam speech at the Wall Saturday—"

"I know that."

"—and Grady's invited me to attend as her guest."

"Wow! That *does* cheer me up." Jane's voice oozed sarcasm.

"And I'm inviting you to be *my* guest."

"You're *her* guest and I'm *your* guest? Can you do that?"

"I don't know. If I ask her, I'm sure she'll get you a seat."

"I get *paid* to cover Hammond's speeches," Jane reminded him. "Why should I go to one on my own time?"

"You got something better to do Saturday?"

"Uh, let's see. Clean out the refrigerator. Root canal work. Getting mugged. You want some more?"

"It's supposed to be a nice day. We'll go to the speech, then drive out to Angler's and have lunch on the terrace. Remember when we ate there last year?"

"I remember."

"How about it? Say yes."

"I don't know, Jerry. I may have to work Saturday. I'll probably end up covering the speech for the Sunday paper."

"You cover the speech, I'll go as Grady's guest, and afterward we'll have lunch at Angler's. Okay?"

"I don't know. Maybe. I've got to hang up. I'm on deadline."

CHAPTER TWENTY-NINE

When A. L. Jones arrived at Homicide's offices on the third floor of the Municipal Center, he found a note taped over his computer screen: "Captain Wheeler wants to see you, honey. Jonetta."

Just what he needed to start the day.

Actually, A.L. wasn't starting his day. The dispatcher had phoned him at three A.M. and directed him to the scene of a multiple murder in an apartment off Bladensburg Road near the Maryland line. A man and woman and a one-year-old baby. The uniformed cops found the baby cradled in the woman's arms, like she'd been trying to shield him. The victims and the apartment had been sprayed with more than twenty shots.

None of the neighbors had seen or heard anything.

A.L. needed coffee before he faced Captain Wheeler.

It was thick as sludge. And tepid.

"How you doing on the McLean case?" Wheeler asked when Jones was standing in front of his desk.

"Okay."

"Yeah? You got any leads?"

Wheeler, a light-skinned black man with close-cropped sandy hair and a pencil-thin mustache, was fashionably dressed, as always. He wore a tight-fitting bright blue suit tailored in a shiny silk fabric, a dark blue shirt with white collar and cuffs, clunky gold cuff links, and a blue tie patterned with gold saxophones.

"Looking to make the boy whacked that waiter, the one served McLean the poison. That might lead somewhere. Also, McLean was a stud. Fucked anything with tits. Lot of activity not involving Mrs. McLean. I'm checking out some angles there. You know, might of been a domestic thing."

"How soon you going to break something? Uncle don't want no part of it. So it's all you, A.L. That dude was high-profile, you know. I'm getting heat on this one. CNN is putting on a special program every day, something like, 'The Dan McLean Murder, Unsolved—Day Twenty.' Mayor ain't happy, A.L."

Oh, yeah. The mayor. Wheeler's benefactor. The word was out that Wheeler was on his way up, maybe to chief, if he didn't screw up. Screw up on a CNN news dude, the captain might be on his way back to riding patrol.

"So, A.L., we need a break here," Wheeler said. "By next Monday? No, Monday's a holiday. I'll be at the mayor's Memorial Day barbecue. By Tuesday?"

"By Tuesday," A.L. promised halfheartedly. "No sweat."

Jones sat at his cluttered desk, covering his face with his pudgy hands, trying to shut out the cacophony of the Homicide offices. He needed to put the jigsaw pieces of the McLean case together. But nothing fit.

"Hey, Jonetta," he shouted. "Go to the deli and get me some coffee I can drink."

"You buy me one?" she shouted back.

"Yeah."

"You got it, honey."

Jones reviewed three different piles of puzzle pieces.

There was the dead gook waiter pile. The waiter definitely put the poison in McLean's soup. The video showed that. But who cracked the waiter? And why? A.L. had no witnesses, or at least none who would talk. No fingerprints. And no clues.

The shooter might have been a neighborhood pipehead the waiter caught robbing his apartment. Jones decided to squeeze his snitches in the Columbia Heights neighborhood.

Then there were the McLean-the-swordsman puzzle pieces. The guy couldn't keep his dick in his pants. Senator Thatcher had been convincing when he claimed he was too busy with his official duties to care that his wife was banging McLean. But how many other husbands of the correspondent's conquests were that understanding? Jealousy was a powerful emotion.

When he was new on Homicide, before the drug thing hit D.C., jealousy had been one of the main reasons people busted each other. Hell, A.L. still felt pangs of jealousy when he thought about his ex-wife married to that doctor up in New Jersey. And Jones had been divorced—what? Eight years?

And there was McLean's widow. A big puzzle piece. In A.L.'s experience, the wives of cheating husbands were a lot more dangerous than the husbands of cheating wives. Willie Wu had reported that McLean was killed by a rare poison found in tropical climates like Africa. Patricia McLean taught tropical medicine at Georgetown University, and she had served in the Peace Corps in Africa. That could be Jones's hottest lead. The poison acted too fast for her to have fed it to him before he left for the dinner. But she could have paid the waiter to slip it into his soup.

He looked through his old notebooks until he found her phone number.

After three rings, a recorded message came on the line.

Hi. This is Pat McLean. The kids and I are going to be at our place in Rehobeth Beach until after Memorial Day. In an emergency, you can reach me there. Otherwise, leave a message when you hear the beep and I'll call you back.

He could drive to Rehobeth in three hours. It was Delaware, and he didn't have any jurisdiction there. But he might be able to bluff her into answering his questions. A day at the beach didn't sound too bad.

Nah. Patricia McLean's kids would be freaked if Jones showed up unannounced to question their mother about their father's murder. He'd visit her next week, when she got back.

If she'd hired the waiter to kill her husband because he was cheating on her, and she was still around, doing the grieving widow number, she wasn't likely to flee now, Jones concluded, unless she thought he was on to her. Another reason not to track her to the beach.

That left one more pile of puzzle pieces. Vietnam. It kept coming up.

The waiter was Vietnamese. Willie Wu said the poison that killed McLean could have come from Southeast Asia. That newsie from the *Post* thought McLean was working on some kind of exposé about Vietnam when he was chopped. When A.L. met her and Jerry Knight at the Vietnamese restaurant in Arlington, the owner acted like he knew something. He said, *"We'll take care of it, we don't need any cops."* Like he knew who chopped McLean, and the gooks were going to settle it themselves.

And then there was that thing came up at a meeting Jones attended in the Secret Service director's office. A warning of some kind from a bunch of former Green Berets, came in on the computer. Couldn't be traced. Something about the President better do something about making Vietnam account for the prisoners. Well, if they were ex–Green Berets, A.L. could believe just about anything. Some of those motherfuckers were crazy.

Once again a long-ago scene from Vietnam invaded the detective's mind.

His platoon was moving down a road, careful to stay in the brush on either side, so if Charlie was waiting for them, he wouldn't catch them in the open.

They came to a cement bridge over a stream. The platoon commander, a young lieutenant who'd been in-country a month, ordered his men to cross the bridge in two columns. Some of the seasoned soldiers protested, warning the lieutenant that he was inviting an ambush. They suggested that the platoon spread out along the stream and cross above and below the bridge.

The lieutenant was lazy, arrogant, and stupid—a bad combination in a combat commander. It had been a hot and unproductive day of patrolling. He was anxious to get back to their base, shower, and have a beer. He ordered the platoon to march across the bridge.

The point man, Scialino, was about five feet from the far end when Charlie opened up on them from the jungle on both sides. A.L. recognized the distinctive chatter of AK-47s and the flat explosion of grenades.

He jammed himself as close as he could against the cement sides of the bridge. They were low, less than two feet high. Chunky even then, A.L. tried to flatten himself, to burrow into the roadbed of the bridge. He felt the shock of VC bullets slamming into the outer side of his scanty shelter. Chips of cement pinged on his steel pot. He was so scared. So fucking scared. He never lifted his head or fired a shot.

It took thirty minutes for air cover to arrive. And another hour for evacuation choppers to land. Out of fifteen guys in the platoon, Scialino and three others were killed, six were wounded, including A.L. A hot shard from a VC grenade nicked his left shoulder. But it wasn't serious enough to get him shipped back to the World.

The lieutenant was one of the dead. Jones suspected he was shot with an M16 by one of his own men.

The detective shook off the memory.

It wouldn't surprise him if McLean's murder had something to do with Vietnam. Anybody who'd been there never got over it. The motive could have been anything. Some of the vets were crazy sons of bitches.

Which made A.L. think of Stump.

Yeah, Stump.

He was fucking crazy, all right.

And if any of the crazy vets had something to do with cracking McLean, Stump might have heard about it.

The legless Stump hung different places in his chrome-and-black wheelchair.

Sometimes A.L. found him with other messed-up vets around the Vietnam Wall, handing out pamphlets about the MIAs and POWs to the tourists.

Other times, Jones encountered Stump in the entranceway of the Farragut West Metro station, shaking a Styrofoam cup, intimidating and shaming the passengers into giving him money.

He had lettered I NEED MONEY FOR FOOD on a piece of cardboard box and propped it on his lap.

Touching. But bullshit. What he needed the money for, A.L. knew, was not food, but malt liquor.

Since it was raining, Jones surmised that Stump was spending the day indoors.

The detective thought he knew where to find him.

On the south side of Massachusetts Avenue, about halfway between the Mount Vernon Square Library and Union Station, stood an abandoned firehouse. It has been closed during some earlier budget-cutting crisis, A.L. recalled, although someone continued to carefully paint the cast-iron fire department emblem—a fireman's helmet above a red, white, and blue shield—embedded high in the brick front wall, above the wide red doors, now nailed closed.

At the library end of this stretch of Massachusetts Avenue, the neighborhood was making a minor comeback, with construction of a convention center and the promised construction of a sports arena, the erection of a conventioneers hotel, and the transplantation of National Public Radio's headquarters.

And at the other end of this stretch of the avenue, the massive, Roman-style Union Station had been renovated—getting it right on the second try, Jones noted—into an appealing center for shopping and dining, as well as catching the train.

But in between, the area was deplorable. Boarded-up stores and town houses. Burned-out buildings. Vacant lots littered with trash and human debris. The abandoned firehouse stood in this stretch.

And Stump lived inside.

A.L. pulled his vanilla-colored detective's car into the alley behind the firehouse, crunching on broken glass.

He shouldered open a rear door. The lock had long since been ripped out.

Inside it was dark and damp. And it stank, of shit, urine, vomit, and unwashed bodies.

A.L. almost gagged. Even armed, A.L. didn't feel secure in there.

"Hey, Stump?" the detective called out. "You here? It's A.L."

Jones heard a scurrying noise. It could have been rats. It could have been winos or drugheads who didn't want to have anything to do with a cop.

"Hey, Stump? You here, man?"

"Yeah, I'm here."

It was a gravelly whisper.

A.L. followed the sound.

The firehouse had been stripped of everything that could be used or sold for cash: lights, wiring, plumbing, pipes, furniture, flooring, stairways. The plaster had been hacked from the interior walls to get at the wood lathing.

Jones found Stump in his wheelchair by the big doors at the front.

He looked worse than A.L. remembered, with filthy, matted dreadlocks, clothes that looked like they hadn't been washed for weeks or months, and an ugly rash on his cheeks and neck. He wore a ragged blanket around his shoulders like a shawl.

Stump's eyes glinted madly in the dark.

Next to the wheelchair, someone reclined motionless under a greasy brown tarp.

"How you making it, bro?" A.L. asked Stump, casually as if the two men had run into each other in a bar.

"How'm I making it? Can't you tell? Didn't you see my new Cadillac parked outside?" He laughed hoarsely.

"Yeah, well."

"So, what brings you around, A.L.? You just come to cheer up your old war buddy? Or you working a case? I'll bet that's it. And you think ole Stump can help you. Am I right?"

"Sort of."

"Yeah, I figured that's it. Ole Stump sees a lot of shit going on as I make my rounds. A *lot* of shit. But A.L., can't you hear my throat? I'm dry, man. My throat's dry as a virgin's pussy. How'm I gonna tell you what I see when my throat's so dry I can't barely talk?"

A.L. walked through the drizzle to a barricaded liquor store on the corner, bought a six-pack of Schlitz malt liquor, with the blue bull on the cans, and carried it back to the firehouse.

Stump downed the first one in a gulp. He consumed the other five methodically while A.L. pumped him for information.

The detective wanted to know if he'd heard anything about McLean's murder through the Vietnam vets grapevine. Had he picked up any rumblings about the gook community in Arlington "taking care" of a problem that might be connected to McLean's murder? Had his vet buddies mentioned anything about an exposé concerning the war that the correspondent was working on?

The more malt liquor Stump drank, the more disjointed his responses were. Sometimes he rambled hoarsely about unrelated matters. Sometimes he didn't say anything for minutes, as if he were searching his memory. If he had any memory left, A.L. thought.

The detective stood the whole time. There was nothing to sit on.

Stump was on the streets, all day, every day, talking to people, listening, watching, seeing things, hearing things. He befriended dozens of other Vietnam veterans, broken in mind or body, who lived on the streets.

Slowly, painfully, over two hours, Jones extracted from the amputee some puzzle pieces that fit together. They didn't make a complete picture. There were a lot of holes in the puzzle, a lot of pieces still missing. But as A.L. emerged from the stinking firehouse into the damp air, he had some ideas about how to complete the puzzle.

"Take care of yourself, Stump," the detective called into the darkness.

"You, too, man," the gravelly rasp came back. "Have a nice day."

On the way back to Homicide, Jones tuned in to WTOP, the all-news radio station. The announcer read a list of activities planned for the coming Memorial Day weekend.

When A.L. heard that President Hammond was making a speech at the Vietnam Wall on Saturday, he thought he knew where all the puzzle pieces would be put together.

CHAPTER THIRTY

SATURDAY CAME, DARK and chilly. Leaden clouds hung low, threatening rain.

Mournful weather. A mournful day for the memorial ceremony.

Walking through the gloomy dawn streets from the ATN studios to his Rosslyn apartment after the *Night Talker* show, puffing the one cigar a day his doctor allowed him, Jerry Knight was weighed down by an ineffable sadness, as he always was when he thought about the war.

At his apartment, Jerry downed his usual sleeping potion, two warm beers, and pulled the blackout drapes over the windows.

Before getting into bed, he rummaged in the bottom of the hall closet looking for an umbrella to place next to the front door so he wouldn't forget to take it to the Wall.

In the back of the closet he came across his Vietnam combat boots, cracked brown leather, olive canvas, lug soles, forgotten for so many years.

Recollections of his years in Vietnam flooded back. Painful scenes he'd kept repressed returned. A sense of loss gripped his heart.

Jerry stared at the dusty boots for a long time. He was transported back to Vietnam. He'd never left it.

After discovering the boots, there was no sleep. Memories of the war wouldn't let him.

He flipped through the Saturday *Post* without really taking in the words.

He put on a CD of old Sinatra ballads. That didn't bring sleep, either.

Finally, Jerry decided to get up, shower, dress, and go to the Vietnam Wall early.

Initially, the wide V of black marble, sunken below ground level and engraved with the names of more than fifty thousand Americans killed in the war, was denounced as a black gash of shame.

The young Chinese-American architectural student at Yale who designed it explained that she intended the memorial to symbolize regeneration. Slash open the earth and, in time, the grass will heal it, she had said.

Indeed, the grass had grown up around the sunken tablets of marble. And people came every day by the thousands, seeking regeneration and healing. From loss, guilt, anger, pain, confusion.

Jerry arrived just before the Park Police closed the memorial to tourists to make ready for the presidential visit.

For the twentieth time, Jerry walked slowly down the sloping path beside the polished black walls, deeper and deeper into the trench, into the earth. The slabs bearing the thousands upon thousands of names of the dead towered higher and higher above him. He was overwhelmed, suffocating, drowning in grief. He'd been a correspondent in Vietnam, not a soldier. But he'd seen more fighting than many soldiers. And more death.

Jerry stopped at the bottom of the V, looking at his sorrowing face mirrored in the marble, merging with the names.

As always, he wept. Without trying to hide it. For all those boys, dying in pain and terror, most of them before they'd lived twenty-five years. For his guilt at coming back alive. For America, which had been unwilling or unable to save the Vietnamese people from subjugation.

Jerry uttered a high, involuntary moan.

"Tran," he sobbed.

And then he climbed up the slope on the other side of the V. The black tablets of names receded. He came out of the symbolic grave, out of the earth, back to the living.

He wiped away the tears.

Jerry bought a Styrofoam cup of coffee and a cellophane-wrapped donut from an Asian vendor in a white truck parked near the State Department. He carried them back to the memorial and sat in the last row of empty folding chairs set up for the ceremony.

Even with the preparations going on around him, the setting was placid.

To the left, the classically columned marble temple to Abraham Lincoln, enclosing the mournful seated statue of the Civil War President. Lincoln was the greatest of all the Presidents, Jerry believed, for leading the nation through that other divisive war.

He noticed a TV camera crew stationed on the long, wide marble staircase leading up to the Lincoln Memorial, panning back and forth between the statue and the Vietnam Wall. No doubt recording video to illustrate some politically correct put-down by a blow-dried anchor too young to remember Vietnam.

Jerry sometimes wondered whether Lincoln would have been able to withstand news-media demands to end the killing if there had been TV cameras at Antietam or Gettysburg. Would Lincoln have been accused of ordering atrocities against women and children if Peter Arnett had been reporting from Atlanta when Sherman burned it?

Through the trees in the other direction, the simple white marble obelisk honoring George Washington, towering over all other structures in the capital. The first President was derided these days as a slave-owning, woman-chasing, fatuous colonial dandy. But, Jerry thought, he had started the new nation down the right path, mostly reflecting his personal commitment to democracy and rectitude. Washington could have been crowned king, but he rejected it. Too bad some of his successors didn't feel the same.

Security for the Memorial Day ceremony seemed heavier than usual. Jerry counted twenty Secret Service agents in suits and sunglasses, talking into wrist microphones, scanning the trees and the growing crowd of tourists held behind orange ropes. Uniformed Executive Protective Service guards set up portable metal detectors through which the invited guests would be made to pass.

Dozens of Park Police and Metropolitan Police disembarked from blue buses and took up positions encircling the ceremonial area. When the side door of an official van parked on Constitution Avenue slid open for a moment, Jerry glimpsed what looked like a black-clad SWAT team inside.

Among the law-enforcement officers milling around the fringes of the ceremonial area was Detective A. L. Jones. But Jerry didn't see him.

The heavy security was probably in anticipation of demonstrations, Jerry assumed. Vietnam still generated strong emotions, even more than two decades after the end of the war and more than three years after Clinton officially ended hostilities by extending diplomatic recognition to the Vietnamese government. The old wounds had been reopened by the recent discovery of a mass grave of American prisoners near Hanoi. Dale Hammond was under pressure to react strongly to the grisly finding.

Jerry wondered what the President would say at the Wall. Grady had told him it would be "major." Jerry hoped the President would put the generation of smug yuppies in their place, so pleased with themselves for dodging the draft. So wrongheaded, in his view.

Jerry looked at his watch. Still an hour before noon.

A Secret Service agent approached and asked his name. The agent found the name on a list attached to his clipboard and placed a checkmark next to it. He directed Jerry to pass through the metal detector.

The other invited guests began to arrive. Jerry recognized the famous faces. Senator John McCain, who'd been held prisoner by the North Vietnamese but had favored Clinton's recognition. Robert McNamara, ghostly, every agony he'd felt and caused etched into his stony face. Henry Kissinger, fat in a dark gray tailored suit, grinning, slapping backs, making self-aggrandizing jokes. Legless Max Cleland, rolling majestically in his wheelchair. Bob Hope, ancient and rheumy-eyed. Neil Sheehan and David Halberstam, two of the first war correspondents in Vietnam. Senator Bob Kerrey, who'd lost part of his leg in the war. General Norman Schwartzkopf, who won his war, chatting with General William Westmoreland, who lost his.

But most of the guests passing through the metal detectors and taking their places on the folding chairs were not famous faces. They looked proud but solemn, a little dazed. Jerry guessed they were the parents, widows, and children of men who died or disappeared in the war.

The guests were escorted to their seats by members of veterans organizations acting as marshals. They wore black REMEMBER THE MIAS/POWS T-shirts, camouflage fatigue jackets and pants, and combat boots. Once trim young troopers, they were middle-aged now, with beer bellies and gray beards.

A military band unloaded from its bus and arrayed itself in a reserved area to the left of the podium.

Jerry heard a commotion from the short street that connected the road encircling the Lincoln Memorial to Constitution Avenue. The noise came from hordes of people pouring out of a bus and two black vans. They came running toward the Vietnam Wall. When they got closer, Jerry recognized them as the White House press corps—TV cameramen, photographers, and reporters, in full gallop.

Secret Service agents herded them into a roped-off pen behind the invited guests. The TV technicians jostled for tripod space on the raised camera platforms. The reporters shouted questions at members of the White House press office staff.

Jerry spotted Jane Day in the pack. He waved at her. But she either didn't see him or pretended not to see him lest her colleagues rib her about her friendship with such a Neanderthal. He imagined that Jane was not happy to be cooped up in a press pen on a drizzly Saturday covering a President she disapproved of. But, as the junior member of the *Post*'s White House team, she got stuck with the assignments the more senior reporters ducked.

Jerry tried waving at her again. Still no response. She'd never given him an answer to his invitation for lunch at Angler's after the President's speech. Well, it was too wet to eat on the terrace anyhow.

As soon as the TV cameras were spotted, chanting erupted from behind the seating area. Demonstrators, Jerry surmised. The security forces had kept the protesters away from the ceremony, back along the Reflecting Pool. A platoon of policemen quickstepped toward the noise. The Secret Service agents looked edgy.

Jerry picked up two competing chants. One was the now-famous *"Hanoi, Hanoi, hey, hey, hey. How many Americans did you bury today?"* The other was a ragged version of the old Beatles song, "Give Peace a Chance."

The TV cameramen snatched their cameras off the tripods, hoisted them onto their shoulders, and headed toward the demonstrators. The chanting got louder and angrier. Another platoon of policemen took off for the demonstration area.

The marshals escorted participants in the program and administration officials to their seats. Billy Graham, who would deliver the invocation. Placido Domingo, director of the Washington Opera, who would sing the "Star-Spangled Banner." The secretaries of Defense and State. Gregor Novasky, the President's national security adviser. The chairman of the Joint Chiefs of Staff, dazzling in full-dress military regalia. The secretary of the Department of Veterans Affairs, beaming on his one annual moment in the limelight.

The heavy presidential podium was set up in an isolated position on the grass so the inescapable shot for the TV cameras would be President Hammond standing all alone against the backdrop of the Wall. Nice photo op, Jerry thought. Of course, the TV crews would be looking for some way to portray the President in an unflattering way, an unplanned slipup, some embarrassing angle.

Suddenly there was a flurry of movement, the roar of motorcycle engines and limousines on Constitution Avenue. The band struck up "Hail to the Chief." Dale and Grady Hammond appeared, smiling, waving, almost hidden in a circle of Secret Service agents. The volume of the rival demonstrations rose.

The First Lady wore a khaki-colored suit tailored to look like a uniform, complete with epaulets and a hat that was loosely patterned after a Vietnam bush cap.

Her detractors were going to have a field day with that outfit, Jerry thought. Dale better give a strong speech, otherwise the reporters were likely to lead their stories with Grady's "affront" to the nation's military tradition.

After the prayers, the anthem, and the warm-up speeches, Dale Hammond waited a dramatic moment, then walked slowly and alone to the podium.

Colbert Clawson had wanted to post agents on each side of the rostrum, and one behind the President. But the press secretary, Garvin Dillon, vetoed that idea because the security guards would detract from the photo op of the solitary President in front of the Wall.

The President pulled his speech text out of his breast pocket and flattened it open. It was full of cross-outs and scribbled additions in red ink. Grady's last-minute edits.

Dale preferred to read his speeches from typewritten sheets, the old-fashioned way, rather than from glass TelePrompTers favored by his recent predecessors. Dillon told him that looking down at the text made him appear scripted and presented the top of his head to the TV cameras. But the President was afraid the TelePrompTer operator would scroll the words too fast or too slow and cause him to lose his place. Anyhow, Dale believed the words were what mattered, not a slick presentation.

He began.

Half a generation ago, this memorial was dedicated. What we say here today in its hallowed shadow will not be long remembered. What the men and women whose names are inscribed on the marble did for the cause of freedom will never be forgotten. They will live forever in the halls of the righteous, and in our memories. How can we, the living, honor the ultimate sacrifice they made? By ending the war that still divides us. We must march forward from those trampled and bloody battlegrounds of yesterday. It is time to make peace, within ourselves, and among ourselves. Let us, a wise people and a proud nation, turn our faces to the tasks ahead, for the sake of those gone, and those yet to come. The warriors we honor today gave their lives in a battle that was lost. But it was only one battle in a war that never ends, the struggle of freedom against tyranny, the struggle of liberty against oppression. From their sacrifice we gain a new measure of devotion to that struggle, and a new resolve that these honored dead shall not have died in vain.

Dale Hammond folded his script, replaced it in his breast pocket, and returned to his seat.

For a moment the only sound in the misty air was sobbing. Even the demonstrators were silent.

He delivered the goddamn Gettysburg address, Jerry marveled.

Grady Hammond leaned over and hugged the President, weeping on his shoulder.

Then the applause began. Hard, approving, sincere applause. It went on for many minutes.

Jerry looked over at the press pen to catch Jane's reaction. He couldn't find her. But he noticed some of the TV correspondents on the camera platform looked panicked. Apparently expecting a standard twenty-minute presidential speech and waiting for a passage that was controversial or made the President sound foolish, they hadn't turned on their cameras yet when Hammond's ninety-second speech ended.

Whatever was going to happen was going to happen soon, A. L. Jones sensed. He waited and watched from behind the band.

A little girl in a purple velvet pinafore, whose grandfather's name was carved on the Wall, left her seat in the family section and toddled to the President. She kissed him on the cheek.

More people started crying.

The applause swelled.

Even the security agents were affected by the emotion.

That's why they were slow reacting when one of the marshals, in black T-shirt and fatigues, slipped up behind Gregor Novasky, the President's national security adviser. The veteran flipped a thin plastic noose around Novasky's neck and yanked, severing his windpipe.

"Man down!" Colbert Clawson yelled when he grasped what had happened. "Move Teddybear! Now! Move! Move!"

Bedlam erupted.

Dale and Grady Hammond were rushed to the presidential limousine by a phalanx of Secret Service agents. The black armor-clad car sped down Constitution Avenue toward the White House and safety.

Other Secret Service agents, Metropolitan Police, Park Police, and bystanders swarmed on the veteran who had garroted Novasky, pinning him on the grass.

The veteran yelled "The prisoners are avenged! The prisoners are avenged!" over and over.

A. L. Jones contemplated jumping into the melee of bodies trying to subdue the man. But he saw that a dozen other law-enforcement officers had him under control. A.L. was too old for that shit.

At Colbert Clawson's first shouted alarm, Secret Service agents throughout the ceremonial area drew their weapons from holsters and canvas bags. At the sight of the guns, many in the crowd screamed in fear and ran.

The fleeing spectators collided with the White House press corps, which stampeded out of its pen and headed for the podium, yelling at anyone who looked official, "What happened? What happened?"

Some of the agents formed a protective ring around the VIP seats, scanning the chaotic scene anxiously.

Novasky lay on his back on the grass behind his overturned chair. A blue-uniformed D.C. Emergency Medical Services team and two Navy medical corpsmen ministered to him. But A.L. knew from the waxy blue-gray color of his face that he was dead.

Jerry Knight stood at the rear of the now-abandoned guest section, following the tumult. He wasn't sure what had happened and he didn't know what he should do.

He spotted Jane Day squatting under a tree, talking rapidly and loudly into her cellular telephone, apparently dictating a narrative of events at the ceremony to the *Post.* Her green eyes had a wild look. With one hand she repeatedly twisted and untwisted a curl of orange hair.

Jerry started toward the reporter. But before he reached her, he was grabbed by Bernard Shaw for a live interview on CNN.

Shaw's first question was, "Mr. Knight, do you think the extreme right-wing rhetoric spewed over the airways by you and the other ultraconservative radio talk-show hosts is responsible for encouraging the kind of violence we saw here today?"

"No," Jerry replied.

He waited serenely while the disconcerted Shaw fumbled for another line of questions.

CHAPTER THIRTY-ONE

FOUR O'CLOCK. THE afternoon had grown darker. A drizzle fell.

The scene at the Wall reminded Jerry of the disorder on a battlefield after the battle.

Park Service workers in green slickers folded and stacked the chairs, then loaded them onto a truck.

The area where Novasky had been killed was roped off with yellow police tape and guarded by a couple of policemen in shiny black raincoats.

TV correspondents jockeyed for position so the yellow tape would show in the background of their standuppers. Stoic producers held umbrellas over the heads of the stars.

Tourists snapped photos.

The emergency NO PARKING signs had been removed from Constitution Avenue, and the white vendor trucks were back, peddling T-shirts, snacks, and soft drinks.

On a knoll overlooking the Wall, aging Vietnam veterans in their fatigues and beards huddled around the card tables where they handed out literature. Some had known the man who strangled Novasky. One had been in his unit in the war.

They speculated among themselves about the aftermath of the killing.

"The goddamn news media will make all vets the villains," predicted a man who ran a dog-tag concession.

"Yeah, I can see the headlines now, 'Vietnam Psycho Killers,' " imagined another veteran, whose black T-shirt sleeve was pinned over the stump of his right arm.

Jerry stayed through the afternoon, mesmerized by the activity. He hadn't slept after his show. But he wasn't tired. Too much adrenaline. Too many questions.

Why Novasky? Did his murder have anything to do with the poisoning of Dan McLean? It must have. A Vietnamese waiter. A Vietnam veteran. McLean working on some kind of Vietnam exposé. Mr. Cao's comments. The scene of the killing, at the Vietnam Memorial.

But how did it all fit together?

Jerry wanted to talk to Jane, find out what she knew. But she was constantly busy, on her phone dictating, conducting interviews, scribbling in her notebook. At one point he handed her a Coke from one of the vendor trucks. She took it, giving him a grateful look, without breaking her dictation.

A. L. Jones nosed his dirty vanilla Ford to the curb on the north side of Constitution Avenue next to the enormous impressionistic statue of Albert Einstein on the lawn of the National Academy of Sciences. He walked across the street to the Wall.

He'd spent almost three hours in the Federal Courthouse at the foot of Capitol Hill participating in the interrogation of the veteran who took down Novasky. It was a federal case, no question, since the victim was a White House official. But Lawrence Frieze of the Secret Service had invited A.L. to sit in, since there was an immediate suspicion that Novasky's death was related to McLean's murder.

After the interrogation, A.L. returned to the Wall to see if any more evidence had been found.

Jerry Knight noticed that Jane seemed to have concluded her reporting duties. She dropped her phone and her notepad into her giant shoulder bag and drank what was left of the Coke Jerry had brought her.

He ducked under the limbs of the tree where she was

standing. The drizzle had turned her normally unruly hair into a bedraggled orange mess. Jerry guessed he didn't look so great himself, damp, wrinkled, and weary.

"Unbelievable," he commented on what had happened.

"Really," she agreed, still sounding wired. "Thanks for the Coke."

"I didn't think you noticed."

"I noticed."

She sagged against his shoulder for a moment.

"My story's leading the Sunday paper," she boasted. "Five-column head. You think it could be Pulitzer material? Breaking news written under deadline pressure?"

Jerry shrugged. He didn't understand the self-absorption of the news media. A man was dead and she was thinking Pulitzer.

A. L. Jones saw them under the tree branches and came over.

"Detective Jones," Jerry greeted him disparagingly. "This is one murder case even the D.C. police can't screw up, huh? Right in front of a couple of hundred cops. Think you can figure out who did it?"

"And a good afternoon to you, too, Mr. Night Talker," the stubby detective replied in a deep rumble.

Jane instantly resumed her reporter mode. She retrieved her notebook from her bag and started firing questions at Jones.

"Are you working on the case, Detective Jones?"

"Sort of."

"What's 'sort of'?"

"It's a federal case, but I attended the interrogation of the perp. D.C. Homicide is working on a few angles."

Jane scribbled faster and faster, not taking her eyes off A.L.'s face.

"Who's the perp?"

"The FBI released it, right?" Jones asked cautiously. "So I ain't giving away any secrets?"

Jane nodded affirmatively. She didn't know if the FBI had released the name. But she didn't want to discourage A.L. from spilling what he knew.

"Guy named Eldon Krohl," the detective intoned. "Vietnam vet. First Air Cav. Went through the Ia Drang Valley deal. He's dying of cancer. From breathing Agent Orange, he says, so he don't give a shit."

"What was his motive?" Jerry interjected.

"Didn't have no motive. He was recruited to do the job."

"By whom?" Jane asked.

She had run out of space in her notebook. She flipped over the pad and started scribbling on the back of her earlier notes.

"Group he belongs to called the Survivors of Cam Hoa. Bad dudes. Green Berets. Rangers. LERPs. And they're pissed because they think the government ain't doing enough to find out what happened to their buddies didn't come home."

"So am I," Jerry said. "So are a lot of people. But they don't kill the President's national security adviser because they're pissed off at the government."

"Well, the discovery of that grave of American prisoners kind of pushed the Survivors of Cam Hoa over the edge. And they're *especially* pissed at Nasky—whatever his name is—because he wrote a paper or a memo, some shit like that, back in the seventies, saying there was no more American prisoners left in Vietnam when he knew there was."

"That was the story Dan told Kristi he was working on when he was killed," Jane said.

"Who's Christy?" Jerry asked.

"Nobody," Jane answered dismissively. She continued her intense interrogation of Jones.

"So Novasky arranged to have Dan poisoned, to keep him from breaking the story, right?" Jane asked.

"Nope," the detective replied. "Nobody arranged McLean's murder."

"What do you mean? He's dead, isn't he?"

"He's dead, all right. But it was a mistake."

Jane's pen was a blur now.

"Mistake?" Jerry cut in, incredulous at what he was hearing. "So Dale Hammond *was* the intended target of the poison? I was right all along?"

"Nope, Mr. Night Talker, you was *wrong* all along. That waiter, Duc Phu something, was hired by the Survivors of

Cam Hoa to kill Nov . . . Novasky at that big dinner because they were so pissed at him about that memo thing. They knew Duc from Vietnam. He'd been a scout for the Green Berets and they helped him get to the States. They showed him a picture of Novasky. But he got Novasky and McLean mixed up. They looked a lot alike, you know . . ."

"Yeah. Yeah," Jane was writing furiously.

". . . and the waiter dropped the poison on the wrong guy."

"And then Krohl volunteered to kill the *right* guy," Jane filled in the rest. "He didn't care if he got caught because he was dying of cancer anyhow. So he strangled Novasky in plain view of thousands of people, in revenge for the memo."

"Hey, Miss *Washington Post,* you ain't a bad lady detective," A.L. said. "But, technically, he didn't *strangle* Novasky. He snapped the guy's windpipe with a cord. Learned it in Nam. Used plastic fishing line so the metal detectors wouldn't pick it up."

Jane shuddered at the vivid explanation.

"Who killed the waiter?" Jerry asked.

"Don't know yet. It's one angle I'm working on. Might of been some street boy he caught ripping off his stuff. But it was probably the Survivors of Cam Hoa, to make sure he didn't talk."

"Who took Dan's notebooks from his house?" Jane asked, cleaning up loose ends now. "Patricia McLean gave them to somebody who said he was from CNN, but he wasn't."

A.L. shrugged. "Dunno. Didn't even know somebody took McLean's notebooks. I'll look into it."

The detective made a note in his own bent pad.

"Maybe the widow didn't really give the notebooks to nobody," Jones suggested. "Maybe she just told you that to get you to stop bugging her."

And maybe the government's computer surveillance program tipped off Novasky that Dan was on to his memo, Jane speculated to herself, and the national security adviser sent somebody to trick Patricia McLean into giving up the incriminating notebooks.

"What about your theory that Dan was killed because he . . . played around?" Jane asked Jones.

"He left one widow and a bunch of husbands who ain't too happy with him," A.L. replied. "But they didn't get a chance to do anything about it."

"If rumors were circulating in the Vietnamese community about Dan McLean working on a story that could stir up old animosities, how come the FBI or the Secret Service didn't hear about it?" Jane asked.

"How do you know they didn't?" A.L. replied guardedly, recalling the mention of the Survivors of Cam Hoa at the early-morning meeting in the Secret Service director's office. Shit, even Stump heard something was going down.

"Did they?" Jane pressed.

"Ask 'em."

"I will."

"Don't be surprised if they play cover your ass," the detective advised.

"Who are the Survivors of Cam Hoa?" Jerry inquired. "Is it a big organization?"

A.L. shrugged. He didn't know.

"Probably a bunch of fat, middle-aged gun nuts who work at the gas station or raise pigs," Jane sneered, "and like to dress up like soldiers because they never got over the war."

"Yeah?" A. L. Jones said in an ominous growl. "A lot of us never got over the war, Miss *Washington Post.* We sure is fat and middle-aged. But we ain't no gun nuts. We went to Nam because we was told to go. And some of us is still trying to figure out what the fuck it was all about. You're so smart, maybe you can enlighten us."

"Amen," Jerry added.

Jane knew better than to taunt them further.

"Dale Hammond could be hurt by this," Jerry suggested, "for not knowing about the memo when he named Novasky to the NSC."

"I wish that was true," Jane replied. "But Novasky's been in and out of government for almost thirty years. He's been appointed by Republican presidents and Democratic presidents. And when he wasn't in the government, he was working as a newspaper and TV pundit. Nobody's going to hold Hammond responsible. Unfortunately."

"Hard as you try to suppress it, your objectivity just keeps breaking through," Jerry gibed.

"I've got to file," she said, punching buttons on her cellular phone. She walked away from the shelter of the tree. The drizzle had stopped.

Jerry and A.L. stood under the branches, not saying anything.

The detective's radio crackled.

"Say again?" He held it to his ear and listened.

"Oh, shit! Oh, shit! Those motherfuckers!" Jones appeared to stagger. He looked like he was going to sag down on the grass.

"How is he?" Jones spoke into the radio. His dark face contorted into an angry scowl as he listened to the reply.

"What's the matter?" Jerry asked.

"LaTroy . . . a boy . . . I been trying to keep him straight. Somebody just shot him. They found him out on Sixtieth Street with two bullets in him. But he's still alive, thank you sweet Jesus. He's still alive."

"What's wrong with this goddamn city?" Jerry asked. "Why can't somebody stop the shootings?"

"Yeah," A.L. said in a whisper. "Why can't somebody stop 'em? Why can't somebody stop 'em?"

"America lost the war in Vietnam and now we're losing the war on our own streets for the same reasons," Jerry lectured the detective. "We lack the will. We're reluctant to use the weapons necessary to win. And we are too soft-headed to recognize the viciousness of the enemy."

A.L. didn't seem to hear him. The detective trudged past the black memorial, crossed Constitution Avenue, and got into his car. He made a U-turn and headed for the Washington Hospital Center, feeling old and useless.

CHAPTER THIRTY-TWO

HAVING UPDATED HER story with the additional details from A.L. in time for the early edition of the Sunday *Post,* Jane searched in the gloom for Jerry.

She was still high from the excitement of the day. She wanted to rehash it with someone. She needed company, somebody to talk to. Her cat Bloomsbury wouldn't be enough.

Jane found Jerry at the Wall, in the deepest part of the trench. His head was pressed against the black marble, his fingers touching a name.

"Did you know him?" Jane asked.

"I was covering his unit," Jerry replied. "He tripped a claymore. It cut him in half. I held him while he bled to death."

Jerry started to cry.

Jane put her arm around his shoulders. She kissed him on the cheek, tasting salt from his tears.

"So many lives gone," he wept. "So many young lives gone."

"I don't understand how you can support the idea that America should have continued the war when you feel this way about so many men dying," she said. "If we'd continued the war, how many more names of dead young men would be on this wall?"

"How many more dead Vietnamese are there—their names aren't listed on a wall anywhere—most of them don't even have tombstones—because we cut and ran on them. This country used to believe there were things worth fighting and dying for. Like other people's freedom. Not anymore."

Jane had never heard him speak so bitterly.

"Wasn't Tran's freedom worth fighting and dying for?" he whispered.

"Who's Tran?"

Jerry turned back to the Wall, leaned his head against the marble again, and cried uncontrollably.

Jane could think of nothing to do but stand beside him, patting his shoulder.

In a few minutes, he took a deep, shuddering breath and turned to face her. His eyes glistened with tears.

"Tran Minh. She was a Vietnamese woman. Owned a restaurant on a boat on the Saigon River. She was so beautiful. Black hair down to her waist. Big black eyes. And smart. Her family sent her to be educated in France. She was . . . I loved Tran. We lived together for almost two years."

"What happened to her?"

"When it became obvious that Saigon was about to fall, the American networks chartered jetliners to fly their correspondents and camera crews out. ABC agreed to let Tran go on the plane with me."

Jane looked puzzled. Was this Vietnamese woman in the United States now, perhaps in Little Saigon?

"But she wouldn't go," he continued. "She refused to leave her family behind, and ABC said there wasn't room for her family on the plane. When I boarded the bus that was taking the network crews to our evacuation flight, Tran stood on the sidewalk in front of the Caravelle Hotel and glared at me through the bus window. To the day I die, I will never forget those two huge dark eyes blazing with hatred."

"Is she still alive?"

"Over the years I've pieced together the story from scraps of information. When the Communists took over Saigon, they sent Tran to a reeducation camp for Vietnamese who were friendly to Americans. They kept her there ten years and then sent her into the countryside to work in the rice fields. In 1988, she and the surviving members of her family somehow scraped together enough money to bribe a fisherman to take them to Thailand. They were never seen again. Maybe the boat sank. Maybe the fisherman took their money and threw them overboard. Maybe they were killed by pirates. Nobody knows."

He paused. "Now you know why I feel the way I do about bugging out of Vietnam."

Jane took his hand. She kissed away his tears. Then she kissed him on the lips.

"Come on," she urged gently.

"Where?"

"I don't know. Somewhere. Dinner, I guess."

"You're not ashamed anymore to be seen with a right-wing kook?"

"No."

"How come? What's changed?"

"You let me see you cry."

"You like me better now because you saw me crying?"

"I *know* you better because you let me see you cry. You let me see that you're more than a celebrity spouting conservative slogans. You are so much more than your politics. You let me see your loss and your anguish, your ability to love, your tenderness. It takes a strong man to let a woman see him cry. And it means you trust me."

She took him in her arms and rocked him like a little boy.

"I have some *other* qualities I hope you'll find appealing, other than the ability to cry in front of you."

"I'll certainly be on the lookout for them."

They walked up out of the trench and left the Wall behind them.